Song of the Lake

Esther Schultz

Backyard Studio Publishing
Harris, MN

Copyright © 2023 by Esther Schultz

All rights reserved. No part of this publication may be reproduced, distributed, or transmitted in any form or by any means, without prior written permission.

Published by Backyard Studio Publishing
Harris, Minnesota (United States of America)

Publisher's Note: This is a work of fiction. Names, characters, places, and incidents are a product of the author's imagination. Locales and public names are sometimes used for atmospheric purposes. Any resemblance to actual people, living or dead, or to businesses, companies, events, institutions, or locales is completely coincidental. Although some real-life iconic places are depicted in settings, all situations and people related to those places are fictional.

Publisher's Cataloging-in-Publication Data

Names: Schultz, Esther, 1978- .
Title: Song of the lake / Esther Schultz.
Description: Harris, MN : Backyard Studio Publishing, 2023. | Summary: Amelia Campbell finds herself in Willow Bay, MN with a new generation of Nilssons. Amelia learns the value of love and family while grappling with family secrets, tragedy, and betrayal.
Identifiers: LCCN 2023915581 | ISBN 9781737908647 (pbk.) | ISBN 9781737908654 (ebook)
Subjects: LCSH: Families -- Fiction. | Family secrets -- Fiction. | Betrayal -- Fiction. | Foregiveness -- Fiction. | Women -- Fiction. | Minnesota -- Fiction. | Boston (Mass.) -- Fiction. | BISAC: FICTION / Women. | FICTION / Family Life / General. | FICTION / Historical / 20th Century / General.
Classification: LCC PS3619.C48 S65 20223 (print) | PS3619.C48 (ebook) | DDC 813 S38—dc23
LC record available at https://lccn.loc.gov/2023915581

Dedication

To my twins: may you always have the same bond and closeness as you have now.

And to my son, Jackson, you are an amazing brother, and you inspire me every day.

Chapter One

Boston 1912

AMELIA CAMPBELL READ THE telegram twice and set it on the table in front of her. The blood drained from her face, and everything blurred. Her ears were ringing as someone called her name.

"What?" she asked, shaking her head.

"Are you okay, darling?" her mother, Charlotte Campbell, asked.

Everything came back into focus, but she had to force her trembling fingers to pick up the paper. She handed it to her mother and pushed away from the table.

"I'm going to my room," Amelia said.

Her mother let out a sharp gasp and hurried to her daughter's side. "Here, let me help you."

Amelia tried to brush her off, but she was not deterred.

"Charles, please get Ivy. Miss Amelia has had a shock, and we need to get her up to bed."

"Yes, ma'am," Charles said, rushing out of the room.

"I'm fine, Mother," Amelia said, trying to move away.

"Nonsense, receiving such news is difficult. We must get you to bed, to rest."

Ivy ran into the dining room, paused, and rushed to help.

"Are you okay, miss?"

"I'm fine, please don't fuss," Amelia said.

"What happened?"

"The Titanic is lost to the sea," Amelia said, tears building at the corner of her eyes.

"What of Mr. Thompson?" Ivy asked.

"He's gone."

"Come, let's get you to bed so you can rest," Ivy said.

She gave in and allowed herself to be led upstairs to her room. Ivy insisted on helping Amelia stretch out on the bed. She grabbed a blanket and laid it across her.

"I will go fetch you some water, miss," Ivy said and disappeared from the room.

Her mother paced about until Amelia, growing impatient, said, "Mother, please. You are making me nervous. Perhaps you should send a message to George. He needs to be aware of what is going on, although he may have already made that determination when he read the newspaper this morning."

"I'm sure he did, but I will send him a note anyway. I, for one, am happy our newspapers were late. It would have been dreadful for you to find out by reading the news of the day," her mother said. She crossed the room, caressed Amelia's cheek, and left.

Amelia let out the breath she didn't realize she was holding and let her tears come. Her sadness was not from losing a great love, but Daniel Thompson had been a sweet man and she had cared for him. She had been looking forward to building her life with him, and now he was gone. She had no direction.

Brushing at her cheeks, she got up and crossed the room to look outside. The view of their small flower garden always brought her peace and comfort. She regained her composure, smoothed out her dress, and sat at her desk next to the window. She picked up a pen and a blank piece of paper, and started to write a note to the woman who would no longer become her mother-in-law.

Ivy walked in with a small tray of toast, water, and coffee just as Amelia finished signing her name.

"I thought perhaps you might want a little something in your stomach before facing what is sure to be a long day," Ivy said.

"Thank you, Ivy. You always seem to know just what I need."

"I know you cared for Mr. Thompson and were looking forward to your wedding in the fall."

"Yes, it was wonderful having a plan with him and not being paraded about any longer."

"He was always so kind to me and the rest of the staff."

"What is Mother doing now?" Amelia asked.

"She was requesting for Charles to send a telegram to your brother in hopes that he will delay his trip to England."

"Yes, I suppose he will. He won't be able to for long, but he will want to be here for the funeral."

"Will his wife come, do you think?" Ivy asked.

"She wouldn't be able to get here in time for any services, so I suppose she will remain in England."

"Traveling back and forth between the two countries must be getting difficult for George," Ivy said.

"I could see him eventually reserving his travel to once or maybe twice a year instead of the four or so times he does now. Especially as he and Violet have more children," Amelia said.

She knew her maid was trying to keep her mind preoccupied by discussing a topic she already knew the answers to, but that was Ivy. She had worked in the Campbell household since Amelia was ten years old and she knew the Campbell's well. Amelia was especially close to her, since Ivy was only a few years older.

Amelia's mother entered the room. "Oh, good. I'm glad to see that you are feeling better. I knew a quick lie down would do the trick."

"I wrote to Mrs. Thompson," Amelia said.

"So thoughtful. I will have Charles make sure that it is sent over right away," her mother said.

Ivy stepped forward. "I will take it to him." She retrieved the envelope from Amelia and slipped out.

"I should probably change into something black," Amelia said. "I would imagine we will be invited to the Thompson's soon, and I must be presentable for the circumstances."

"Quite right, darling," her mother said. "I shall send Maria up to help you."

"Thank you, Mother."

"I'm sorry this happened to you, Melia," her mother said, and left the room.

Surprised by the pet name, she wondered at the emotions her mother must be feeling to call her that. Melia was what her brother called her, and she couldn't remember her mother ever using it before.

Their relationship had always been complicated. Her mother was rigid with a focus on protocol and was afraid of what others in society thought. This clashed with Amelia's strong opinions and independent nature. She rarely measured up to her mother's expectations and often believed she didn't belong in her own home.

Forcing herself to think about other things, she threw herself into the task of changing her clothes. As she fastened the last button, she received a note from Mrs. Thompson. She was inviting Amelia and her mother to stay with them at the Thompson family home outside of the city. Since it would take about an hour to get there, and she needed to purchase new items for proper mourning, she wrote back, saying they would be there first thing the following day.

Her mother already had plenty of mourning clothes, as she was a widow and liked to remind people of it by the way she dressed. However, since Amelia's father had passed away when she was in her teens, Amelia no longer had any of those clothes. Maria helped her put together a list of options and sent another maid to their favorite dress shop to purchase them.

Amelia helped pack throughout the afternoon and was happy when she was almost done. She tucked the last few items neatly inside and shut the trunk. She pressed her hand against her chest at the pang in her heart. She wondered what her next steps would be after the funeral when life went back to whatever normal was left. Her mother would want her to be back on the market as soon as possible, and Amelia shuddered. She had always hated being presented to others as possible wife material, like she was an animal at auction.

Her mother rushed into the room, her cheeks flushed, wringing her hands. It surprised Amelia, since her mother always appeared calm and cool-headed.

"What is it?" Amelia asked.

"I've just heard from George, and he isn't sure when he can get here. He isn't even sure if he can delay his trip. What will the Thompsons think? What will everyone else think?"

"I'm sure everyone else has things to focus on other than what George is doing."

"Don't be foolish, Amelia," her mother snapped. "You are Daniel's fiancé and people will wonder at your brother's absence."

Amelia tried to keep her annoyance from showing. "Perhaps we should be focusing on the fact that you and I are rushing over there as soon as possible and that we will be comforting Mrs. Thompson and Daniel's sister."

"I just don't want Mrs. Thompson to feel slighted, especially during this time."

"I'm sure she won't. Come on now, let's finish our preparations for our trip in the morning."

Her mother let out a long breath, and her shoulders drooped. "Always so strong, Amelia."

"I get that from you, I'm sure."

"You are too kind, but we both know that isn't true."

Amelia squeezed her mother's hand.

"We should head down to dinner," her mother said, pulling away to leave the room.

"I will be down shortly."

Her mother disappeared into the hallway, and Amelia went to grab her gloves. She was consumed with the upcoming funeral, and worried about what would come after. She hoped she had the strength to endure it all.

Chapter Two

Mrs. Thompson dabbed at the corners of her eyes and sprinkled dirt over her son's empty casket, which had just been lowered into its freshly dug grave. Johanna, Daniel's sister, helped keep Mrs. Thompson steady as they moved back to their seats.

Johanna elbowed Amelia, signaling it was her turn. Amelia stood, glanced around, and forced herself to move. Her cheeks grew warmer with every step forward until she teetered on the edge of Daniel's grave. As she peered into the dark hole, thoughts of their last dance together flitted through her mind.

They had been making plans for their future together as a married couple, and Daniel had valued her input. He had understood her so well. And now she was helping to bury an empty box in his memory. Her stomach churned, and she swayed on her feet. The movement brought her back to the present, and she realized she was taking longer than intended. She reached out her trembling hand, let the dirt slide through her fingers, and hurried back to her chair.

Once Amelia was settled, she squeezed Johanna's hand, but her cheeks were flaming hotter than before. As independent as she was, she hated attention, and now everyone was watching her every move. Thankfully, the reverend cleared his throat, and the focus was back on him. He said a final prayer and dismissed the crowd of mourners. Amelia started sweating as she walked with the Thompsons back to the waiting vehicle. It would be a short drive back to Thompson's home, but she dreaded the confined space.

She requested to walk back, offering her seat to her mother. Johanna said she would go with her, but they were met with protests by both mothers. George popped out from the crowd, saying he would escort the ladies back.

Amelia's eyes widened at the sight of her brother. She smiled and mouthed the words, "Thank you."

"George," their mother said, leaning in for a kiss on the cheek from her son. "I'm so thankful you were not delayed further. I know it was difficult for you to get here so quickly."

"Yes, it took a few days to change around my travel plans, but I wouldn't have missed this. I needed to be here for Melia," George said.

George once more offered to escort Johanna and Amelia, which appeased Mrs. Thompson. Amelia could tell her mother still wanted to give a quick lesson in proper etiquette at a fiancé's funeral, but didn't say anything else. Relief flooded through her as her mother and Mrs. Thompson climbed into the car and drove off.

George commented on how sharp the vehicle looked, and Johanna bragged it was the latest Stevens-Duryea Model AA. George asked a question about it, but Amelia rolled her eyes. Ignoring the conversation between her brother and Johanna, she started the procession toward the Thompson home. The subject eventually tapered off, and she reveled in the silence. She looked up toward the sky and enjoyed the sunshine on her face.

"So, what now for you, Amelia?" Johanna asked.

"I don't know."

"Surely you won't be in mourning for long, especially since Mama says you shouldn't waste your time on that. I know she was right in saying it. Daniel wouldn't have wanted that for you."

"Perhaps, but I know Mother will want to make sure we are meeting society's standards."

"Well, maybe I can spread around what Mama said to you, so your mother won't put such pressure on you."

"That would be kind of you, but I'm okay not going back on the market so quickly," Amelia said.

"I know. We all miss him," Johanna said.

"Yes, we do indeed," George chimed in.

He quickly changed the subject to the warmth of the afternoon sun. Amelia was sure he did it to rescue her from a conversation she didn't want to have. Johanna linked arms with her and thanked her for being such a strong support while the funeral arrangements were made.

"I was happy to be of service during such a dark time."

"I would have loved having you as a sister."

"I feel the same," Amelia said. "Perhaps we can be honorary sisters. Besides, I will always be your friend."

"That sounds lovely."

The conversation lulled, and the trio walked the rest of the way in silence. Once they arrived at the Thompson home, Johanna went to look for her mother, and George asked Amelia for a few private moments to talk.

She agreed and led the way to the back patio where they would be alone. Being outdoors allowed her to breathe easily for the first time since arriving at the Thompson's, and she wasn't ready to leave the outdoor air.

"What is it?" Amelia asked, sitting on a bench that overlooked the flower garden.

"Mother and I have been corresponding, and she is worried about what will happen to you now."

"Financially or going back on the marriage market?"

George chuckled. "If I didn't adore you so, I would admonish you for being so crude."

"I don't believe I'm being crude, just explaining how I see it."

"Perhaps, but Mother would roll her eyes, clear her throat as she does, and give you *that* look if she were here."

"Yes, I suppose you're right."

"Proper behavior aside," George said. "I followed up with my financial advisors and our family attorney, and I'm setting aside a larger sum for you to live on until you can make a proper entrance back into society—after your mourning period is over."

"So that I may find another suitable husband," Amelia said with a sigh, staring down at her hands.

"Why is that such a bad thing, Melia?"

"Because I want to make my own choices in life. I want to live as I see fit. I want to go on adventures and see new things. And if I decide I want to marry, I want it to be because it is more than just a good societal or financial match."

"Such a speech," George said. "You know Mother would worry over it."

"Of course she would. She always worries about what I will do or say next, but I can't stop being me just because I was born a Campbell."

"Some would say being a Campbell is a large part of who you are."

"Father would understand if he were here."

"Maybe, but he did indulge you more than he probably should."

"You can't be serious, George. Father didn't indulge me, he just understood me. And I would like to think you understand me, too."

George shook his head and stifled a grin. "You know I do."

"So now what?" she asked.

"Well, as I said, you will have a nice sum to live on, separate from Mother's monthly allowance, for as long as you need. Given the circumstances you can take a little longer to return to society if you see fit."

"Thank you, George."

"Look, I know it was hard for you to settle on Daniel. And his passing makes things even more difficult for you, but please try to behave and not stress our mother more than necessary."

"I will try," she said. "I suppose I can't travel?"

"Actually, I'm going to discuss with Mother that a change of scenery might be good for you both. I know going to England would be ideal for Mother, but since this was your fiancé who died, I think I can convince her to support a choice more suited for you."

"Which would be where?"

"I was thinking maybe you should go visit Aunt Lucille. Mother hasn't seen her sister for some time, and they will be starting their trek to their new summer home soon. The northern country air might do you good. It might allow you to breathe a little, regroup, and prepare for what's next."

"And what about you, George?" Amelia asked.

"I will be in England all summer with my family. I hope to be back here by Thanksgiving."

"Your visits to America are going to become fewer and fewer I'm afraid," Amelia said.

"Most of my business ventures have been in London lately. I still have a few holdings here in America, though, so I will continue to go back and forth, but I just hired a man to help with that, so I won't be returning as often," he said.

"I suppose that is to be expected, since you married someone from another country."

"It made good business sense. I also took a page from your book and married her because I adore her."

"All is not lost on you, I guess," Amelia said, giggling.

"Children, it is nice that you are getting along so well, but must I remind you that we are guests in someone else's home, and that we just buried who was to be your husband, Amelia?" their mother asked.

"Why am I the one in trouble?" Amelia asked, her forehead creasing. "George is the one who asked to speak with me."

"The conversation needs to be tabled for now. We are about to receive more people, and Mrs. Thompson is expecting you to be by her side."

Amelia glanced at George, who nodded slightly. She stood and followed her mother into the house. She paused in the shadows to brush at the wrinkles in her dress. She plastered the most appropriate look of mourning on her face and crossed to Mrs. Thompson. Amelia caught her mother's look of approval before turning to her duties.

Chapter Three

Stepping onto the platform with ease, Amelia turned to check on her mother, who was shaking her head at her. They had just arrived in Saint Paul, Minnesota after a long train ride. She knew her mother was irritated with her for not accepting the assistance offered to help her down the stairs. She rolled her eyes but smiled at her mother and turned toward her name being called.

Amelia scanned the area and found her cousins, Madeline and Henry Granger, waving wildly at her.

Letting out a laugh, she turned to her mother. "Look, Maddy and Henry are here to fetch us."

"I can see that, darling."

"Always so grumpy when we travel."

"Nonsense, what you see is frustration at your behavior when we travel."

Amelia started to retort but was interrupted by Maddy pulling her into a hug.

"It's so wonderful to see you, cousin, and of course you, Aunt Charlotte. I hope you're not too tired after your journey."

"A nice rest will be all that is needed, Madeline, to become refreshed for the rest of the day," Charlotte said, hugging her niece and nephew.

"Come along with us. We'll have Martin get your things and follow along directly. I will drive us home in a separate car," Henry explained.

"How marvelous that you can drive," Amelia said. "Perhaps you can teach me."

"That sounds like a dreadful idea, Amelia," her mother chimed in before Henry could respond.

"Well, maybe when Mother isn't looking," Amelia said.

Her mother started to retort, but Henry cut her off by offering his arm to escort her to the car. Over his shoulder, he said, "I think perhaps I should listen to your mother, Amelia. After all, a woman of such delicacy should be driven around and not the one doing the driving."

Amelia bristled at the remark and was ready to share her thoughts on the subject, but noticed the twinkle in his eye before he winked at her.

"Of course, you're probably right," Amelia said with a giggle.

"Why do I feel like you are making fun of me?" her mother asked, with a pointed look at Amelia.

She shrugged and followed her mother and cousin.

Madeline fell in step beside her. "I'm so excited that you're here. We delayed our trip north just so that we could receive you here, but we're still going to Duluth, where we plan to spend the rest of the summer."

"I'm excited to visit your summer home," Amelia said. "I don't believe I have ever been there."

"No, darling, we haven't," her mother said. "This home was built only a few years ago."

"Yes, it was completed around the same time as the Congdon's home," Madeline said. "Mother is friends with Mrs. Congdon, and we have been invited for several picnics and parties there this summer. It should be a grand time."

"Is your home located close to your friends?" Amelia asked.

"Yes, we're only a few miles away," Madeline said. "But alas, our home is not on the banks of the lake."

"I have been told it is still a beautiful home," Charlotte said.

"It is indeed," Henry said.

After assisting Charlotte into the car, Henry turned to assist Madeline and Amelia. It didn't take long for Henry to pull onto the main road. Amelia listened to the chatter of conversation while she took in her surroundings. She gazed at the city as they drove toward her aunt's home. The last time she had been there was when she was a child, so was surprised at a few landmarks she remembered. Henry pulled onto their half-moon driveway, where Aunt Lucille stood on the front stoop waiting to greet them.

After climbing out of the car, Amelia hugged her aunt and followed the small party into the grand home. She was led upstairs to the guest room designated for her and was thankful when everyone left her. She needed time to recharge before dinner. Amelia looked out the window at the grounds below. The view reminded her of her own gardens at home, perfect for entertainment during parties, but an even better spot for relaxation when there was downtime.

Amelia stretched across the bed and allowed her eyelids to flutter closed. She listened to the distant hum of a busy household, and it didn't take her long to fall asleep.

A gentle voice woke Amelia. She opened her eyes and smiled. She sat up and looked around, wondering how long she had been asleep.

"When did you get here?" she asked.

"About thirty minutes ago," Ivy said. "Maria and I tried to make it onto your train, but unfortunately, we got stuck in Boston's downtown traffic."

"That's okay," Amelia said. "You're here now."

"Yes, and it's a good thing, too. You may be late getting down to dinner as it is."

"What time is it?" Amelia asked, climbing off the bed.

"Time for you to be going down to dinner, so we must hurry and get you dressed. I already have your clothes set out for you and there is a washing bowl full of water with a rag. Wash your face while I unfasten your dress."

"Yes, ma'am," Amelia said with a chuckle.

"What would your mother say?" Ivy asked with a twinkle in her eye.

Amelia laughed harder, but complied with Ivy's instructions. It wasn't long and the two of them had Amelia looking presentable. She rushed to join the rest of the dinner party, and her cheeks warmed when she stumbled into the drawing room. She immediately received a disappointed look from her mother.

"My apologies for my tardiness, Aunt Lucille," Amelia said. "I was resting so well in my accommodations that I lost track of time."

"Nonsense, child," Aunt Lucille said. "You are right on time."

"Mother," Amelia said with the hopes she wouldn't be too cross with her.

"Dinner is ready for you, ma'am," the butler said, standing in the doorway Amelia had just rushed through.

Amelia followed everyone into the dining room and found her seat next to a stranger. She smiled at the man and looked across the table at her cousin Madeline.

Amelia mouthed, "Who is this?"

"Fiancé," Madeline mouthed back.

Amelia nodded and turned to her dinner companion to introduce herself.

"Nicholas Nilsson," the man said. "It's nice to meet the cousin that Maddy has been talking about since we learned of you coming to visit."

"All good things I hope, Mr. Nilsson," Amelia said.

"Please call me Nick, Miss Campbell. And yes, I assure you all good things."

"Wonderful. And please, call me Amelia."

The conversation started lightly but quickly changed to a deeper one. They discussed the business ventures of the Nilsson family, and a place called Willow Bay, along the shores of Lake Superior. Amelia made a few comments on the Nilsson entrepreneur strategies and Nick's eyes lit up.

"You didn't tell me that your cousin would be such a great conversationalist," Nick said to Madeline.

"I don't think I realized it myself," Madeline said, staring at Amelia with envy.

"I hope you don't mean that as a slight against me," Amelia said, growing irritated at what she perceived was a rebuke from Nick for being smart.

"On the contrary, cousin," Madeline said. "Nick loves to chat with individuals who can keep up with his level of intelligence."

Amelia's face softened. "Which is why you get along so well with him, Maddy."

"Actually, I help to distract him from the stress of his busy life by talking about lighter things," Madeline said.

Looking over at her mother, Amelia realized she had taken a misstep somewhere. She always struggled to stay on proper topics, especially in social engagements. Her face grew hot, and she looked down at her plate.

Nick leaned over and said, "Please don't be upset. I've enjoyed talking with you. It reminds me of conversations with my grandmother."

"That is kind of you to say," Amelia said, taking a bite of food, wishing she could run upstairs and hide.

"Yes, she always likes to engage in conversations that most women of your standing don't."

"I prefer to avoid talking about nonsense," Amelia said.

Madeline clanged her fork down on her plate, and Amelia wanted to crawl under the table. She realized what she said must have hurt her cousin's feelings and feared she was ruining her first dinner in her aunt's home.

Amelia couldn't think of a way to fix the situation so blurted out the first thing that came to mind. "I'm not myself right now, Madeline, since Daniel's passing. Please forgive my rudeness."

The statement did the trick because Madeline's expression softened when she said, "But of course, that makes sense. I know I would be having a difficult time if I were going through the same thing."

Amelia started to respond but was cut off by Nick's question.

"Who is Daniel?"

"He was my fiancé," Amelia said. "He went down in the Titanic."

"That's just awful. I'm so sorry," he said.

"Thank you."

Madeline cut in. "I'm surprised that you're not still wearing black."

"Mrs. Thompson insisted I not practice the normal mourning customs as Daniel wouldn't have wanted it," Amelia said.

"That was rather kind of her," Nick said.

"Yes, indeed," Madeline said. "I suppose it's so you can get back out there again to find a husband."

It took everything in Amelia not to roll her eyes. "I don't plan to try and find a husband anytime soon."

"No, but you *are* getting older, dear cousin."

Amelia couldn't believe how snobbish her cousin sounded. She wondered if she would have acted the same way if her father hadn't taken the time to nurture her brain. He had often encouraged her not to settle for the normal customs in society.

"Yes, I suppose I'm getting older, cousin, but I appear to be younger than the men at this table, so it appears I still have time if I ever feel so inclined to get married."

Madeline started to retort, but Nick cut her off.

"Perhaps we should allow your cousin some grace since she is going through a difficult time. She may have too much love in her heart to want to immediately marry someone else."

Amelia glanced at Nick but caught her mother's horrified expression, and her cheeks started to burn again. She focused on her plate, wishing for anyone else to speak up and change the subject. Thankfully, her cousin Henry came to her rescue.

"Amelia, please tell us about your trip to London with George last year. I heard you visited quite a few museums and attended several operas while there. Didn't I hear you even got to see royalty?"

Nodding a thank you to Henry, Amelia shared about her time in London and how the Prince of Wales was in the balcony, across the auditorium from her. She described the art galleries she visited and the museums she toured.

When she was done with her stories, Nick leaned over and said, "Wow, that sounds like quite the time for you."

"It was enjoyable and educational, but I would rather not go back," Amelia said.

"Yes, this would surprise most. My daughter does not appreciate the luxurious life my son and I try to give her," her mother said.

"What kind of life do you prefer?" Henry asked.

"I'm not sure," Amelia said, taking a sip of Chardonnay.

"I think you do know," Nick said.

Setting her glass down, Amelia said, "I prefer using my mind. Being a companion of someone who values my opinion. I'm not even afraid of a little bit of hard work. And I want to spend as much time as possible outdoors."

"Sounds hellish to me," Madeline said.

"Sounds hellish to most women," Charlotte said.

"Where is George now?" Aunt Lucille asked.

"He's in London," Amelia said. "We will probably not see him again until Thanksgiving."

"Who is George?" Nick asked.

"My big brother and my mother's favorite child."

"Amelia, such utter nonsense, darling. A mother does not have favorites."

"Perhaps, but he does seem to get in less trouble than I," Amelia said and took another bite.

Her frustration was evident, but she didn't care. She sensed Nick was studying her and turned toward him to say something witty. She didn't expect his face to be so close to hers. It caused her to pause, and she had to force her food down her throat.

"I think you should meet my grandmother. She would be delighted by you. I know I am," Nick said.

Madeline gasped. "Why have you never said that to me? Plus, I have been dying to meet your grandmother."

"My apologies, Maddy. The thought never entered my mind, especially since you prefer the city so much," Nick said, turning to his glass of wine.

"Perhaps while we are in Duluth, we could make a small trip up the shore to Willow Bay?" Henry asked.

"That is a grand idea," Madeline said. "What do you think, Amelia?"

"Whatever you wish to do will be fine with me," Amelia said.

"I am sure my family would love to have you all," Nick said.

The rest of the dinner turned to conversations of their upcoming trip to Duluth, and their first party at the Congdon's once they got there. Amelia didn't participate for the rest of the evening and couldn't wait for the night to be over. She was hoping she could escape to her bed before her mother had a chance to give her another lecture.

Thankfully, she was dismissed by her aunt, who indicated Amelia must be exhausted. She didn't care if her aunt pitied her. She yearned for the confines of the guest bedroom away from her mother's disapproving scowl. Later, when her mother eventually knocked on the door, Amelia pretended to be asleep.

Chapter Four

THE PASSING COUNTRYSIDE WAS breathtaking, and Amelia couldn't wait for what was described as the magical moment when cresting the hill. She had been told the first glimpses of Duluth and Lake Superior could be seen there, and she was excited to experience it.

When the lake came into view, she gasped and couldn't hold back her enthusiasm.

"How splendid it is, Mother," Amelia said.

"Yes, I suppose it is," her mother said and returned to her conversation.

Amelia returned her focus to outside her window, and her grin widened with every mile closer to her aunt's summer home. The cousins were in the car behind her, which she was thankful for. The more she got to know Madeline again, the less they had in common. She had loved her cousin when they were kids, but was disappointed at how different they were now. She had a hard time conversing with Madeline, and all Amelia wanted to do was read or go for a walk outside.

The car eventually pulled into the driveway of the smaller summer estate, and Amelia was ready to stretch her legs. She was ushered into the house and to her rooms before she had a chance to steal away to the grounds to see a partial view of the water. She had barely settled when there was a knock on her door.

"Come in."

Madeline walked in and circled the room. "I forgot about this room. It's so...out of the way."

Realizing her cousin was trying to goad her, Amelia said, "You know, cousin, jealousy and pettiness are really not good looks on you."

"What a dreadful thing to say," Madeline said.

"Is it? I'm sorry if I hurt your feelings, but we both know what you were trying to do with your comment about my room."

"Oh, alright, perhaps we should make up our minds to just be friends. After all, we are cousins."

"I'm game if you are. So, what is on the agenda for the rest of the day?"

"We will have a light luncheon, then later we are going to the Congdon's for a small dinner party."

"Since their home is so grand and I'm usually not good at picking the right thing to wear, perhaps you can help me pick out an outfit for the occasion."

Amelia knew exactly what she should wear but was trying to make peace with her cousin. It was hard for her to stay engaged in conversations about clothes, but she was committed to finding peace with Madeline. Plus, she was confident she wouldn't get another lecture from her mother on how to behave in someone else's home.

They went through her dresses and settled on an outfit that matched one of Madeline's. When they left to go down for lunch, they were talking as though they had been lifelong friends.

The rest of the day passed quickly and they were off to the Congdon dinner party. As they drove up to the house, Madeline chattered about the interior of the home and how it was decorated. It was difficult not to become irritated again while Madeline prattled on, as though Amelia wasn't accustomed to such a grandiose home. Her own home in Boston was just as fine, as were the mansions within the circles the Campbells kept.

She was about to enlighten Madeline, when her mother overtly pinched her arm, and she kept her mouth shut.

She glared at her as her mother whispered, "It never hurts to be gracious, darling."

"I suppose you're right," Amelia said.

Amelia reminded herself of her commitment to be friends with Madeline, even though it was difficult to overlook her cousin's need to criticize her at every opportunity. She promised her mother she would be polite going forward no matter what.

Charlotte and Amelia were escorted in, introduced to the party hosts, and a polite conversation ensued. Amelia remained quiet until she spotted Nick. She excused herself and made her way across the room to greet him. As she approached, she realized he was talking with a man who looked just like him.

"Surely this must be your brother, Nick," Amelia said.

"How perceptive you are, Amelia," Nick said. "This is, in fact, my twin brother, Nathanial. He came down from Willow Bay to join me this evening."

Nathanial smiled and stretched out his hand. "Ah, the cousin I've heard so much about. A match for his wit, I've been told."

"Are you not as much of an expert on the art of conversation as your brother?" Amelia asked.

"On the contrary, I think I'm better at it."

Amelia laughed as Madeline joined them.

"I see you wasted no time being the center of attention, cousin."

Nathanial lifted his eyebrow, and a flash of annoyance crossed his face.

Forcing a smile for his brother's wife-to-be, Nathanial said, "Pleasure as always, Madeline."

"Likewise, sir," Madeline said with a flirtatious giggle and turned to Amelia. "Isn't it simply uncanny how much they look alike?"

"It is something," Amelia said.

Madeline excused herself, taking Nick with her, leaving Amelia to talk with Nathanial alone.

"You don't much care for your brother's fiancé, I see," Amelia said.

"I was hoping I covered my expression," he said.

"I doubt she noticed."

"She is nice enough when she wants to be. Has the right connections, which is good for the family, but sometimes I wonder at my brother choosing her."

"I think he genuinely likes her," Amelia said.

"I used to believe the same thing," Nathanial said. "When they first started courting, she was much sweeter of nature, but once he asked her to marry him, her character seemed to change."

"Or perhaps her true character finally came out," Amelia said.

"Such a harsh critique for your cousin."

"I only call it as I see it."

"Amelia, please introduce me to the gentleman you are discussing your family with," her mother said from behind.

Amelia grimaced. "Forgive me. Mother, I am pleased to introduce Nathanial Nilsson. Nathanial, this is my mother, Mrs. Charlotte Campbell."

"It is a pleasure, Mrs. Campbell," Nathanial said.

"You must be related to the other Mr. Nilsson," Charlotte said.

"He is his twin brother," Amelia said.

"Twins," Charlotte said. "Your poor mother. Bless her."

"Yes, I'm sure twin boys were a challenge for her, but she met it graciously," Nathanial said.

"I have no doubt she would have," Charlotte said.

A voice from across the room called everyone to dinner and Nathanial offered to escort Amelia and her mother into the dining room. Her mother glanced at her approvingly, but Amelia pretended not to notice. The last thing she wanted was for her mother to push her into something she wasn't ready for. But at least her mother approved of her having conversations with him, even if Amelia never planned to take it further.

Amelia found her designated seat next to Nick again, with Madeline across from them. She hoped this time she wouldn't ruin the dinner conversation by speaking her mind. Thankfully, she was flanked by Mrs. Congdon and was able to ask questions about the house and the food.

As the dinner neared the end, Nick leaned closer. "I can't help but feel like you are ignoring me, Amelia."

"No, I'm just simply trying to behave by not talking about things of more importance."

Nick chuckled. "Did you have a nice chat with my brother?"

"I did," Amelia said.

"Madeline will be pleased. She insisted you two should meet," Nick said.

"Please, not you, too," Amelia said.

"Not looking to find a husband, then," Nick said with a teasing smile.

"No, I'm not."

"I'm happy to report that I didn't invite him at Madeline's insistence, but rather I wanted him in Duluth to help me with some business meetings. We head up to Willow Bay in a few days, and I've finalized the arrangements for you all to come with us. You get to drive while my brother and I take our boat."

"Do we have to ride in the car?" Amelia asked.

"No, but it will take longer by boat."

"I don't care. Riding in the boat sounds much more fun."

"Madeline will most likely not want to come along," Nick said.

"I can be Amelia's escort if she wants to go by boat," Henry chimed in from the other side of Nick.

"How thoughtful of you, Henry," Madeline said. "Are you sure you want to do that, Amelia? It will be a long day."

"Yes, I'm sure," Amelia said. "I only have to convince my mother."

"Have her talk with me," Mrs. Congdon said. "A boat ride can be good for the soul at times."

Amelia's smile widened, and for the first time since Daniel's passing, she was looking forward to something.

"I guess it's settled."

"You are positively glowing, cousin," Madeline said. "Perhaps this is just what you need after all. And maybe it will lighten your mood and you won't be so stuffy."

"Perhaps you're right," Amelia said, taking another sip of cabernet.

Chapter Five

Amelia leaned over the railing as far as she dared to look at the water below. She had been on cruises across the Atlantic but never a boat this small, and she loved it instantly.

Henry grabbed her arm. "Careful, cousin. Aunt Charlotte would kill me if I lost you to the lake."

"I'm fine, Henry."

She straightened and looked around, taking it all in. Nick encouraged them to find a place to sit as they were about to cast off.

"Do I have to sit?" Amelia asked. "I mean, you won't be sitting, right?"

"Right, but I would wager my sea legs are a bit sturdier than yours," Nick explained.

Amelia couldn't argue, so found a place out of the way but where she could still see views beyond the boat. It didn't take long for them to cast off, and her heart began to race. She was unable to contain her grin and craned her neck to get a better view of the water. She tried to keep from laughing as she shifted in her seat and lifted off the bench. She straightened, took a step forward, chided herself, and forced her body back into the seat.

I can't take this any longer.

Taking a deep breath, she bounded out of her seat and wandered about the boat.

"Do you struggle with following directions, Amelia?" Henry asked, trailing behind her.

"I just don't want to miss anything. Have you ever seen anything so beautiful? The water. The land. The boat. It's all so breathtaking."

"She is magnificent, isn't she?" Nick said, coming to stand next to her.

"Thank you for allowing me to ride on the boat with you," Amelia said. "How could I ever repay you?"

"Perhaps we can think on that for a time," Nick said with a twinkle in his eye.

"If I didn't know any better, I would think you're flirting with me, Mr. Nilsson."

"So formal, Amelia. I thought we were past that."

"Only when I think it might be necessary to avoid giving anyone the wrong impression. After all, you are to be married to my cousin soon."

Nick's smile faltered. "I wouldn't say soon. But you are correct. I'm supposed to marry her eventually."

Nathanial called for Nick to help, giving Amelia more time to scout her surroundings.

I could stay here forever. This place calms me somehow.

"Penny for your thoughts?" Henry asked.

"I was just thinking how much I love where you get to spend your summers, Henry."

"I love it too, but I won't be spending many more summers here."

"That's rather tragic," Amelia said.

"We have offices opening in New York, which is where Father is, and he plans for me to take over for him once the summer is over."

"Just like that?"

"We've been planning this for a year now. I requested one more summer here, and he agreed."

"That was kind of him."

"He loves it here as much as I do. But I'm also looking forward to a new start in New York. Perhaps you can come visit me there once I am settled. Boston is closer to New York than here."

"That would be lovely."

"Have you ever been to New York?" Nathanial asked, joining the conversation.

"Oh yes. We spent many summers there. Mother loves New York in the summertime," Amelia said. "And when Father was alive, he spent a lot of time there. Now, of course, George spends most of the time there when he is in America, so he took over our apartments."

"Who is George?" Nathanial asked.

"The favored son," Nick said.

"Listening in on our conversation is rude, Nick," Nathanial said.

"Perhaps, but I couldn't resist the chance to get under Amelia's skin."

"Maybe you should think more on how you can get under Madeline's skin and leave Amelia to me."

"Or you both can stop teasing me, and I will take care of my own skin," Amelia said.

Everyone laughed at her response, and the conversation turned to a boat passing by. Nathanial pointed out a moose that slipped from the trees to sip water along the shoreline. As they passed a treacherous area, Nick shared what to look for to avoid running aground on rocks sticking out of the water. Henry showed Amelia a lake trout before it slipped out of sight. He continued with stories about his fishing excursions catching walleye and lake trout one summer.

She asked about the purple and yellow flowers dotting the landscape, and Henry shared they were most likely marsh marigolds and violets. Enjoying the conversations, time slipped by too fast for her. She could have stayed on the water all day.

As the boat neared its destination, her thoughts drifted to how she could manage to stay in Duluth after her mother decided it was time to leave. Nick moved to stand next to her again, and he had an adoring look on his face. She couldn't stop studying him instead of the water.

Nick turned his look of adoration on Amelia. "Might I suggest you look ahead, Amelia, for we are here. Welcome to Willow Bay."

Amelia gasped. The beauty of the coastal town took her breath away. Rows of buildings and homes dotted the hillside. A well-cared-for marina was on the left side of the bay, while a wooded area with a brownstone home peeking through the trees of the point on the other.

"How do you ever leave here?" Amelia asked.

Nick chuckled. "It is always difficult."

"Yes, it is. Which is why I never plan to leave, unlike my dear brother here," Nathanial said while getting ready to dock.

Nick joined the activity, and as the boat slowed to a stop, he hollered at a gentleman standing next to a piling.

"Tie her off."

"Was your brother telling the truth, and you plan to leave here someday?" Amelia asked.

"It isn't my first choice," Nick said, "but Madeline doesn't want to live here. She wants to live in the city."

"Duluth?" Amelia asked.

"No, Saint Paul. It's what she wants, and it's what she's used to, I guess. Plus, the hope is it will allow our own business holdings to expand a little more there."

"Is that so necessary?" Henry asked. "After all, you do own the entirety of Willow Bay."

"You own the town?" Amelia asked.

"Yes, you could say it makes up the bulk of the family business," Nathanial said, his grin lighting up his face.

"Gracious," Amelia said.

"Time to disembark," Nick said with a hint of sadness in his voice.

She wondered if it was due to the conversation about him leaving the lake or Willow Bay. She was experiencing this place for the first time and was saddened by the thought of having to leave in a few days. She couldn't imagine the depth of emotions if one lived here their whole life.

Henry escorted her down the ramp and across the docks to a waiting car. Nick and Nathanial stayed back, explaining they would be along shortly. They needed to provide instructions on what to do with the supplies and goods they had brought with them.

Amelia asked Henry a few questions about the town as they drove along, but he admitted this was his first time coming to Willow Bay, too. He didn't know much about it, other than the Nilsson family had founded it. It didn't take long to reach the other side of the bay, and they were driving toward the big brownstone home she had seen from the water.

"What a spectacular house," Amelia said. "It appears to be a brownstone mansion and not a smaller house, as I originally thought."

"We actually call this redstone, for the hue is more of a reddish color than brown," Henry said.

"It looks like they have three or four stories. And look at that wrap-around porch leading to the front of the home. I was not expecting a place of this stature in a small town. It is beautiful."

"The carport is quite impressive as well," Henry said.

"And the large windows are glorious. I bet the views are incredible," Amelia said.

"Oh look, Amelia," Henry said. "There is a tower rising toward the sky on the front of the house with a lookout at the top. I bet those views are the best."

"I see lots of brownstones back home, but this place is quite something. The ornate dormers and gables really send it over the top," she said.

"Nick told me that his father, Mr. Billy Nilsson, was the one who built it for his wife when the twins were young," Henry explained.

The car slowed to a stop under the carport, and the driver opened the rear passenger door, allowing Amelia and Henry to climb out.

"Your luggage will be taken inside for you, Mr. Granger, Miss Campbell."

"Thank you so much, um, Johnston, was it?"

"Yes, Miss Campbell," Johnston said.

"Have you been their driver long?" Amelia asked. "I only ask because you did such a splendid job."

"My primary position is to care for the Nilsson family horses and carriages. I only just recently learned to drive."

"Perhaps you could teach me," Amelia said.

"Not giving up on that, are you?" Henry asked with a chuckle.

"Oh, never mind," Amelia said.

"Yes, Miss Campbell," Johnston said.

A door off the carport was opened by a young gentleman who welcomed Amelia and Henry. He introduced himself as Sundgaard, the butler. He explained he would assist with anything they needed during their stay.

"Thank you, Sundgaard," Amelia said and followed him indoors.

Henry was on her heels as they walked through the house to the sitting room. She noticed her mother, aunt, and a stranger, who resembled the Nilsson twins, huddled together discussing parties planned for the summer. They grew quiet when they noticed her.

"Ah, Miss Campbell and Mr. Granger, it is a pleasure to have you in our home. I am Mrs. Wilhelm Nilsson, Miss Campbell," Mrs. Nilsson said, crossing the room to greet her.

"The pleasure is mine, Mrs. Nilsson," Amelia said. "I just love your town and the bay here."

"Yes, it is one of those places that one could fall in love with," Mrs. Nilsson said.

Henry greeted Mrs. Nilsson, and as they talked, Amelia excused herself to go embrace her mother.

"Mother, I hope it was a pleasant ride up."

"It was, but my goodness, child, you are positively windblown."

"Perhaps we should have our new guests taken to their rooms so they can freshen up before dinner. Sundgaard, show them where to go, please," Mrs. Nilsson said.

A small commotion near the front of the house announced Nick and Nathanial's arrival. When they walked into the room, they scanned the area, saw their mother, and went directly to her. Amelia noticed the delight on Mrs. Nilsson's face. They obviously had a close relationship, and Amelia couldn't keep from smiling.

They started discussing the boat ride when Amelia yawned. She tried to stifle it, but the fresh air and journey on the water caught up to her. Her mother gave her usual look of disapproval, and Amelia's cheeks flamed.

"We must not keep our guests from getting settled," Mrs. Nilsson said, rescuing Amelia. Sundgaard, please show Mr. Granger and Miss Campbell their rooms."

"Yes, Mrs. Nilsson," Sundgaard said. Turning toward Amelia, he said, "If you wouldn't mind following me, miss."

Amelia and Henry excused themselves and followed the butler. She could hear Nick and Nathanial explain they were going to freshen up as well. She had just reached the top of the stairs when she caught Nick watching her from below. She flashed him a grin before disappearing around the corner.

Sundgaard deposited Henry first, then led Amelia to a corner room. It had views of the bay, the front yard, and the lake beyond. She leaned against the glass on one of the windows as she stared at the sparkling water.

"I wish I never had to leave."

Chapter Six

Amelia let her mind wander while Ivy secured the last stands of hair.

"Have you ever seen anything like this place?" Amelia asked.

"I would say you are quite smitten," Ivy said.

"Of the lake and Willow Bay, absolutely," Amelia said. "I don't think I have ever been more in love."

Ivy giggled and said, "There now. You're all set."

Amelia glanced at her reflection in the mirror. "Looks perfect as always, Ivy."

"You'd better make your way downstairs."

"You're probably right." Amelia stood to leave and asked, "Do you have good accommodations?"

"They are great for what I need, and the view from my room is pretty."

"I'm glad to hear that," Amelia said. "Perhaps sometime later today, you and I can go for a walk, maybe go down by the water."

"I would like that, but only if you have time."

"I will let you know," Amelia said and left to go down to lunch.

When she entered the room, she spotted her mother and crossed to greet her.

"How was your morning, darling?" her mother asked.

"It was just what I needed after yesterday's travel. I wrote letters to George and Mrs. Thompson and ate a light breakfast in the morning room. What about you? Were you able to get some rest?"

"I was able to sleep in a little. I also wrote some letters. I think Aunt Lucille and I will be attending a small reception with Mrs. Nilsson later for some women in town. Apparently, she holds one once a month."

"That sounds lovely. I'm hoping to take a walk along the water this afternoon if you don't mind. I've asked Ivy to be my escort."

"Very well. Just be sure and wear a hat."

"Yes, Mother."

They were called into lunch, and after getting settled at the table, Amelia made small talk with Madeline. Amelia discovered Madeline had a room just down from her, but it faced the backyard. It didn't have a good view of the lake, but Madeline didn't seem to care.

"I would think with you becoming a Mrs. Nilsson someday, you would want a better room," Amelia said.

"I don't really care for the views as much as you, Amelia. I only care for the size, which is amply large enough and very luxurious," Madeline said. "Besides, one day I will be part owner of this home and will have a pick of my room, so it doesn't matter which room I'm in now."

"That is one way to look at it, I guess."

Madeline's words grated on her. She decided to change the subject and asked how long they planned to stay in Willow Bay.

"Only for a day or two. We have plans with the Congdons on the weekend, so we are going to head back in time for that," Madeline said.

Amelia's shoulders drooped, and she tried to hide her disappointment. She didn't trust her cousin not to give her a hard time about it. She didn't talk for the rest of lunch, and when she was able to get away, she went in search of Ivy. She found her arranging a bouquet of wildflowers on Amelia's nightstand.

"Oh, how lovely," Amelia said.

"They are not from me. Mr. Nick and Mr. Nathanial wanted to make sure you and Miss Madeline had flowers in your room."

"That was nice of them."

"I agree," Ivy said. "I hear you were searching for me."

"Yes, are you ready for that walk?"

"Oh goodness, that sounds lovely. I will go fetch my hat and meet you out front."

"See you there," Amelia said and went to rummage for her own hat.

She found it quickly, then wound her way downstairs and out to the front porch. She watched a few people working in the yard but turned to the sound of a door opening and closing. She stood more at attention when she saw it was Mrs. Nilsson.

"Expecting someone else, Miss Campbell?" Mrs. Nilsson asked.

"Please call me Amelia, and yes, Ivy and I are going to walk along the lake."

"You seem quite taken with our Willow Bay," Mrs. Nilsson said.

"I suppose you could say that."

"I heard of your poor fiancé. How tragic for you."

"Yes, it was quite a shock, Mrs. Nilsson."

"Please, I wish you would call me Kathleen. My late husband, Billy, and I always tried to keep up with the protocols and societal norms only when entertaining out-of-town guests or business acquaintances, but at the end of the day, we are just bay people."

"Bay people?" Amelia asked.

"Yes. Well, Billy was born and raised here, of course. And he met me when I was very young when he was on a business trip to New York City," Kathleen said. "We wrote letters for a year before he came back to the city. He proposed, and about a year later, we married."

"What a lovely story," Amelia said. "How long after you were married did you move here?"

"I actually moved here about six months before we got married," Kathleen said. "My mother was struggling with the death of my sister. She had always been ill, but it was still tragic when she died. And my father, well, he was always busy working. So, when I came here for a visit, I didn't want to go home, and Mamma told me I could stay."

"Mamma?" Amelia asked.

"Yes, you have not met her yet. She is quite wonderful. It's interesting really."

"What's interesting?"

"My boys say you remind them of her."

"Oh, I will consider that a compliment."

"It is a high compliment. Now I do believe Ivy is walking toward us. Enjoy your walk."

"Thank you. Have a pleasant time at your reception."

Amelia watched Kathleen walk away and was puzzled at their exchange.

She shook her head and turned toward Ivy. "Are you ready for our walk?"

"Yes, let's go."

They wandered down the side of the ridge toward the lake and walked along the water's edge. Amelia would stop and stare or skip a rock. At one point, she sat on a boulder to watch the boats coming and going out of the bay. She listened to the small waves slide over the rocks along the shore and breathed deeply. She was thankful Ivy knew her well enough to know she wanted the quiet while she was taking it all in.

"I can't get over the beauty of it, Ivy. I keep trying to come up with a plan that would allow me to stay longer. I wonder if there are some rooms I can rent in town for a bit."

"How long are you thinking? I'm not sure your mother would go for you staying by yourself in a rented room."

"I want to extend my time here for as long as I can. I suppose you're right about Mother not wanting me to stay in those types of accommodations." Amelia paused, let out a sigh, and said, "I know I can't remain here forever, but I believe this is the best place to help me recover, so to speak."

"It truly is beautiful. And after a loss such as yours, it is understandable that you would need some time. Perhaps a rejuvenation of the soul is needed. And what better place than this I suppose."

"I couldn't have said it better myself," a female voice said.

Amelia turned and discovered an elderly woman who had a look of strength about her. Her gray hair was pulled back into a tight bun, and she had a twinkle in her eyes that reminded Amelia of Nick's. The woman studied Amelia before looking out at the water.

"She is quite something, isn't she?" the woman said.

Amelia stood. "It is one of the most beautiful things I have ever seen. And I live close to the ocean on the east coast."

"You must be Miss Amelia Campbell. But forgive me. My name is Tuva Nilsson. Welcome to my Willow Bay and our gichi-gammi."

"Oh yes, of course, Mrs. Nilsson," Amelia said. "It's such a pleasure to meet you. Mr. Nilsson mentioned we should meet, so I'm excited we came upon you during our walk.

"Please call me Tuva. I'm going to take a guess that the Mr. Nilsson you are referring to is Nick."

"Please call me Amelia. And yes, what a perfect guess."

"Well, he mentioned you to me. So, it was purely an assumption on my part."

Amelia's cheeks warmed, and she looked out at the water.

"No need to be embarrassed, my dear," Tuva said. "They were all gracious and lovely things. He admires you. But he admires anyone who keeps up with his conversation."

"Is he a bit arrogant, then?" Amelia asked.

Tuva laughed. "That is a possibility. Or perhaps he is just confident and knows who he is and what he wants."

"To have the freedom to have such confidence."

Tuva's eyebrow lifted. She acted like she was going to say something more but looked out at the water instead.

Ivy shifted, causing a stone to tumble down the bank into the water.

"Oh, Ivy. Please forgive my rudeness," Amelia said. "Mrs. Nilsson, this is Ivy."

"It's a pleasure to meet you, Miss Ivy."

"Likewise, Mrs. Nilsson," Ivy said with a half curtsy.

"Such formality," Tuva said. "It's not needed here, for we are among friends."

Amelia linked arms with Ivy. "Something I tell her often."

"So, you wish to stay in our bay?" Tuva asked.

Amelia nodded. "I do, but I'm not sure it's possible."

"Well, one never knows what the future will bring," Tuva said. "I never would have believed I would end up living in such a place as this. And yet, here I am, and the matriarch of the bay at that."

"Such a splendid perspective," Ivy said.

"I agree," Amelia said. "Perhaps something will open up for me."

"You must come have tea with me one afternoon before you leave," Tuva said.

"We should confirm those plans soon, I'm afraid," Amelia said. "We are leaving in two days."

"How sad," Tuva said. "I will plan something with you soon."

Amelia agreed. Tuva made a final comment about the beauty of the day before walking on. When Tuva disappeared around the point, Amelia turned to Ivy and suggested they continue their walk before the day got away from them. They kept quiet for the rest of their outing until they approached the house.

"Thank you for always treating me as a friend and not a servant," Ivy said.

"You are my friend. I don't know what I would do without you."

"One of these days, protocol may interfere, but I will always remember these moments when we walk as equals," Ivy said, and disappeared into the house.

Amelia walked onto the porch and sat on a nearby bench to gaze out at the water. She thought more about her conversation with Tuva. She wasn't sure how much time had passed, but the butler appeared and handed her a note from the very woman she had been thinking about.

It simply said.

Our afternoon tea has been confirmed. Tomorrow at two. I look forward to our conversation. Tuva.

Chapter Seven

Nathanial leaned toward Amelia as she lifted her fork to her mouth. "I heard you met our grandmother?"

Amelia paused and smiled. "She is quite the woman."

"I also heard you are meeting her for tea tomorrow."

"That is true," she said. "I'm looking forward to it."

"As you should," Nathanial said, taking a sip of pinot.

"How is it that *you* are having tea with their grandmother?" Madeline said, her sharp tone competing with her dark glare.

Amelia closed her eyes briefly, taking a deep breath. "I met her yesterday, and she asked me to tea."

"This just isn't fair," Madeline said.

"This isn't a competition," Amelia said. "Plus, you are to be wed into this family, so I'm sure you will have lots of opportunities for tea with their grandmother." She caught her mother's disapproval, and her ears burned as she apologized with her eyes.

Turning toward Madeline, she said, "Come now, cousin, let's not quarrel."

"Easy for you to say. You're getting all the attention," Madeline said.

Amelia struggled to keep her annoyance in check and contemplated a brusque retort, but focused on chewing her food instead. Madeline attempted to continue the conversation but was stopped by her own mother.

Nathanial leaned close to Amelia. "I worry for Nick."

Her head whipped around, stopping inches from Nathanial's face. They stared at each other longer than was appropriate. She abruptly turned away, reaching for her wine. She took a bigger gulp than intended, but managed it without causing a scene.

She leaned toward Nathanial. "As we have discussed before, you really don't seem to care for the match."

"No, I don't."

"Whispering at the table isn't very polite, Nathanial," Nick said from across the table.

"We can finish this conversation later," Nathanial said to Amelia. Turning to his brother, he said, "We are just bonding over something we might have in common."

"And what is that?" Nick asked.

"How much we don't care for people's poor attitudes." Madelina gasped.

"Boys, for heaven's sake," Mrs. Nilsson said. "You must stop being so rude. What will our guests think?"

Amelia tried hiding her grin, focused on her food, and didn't look at her mother. She could feel her mother staring at her unapprovingly, so kept her head down for the rest of dinner. As soon as she was able to escape, she went for a walk outside.

The sun was just setting as Amelia reached the edge of the point. She loved watching the oranges and pinks of the sky dance across the waves of the water.

"Beautiful sunset tonight."

Amelia turned around, expecting to see Nathanial, but saw Nick walking toward her. Her heart skipped a beat, which caught her off guard, and her eyes widened. Fearful of any unwanted feelings, she forced away any thoughts on what it could mean.

She looked back out at the water. "That it is. It makes me want to paint. Which is something I haven't done in so long."

"You should paint," Nick said. "This place gives lots of opportunity for inspiration."

"Where is Madeline?"

"She said she had a headache, but I think she's trying to punish me because of the conversation at dinner."

"Which is why I worry for Nick," Nathanial said from behind.

"I don't want to get in between whatever is going on here," she said.

"It's nothing. It's no secret that Nathanial is not overly fond of my fiancé," Nick said.

Nathanial shrugged. "Perhaps it's true, but you both know this, so why is it news?"

"I came out here for peace and quiet, not to get in the middle of a row between brothers," Amelia said.

Nathanial offered his arm to her. "My apologies. Come along. Let's walk across the ridge and enjoy the quiet and beauty of the evening."

She accepted the offer but felt bad for Nick and glanced back at him. He had a strange look on his face as their eyes met before Nick looked away and out toward the water.

"He seems upset," Amelia said.

"I think he's realizing he has committed himself to someone who wasn't honest about who she really is, and he isn't sure what to do with that knowledge now."

"You're probably right. Let's not talk about it any longer, though."

"Good idea," Nathanial said. "I would like to honor my promise of a quiet and peaceful walk, so I won't say another word until we find our way back into the house, and I bid you good evening."

Nathanial kept his word until a sigh escaped her lips.

"Is everything okay?" Nathanial asked. "Oh, I promised I wouldn't say anything. Sorry."

Amelia's lips lifted in response. She squeezed his arm and giggled. He joined her until their laughter faded into the quiet of the evening. Their comfortable silence remained until the evening light changed to darkness, and they moved indoors.

Nathanial kissed her hand softly, said good night, and disappeared to a different part of the house. She went to her room, shut the door behind her, and rested against it. The soft glow of candlelight only lit part of the room, so it took her a moment to realize a woman was sitting in the shadows.

Amelia slammed her hand against her chest. "Mother, for heaven's sake. You startled me."

"Sorry, my darling. I had no idea you would be out walking for such a length of time."

"I was enjoying the fresh air and the beauty of the sunset," Amelia said as she went to sit across from her mother.

"And perhaps enjoying the conversation and attention of a certain gentleman."

"Please don't do that. I'm not ready for a courtship or another engagement or anything like it right now."

"I'm only thinking about your future."

"Yes, I know. But George set up funds for me to be a little independent while I get my bearings again."

"Let's not pretend you're mourning a great love."

"That is low, even for you."

"My apologies, but we both know it's true."

"Was he the love of my life? Perhaps not," Amelia said. "I did care for him, though, and I was excited about the future we were going to build together. He understood me, and he would have at least allowed me to be myself. He was a wonderful man, and I'm so very sad for losing him and losing the life I would have had with him."

"I'm sorry. I guess I didn't realize how much you cared," her mother said.

"I'm not heartless, Mother."

"I know. It's just you keep your true inner feelings from me."

"Only because I'm never allowed to show them to you."

"That's not fair."

"Maybe, but it's how I feel."

"Then I have failed as a mother," her mother said while standing.

Amelia stood watching her warily as she walked toward her. She paused briefly to caress her daughter's cheek and left the room.

Amelia sank to the floor, burying her face in her hands. She let her grief dampen her fingers until an unexpected weight was lifted. She wiped her face and moved to a chair. She stared at the water through the window until the shadows of the room darkened. She readied for bed, crawled into the coolness of the sheets, and dreamed of a lost love sinking below the sea.

Chapter Eight

Amelia followed the path to a smaller home that mirrored the red stone mansion. It didn't have a tower, and it was only two stories instead of three, but it had a matching wrap-around porch along with other similar features. She walked onto the porch and started to knock when the door flew open to a laughing Tuva.

"I'm so delighted you could make it," Tuva said. "Come in, please come in."

Amelia was led to an enclosed back porch. Massive, screened windows graced three walls allowing a gentle breeze to cool the room. Tea was already set up on a small table, with cookies and sandwiches adorning the tray. Tuva showed her where to sit and she settled into the cushions of the couch. The sound of waves crashing against rock caught Amelia's attention, and she looked across the well-manicured backyard to the lake beyond. The view of the water here was breathtaking.

"This is my favorite spot in the house," Tuva said.

"I can see why."

"She speaks to me here. Sometimes, it's like she's singing."

"She?"

"Lady Superior," Tuva said. "I'm sure I sound like an old fool. But her waves crashing against the rock and the wind rushing over her are like an old friend singing the joys of a good life."

"That's beautiful."

"It always calms me."

"I know how you feel," Amelia said.

"Ah, so she sings to you too."

"I guess she does."

Tuva sang her favorite song about the lake. It told of the lake's fury and a hope for calm. When the song came to an end, Tuva explained that her brother-in-law had written it years ago. Tea was served with a bite to eat, and a peacefulness nestled around them as they watched the dark blue waves dance. Amelia hummed the song she had just learned and thought of a boat caught in a storm.

Pulling herself out of her reverie, Amelia said, "I must thank you for inviting me."

"It's my pleasure. I believe you and I were meant to be friends."

"I like the thought of that."

"I felt that connection much the same as I did with my dear friend Minwaadizi long ago."

"Is that her?" Amelia asked, pointing to a portrait of Tuva standing next to another woman.

"Yes, that's her. She was my friend. My sister. My companion after my husband died. And when she passed on, I believed I would not find another friend like her. Then you walked along the banks of my bay, and I knew Minwaadizi sent you to me so that I wouldn't die alone."

Amelia sipped her tea quietly, contemplating what Tuva had just said. Thoughts of leaving drifted into her mind and she frowned.

"Is everything okay?" Tuva asked.

"I'm saddened by the realization that I'm leaving soon."

"About that. I have a proposition for you."

"A proposition?"

"Yes. You see, I know I appear spry, but in reality, I'm limited on what I can do some days. The family is busy with their lives, and I could use someone to come visit me. Check on me. Take me into town. Help me with my correspondence. My housekeeper assists me with those things, but it would be nice to give her a break."

"You're really looking for a companion to help you?"

"We can make that our excuse."

"I'm not sure what to say."

"You don't need to respond right away. I know a woman of your station doesn't need a job, and perhaps having you as my unofficial companion is beneath what is expected of you. I was hesitant in offering such a position to you. But I know you are trying to find a reason to stay, and I would like to think helping an old woman is a reason worth contemplating."

"Could Ivy stay?" Amelia asked.

"Of course," Tuva said. "You could remain in the big house. I've already discussed this with Kathleen, and she has agreed."

"I don't want to be an inconvenience to anyone," Amelia said.

"You wouldn't be an inconvenience. I only ask you to come visit me every day, and you can always bring Ivy with you."

"I will need to discuss this with Mother, but I would love to stay if it works out for me to do so."

"Splendid," Tuva said. "I will be at dinner tonight and will discuss it with her as well."

The conversation turned to other things. Tuva shared about her journey to Willow Bay and its founding, and Amelia talked about her fiancé and losing him to the Titanic. Amelia realized she could talk about anything with Tuva. The hour passed quickly, and when it was time for her to leave, she was excited about the prospect of staying in Willow Bay.

Chapter Nine

Madeline spun around, glaring at Amelia. "You can't be serious."

The cousins and the Nilsson brothers had gone for a walk after breakfast, and Amelia had shared her exciting news with the rest of them. Tuva had kept her promise and talked with her mother the night before. They had agreed it might be good for her to stay for the rest of the summer, and Amelia had received confirmation of her mother's agreement right before their walk.

"Of course, I'm serious. And I'm excited about staying here," Amelia said. "I don't understand why you're so upset with me about this, or ever for that matter."

She studied her cousin while she waited for a response. Madeline started and stopped her sentence several times, and her lower lip stuck out in a pout. Not missing the exchange of glances between the Nilsson brothers, Amelia almost said something to encourage her cousin, but was cut off.

"I was so excited when I heard my favorite cousin was coming for the summer," Madeline said, fidgeting with the front of her dress. "I thought we would be planning parties and picnics. But instead, I've had to compete with you for the attention of my fiancé and my fiancé's family."

"I'm not your competition, Maddy," Amelia said, reaching out to squeeze her cousin's hand. "I've barely even seen Nick. And I'm not taking your place in this family. I'm just helping Mrs. Nilsson for a few short months. It's almost like a job."

"You and I both know Aunt Charlotte would never allow you to stay if it was for a job."

"Perhaps you're right. But I'm only staying to help Mrs. Nilsson, Nick's grandmother. Not to spend time with Nick."

Madeline only nodded and clasped Nick's arm as the group walked on. A bend in the path brought the house into view, and Amelia sighed, hoping the conversation was over. Amelia noticed a clump of purple flowers and paused to pick one, causing the procession to halt again.

"I, for one, think it's a grand idea," Henry said, breaking into the silence.

"You would take her side," Madeline said, turning to face her brother.

"What side?" Henry asked. "There are no sides."

"Madeline, if you want to stay, you can stay as well," Nick said.

"Why haven't you asked until now?" Madeline asked.

"I've asked in the past, and you always said you couldn't handle being away from the city for so long. I honestly didn't think you would want to stay," Nick said.

"He has a point, sis," Henry said.

"Well, that was before I thought I needed to worry about anything," Madeline said, sending Amelia a look of resentment.

Amelia moved to give her cousin a hug. "I would never try to take your fiancé away, Maddy. It hurts me that you would even think I would do such a thing."

"You just seem to be able to talk with his family better than I," Madeline said, leaning into Amelia's embrace.

"I will try and take up all her time when she isn't spending time with Gram," Nathanial said.

"See, there is nothing to worry about," Henry said. "Not that I think you have anything to worry about anyway.

"I would be happy to trade rooms if you wanted to stay," she said, looping her arm with Madeline's as they continued their walk.

"You just want the bigger room," Madeline said.

Amelia stopped, let go of her cousin, and threw up her arms. "No, I'm just trying to give you a room with a great view."

"My view is just fine," Madeline said, stopping as well.

"You're just being difficult, as always," Henry said, moving to stand next to his sister. "Do you want to stay or not? I could talk with Mother and see if you and I can stay on for a little while longer."

"The Congdons are having their big party this weekend to kick off the summer activities. I don't want to miss it," Madeline said.

"We could go to Duluth for the weekend, and I would be happy to escort you back," Henry said.

"You would do that?" Madeline asked.

"Yes, but you and I both know once you get to Duluth, you will just want to stay there. So why are you giving everyone such a difficult time?" Henry asked.

"I suppose you're right. I don't mean to be difficult. I just want to make sure my concerns are shared. I'm sorry, Amelia," Madeline said.

"Thank you, Maddy. I'm sorry too. I didn't mean to make you feel bad," Amelia said.

Nick held out his arm. "Come, Maddy. I will escort you inside before I must head to the docks."

"Why are you going to the docks?" Amelia asked as they neared the porch.

"He goes there often," Madeline said.

"We have a shipment coming in," Nathanial said.

"Oh, that seems like a lot of work," Amelia said.

"It's just some supplies we ordered but couldn't get here until today," Nick said.

"I thought maybe you would be heading out on the water," Amelia said.

"Not today, but I can let you know when we are going out again, and you can come with us," Nathanial said.

"That would be fantastic," Amelia said, unable to keep her excitement from showing.

"Amelia," Ivy called from the porch. "Your mother is looking for you."

"Thank you for a lovely walk, but I must go. Please excuse me," she said and walked toward Ivy.

She followed Ivy into the house and caught up with her on the stairs.

They were almost to her room when Ivy asked, "What was that all about?"

"What was what about?"

"Miss Madeline was shooting daggers into your back. Mr. Henry was looking annoyed watching his sister. And the Nilsson brothers were both watching you walk away with a look in their eyes."

"A look in their eyes?"

"You know, almost like a look of desire," Ivy said.

"No, please, not that. At least not from Nick."

"Maybe, but Mr. Nathanial Nilsson sure had that look."

"I'm not ready for that," Amelia said.

"I know, but I think when you are ready, you could have someone," Ivy said.

"Maybe, but I could use some time before we talk about such things again," Amelia said.

"Of course, Amelia," Ivy said.

"Are you excited about staying in Willow Bay?" Amelia asked. "I guess I never asked if you wanted to stay."

"I'm very much looking forward to it. I enjoy it here too."

Amelia walked into her room, and her mother asked Ivy to give them a minute. When the door shut, her mother dove into one of her favorite lectures about proper etiquette. She added a reminder on the importance of Amelia staying above reproach in all things. Amelia settled in because when her mother started in on such a lesson, it could take a while.

Ivy pinned the last strand of Amelia's hair in place before Amelia's mother walked into the bedroom.

"You always do such lovely work, Ivy," Charlotte said.

"Thank you, Mrs. Campbell."

"What do you think of my dress, Mother?" Amelia asked, standing to twirl around slowly.

"Goodness, child. Don't twirl. It isn't ladylike, and you will mess up Ivy's great work."

"My apologies, Mother, but still, what do you think?" she asked, smoothing out the front of her dress.

"It's lovely, darling," her mother said, and turned to Ivy. "Can you leave us please, Ivy?"

"Yes, Mrs. Campbell," Ivy said and left the room.

"What have I done now?" Amelia asked as she put on her gloves.

It was the night before the Grangers and her mother were returning to Duluth, and the Nilssons had planned a party. Some of their friends from Duluth had come into town to join the festivities. Amelia thought this was the perfect night to wear her new party dress. She hoped her mother might be pleased with it, but based on her response, she started to second guess her choice and contemplated picking a different one.

"Why do you always think I'm going to criticize you?" her mother asked.

"Because when you ask to speak to me alone, it's usually because you want to admonish me for something," Amelia said.

"That hurts my feelings, Amelia."

"I don't mean to hurt your feelings."

"Well, just the same, the reason I wanted to speak with you is just to remind you to behave at tonight's function."

"Wasn't that the reason for your speech earlier today?"

"Oh, Amelia," she said, throwing her arms in the air. "What is a mother to do? It is my job to make sure you are raised properly and presented to the world correctly. When you push back, it makes my job that much more difficult."

"I don't mean to push back. But I also can't pretend to be something I'm not."

"Like it or not, you are a Campbell. That is a part of who you are. And as such, it's important you represent yourself in a way that makes a Campbell proud. That would make your father proud."

Amelia studied her mother and noticed the sadness wash over her face before it was replaced with the empty expression she usually had.

"You're sad."

"I am not," her mother said, waving her off.

"Mother, you are sad. It's because of me, isn't it?" Amelia tilted her head. "Is it because I'm staying?"

"I understand why you're staying here, Amelia. I just can't help but feel like part of the reason you're staying is because you are running away from me as well."

"That isn't it. I swear it isn't. And I know you don't like me to swear. I just haven't felt like I could breathe since Daniel died. That is, until we came here."

"I know. A light went out in you after his death. A light that seems to be trying to come back here. I just don't want to lose you."

"Do you want to stay?" Amelia asked. "I'm sure they would understand."

"Goodness, no. My schedule is full, and I will be needed back home in Boston in a few weeks for my charity duties there. But I will miss my companion."

Amelia was stunned by her mother's vulnerability. For all her pomp and protocol, she still had feelings. She tried to comfort her mother, but she brushed her off. Trying to hide her hurt, Amelia suggested they join the party.

As they walked into the hallway, her mother flung her arms around her. Shocked, Amelia hesitated but wrapped her arms around her. A lump formed in the back of her throat, and she wanted to prolong the connection between them.

She started to say something but was cut off as her mother pulled away, smoothed the front of her dress, and rushed off. Amelia wiped a tear away, and caught her mother dab at her own eyes before she disappeared around the corner.

Chapter Ten

THE SOUND OF THE water slapping against the boat lulled Amelia to sleep. A month had passed since her decision to stay in Willow Bay, and this was only the fourth time she had been allowed back on the water. This time, though, Tuva had come with her.

"As much as I enjoy a good nap on the water, I would recommend not falling asleep just yet. I think Nathanial has prepared a light lunch," Tuva said.

Amelia opened her eyes and smiled. "I can't help it. She relaxes me."

"Yes, the lake is one that can soothe, but she can also be fierce and take away."

"I have seen some of her waves crash against the bay, so I can only imagine what it must be like out here when a storm hits."

"When we first moved to Willow Bay, before it was Willow Bay, our homestead was destroyed by her waves in a storm," Tuva said.

"Wow, I can't imagine, and yet you stayed. Look at all you created," Amelia said, sweeping her hand toward the cove in the distance.

"Gram, Melia, Nathanial has a few things set out to eat if you're hungry," Nick called.

Amelia sat up straight at the nickname. "What did you call me?"

"Oh, I'm sorry. It just slipped out," Nick said. "I don't have to call you that, though."

"No, it's fine," Amelia grinned. "It's just my brother is usually the only one to call me that. I was surprised to hear it, is all."

"Okay then. Melia it is," Nick said with a nod.

Nathanial popped on deck from the galley below, carrying a bottle of wine and some glasses. He raised the beverage, winked at Amelia, and said, "Your favorite."

Laughter bubbled out of her as she helped Tuva to the waiting meal. "What a splendid addition."

Tuva squeezed Amelia's arm in thanks as they both settled to eat. The conversation stayed light until Nathanial asked Nick how Maddy was faring in Duluth.

A wave of annoyance washed over Nick's face. "You know the answer to that, so why are you bringing it up."

"Is she not doing well?" Amelia asked.

"She continues to complain that Nick is here instead of Duluth. Nick offers to have her come here since he has work to do. She refuses and says she doesn't understand why he can't just make some excuse to get away to see her. The strange part is she never cared until a certain cousin took up residence here," Nathanial said.

"Nathanial, I don't think it's fair for us to judge," Tuva said. "Perhaps we should change the subject and talk about something different."

"Thank you, Gram," Nick said.

Amelia's cheeks grew hot while she tried to concentrate on her food and not the conversation.

"You are embarrassing our guest, boys," Tuva said.

Amelia waved her hand in the air. "No, I'm fine, really." Changing the subject, she said, "This fish is exceptional today. Perhaps it's because we are on the water."

"Or perhaps you are a lucky charm, and I was finally able to prepare it properly," Nathanial said.

Amelia grinned at him but turned to Tuva to say, "Tell me more about the beginning days. I can only imagine how isolating it must have been for you."

"Yes, it was isolating but we didn't feel lonely. We had each other and Isak's parents and brothers. Sometimes I long for the solitude of those days. But I'm mostly thankful for what my Isak and I built together."

"Something worth passing on," Nick said in between bites.

"Yes, partly," Tuva said. "But mostly, a place where anyone can live and work and be. A place that is truly special."

"What an amazing gift of a life so full of love and community. Plus, your creation of something so wonderful," Amelia said.

"Yes, my dear. You are so right," Tuva said. She paused, studying Amelia, and asked, "What are your plans next, Amelia? After you leave us."

"Oh my, I couldn't say," Amelia said. "I hope to stretch out my stay here longer and longer if I can get away with it."

"You seem to fit here, that's for sure," Nick said.

"I agree," Tuva said. "We will just work something out."

"Sounds wonderful to me," Amelia said.

The conversation turned to their hopes for weather for the rest of the week and plans for another boat ride soon. Amelia watched her companion and how she interacted with the brothers. The love between the three of them was obvious, but Tuva seemed to enjoy teasing Nick the most. Amelia was envious of their relationship and wished she had a relationship like theirs with her mother.

Forcing away thoughts of her mother, Amelia looked at the sky and noticed darker clouds approaching. She started to say something but realized the brothers had already sprung into action. They packed up the food provisions and prepared to head back to the bay.

"You never know when she will turn on you," Tuva said. "Perhaps she is matching the sudden sadness you seem to be feeling."

Amelia tried to hide her shock. "Sometimes I think I hide my feelings so well until someone reads me so perfectly."

"Never apologize for being real, my dear," Tuva said.

"Wise words, Gram," Nick said with tenderness.

Amelia's heart skipped a beat, and she hid her face.

"I think you and Melia should head inside soon," Nick said. "We may beat the rain back, but if not, I wouldn't want you to get soaked."

"I've been watching the sky and water longer than you've been alive, my boy," Tuva said. "I think I will make up my own mind on the matter."

Amelia chuckled. "And I will follow Tuva's lead, Nick. I trust her. Besides, you never know when learning to read the sky and water may come in handy for me."

Nick rolled his eyes playfully at her, grinned, and turned back to his chore.

The breeze turned into gusts of wind, and waves started to build, but the boat sailed steadily toward the cove.

Tuva closed her eyes, and Amelia studied her instead of the worsening weather.

"What are you thinking about?" Amelia asked.

Tuva opened her eyes, and Amelia caught a hint of sadness before Tuva's normal twinkle returned.

"I was thinking of rougher seas," Tuva said.

"No doubt the crossing, eh, Gram?" Nathanial said, walking past to secure a rope.

"The crossing?" Amelia asked.

"Yes, my Isak and I crossed the ocean from Sweden. There was a moment that we thought we weren't going to make it."

"That must have been so scary," Amelia said. "I sometimes wonder what Daniel's last thoughts were."

"No doubt they were of you," Nick said with the same gentleness as before. A strange look flashed across his face, and he turned back to his duties.

"How unkind of me to talk of my crossing when your beloved didn't make it," Tuva said.

"He wasn't my beloved," she said without thinking. "He was a wonderful man and I adored him, and I was looking forward to our life together, but it wasn't a love match. I was content with it at the time, though. Now, looking back, things seem so different somehow."

"Perhaps we should talk of something else if it's upsetting you," Tuva said.

"No, it's okay. Strange enough, it helps to talk about it."

"One must never keep their feelings bottled up, I always say. Talking about things helps heal."

"A philosophy that is in direct contrast to my mother's."

"Yes, I suppose she adopts the adage of keeping things close and your feelings ever closer. That same way of handling things is often the case for most. But I'm not like most, and I would wager neither are you," Tuva said.

Amelia laughed outright. "You could say that. I stand out when I shouldn't. I stand back when I shouldn't. I'm always in trouble. I often get irritated with society's way of handling things. So, yes, I suppose I'm not like most."

"I like it that way," Nathanial said.

"I think we all do," Nick said.

A warmth rushed through Amelia at being accepted for who she was without question. Something she only experienced with Ivy and occasionally her brother.

I think I finally found a place I belong, popped into her mind as she took in her surroundings.

Tears welled up as the boat slowed. If she could only stay here forever, she absolutely would.

Chapter Eleven

The breeze across the water was warm while Amelia walked along the shore. It was a clear night. The moon was bright, and it had pulled her outside. She was amazed at how quickly the summer had flown by. She was thankful for the extra time there but knew her mother would be expecting her to return home soon.

She spun around at the crunch of pebbles behind her. Her heart pounded as a dark figure moved. She froze but contemplated running. Perhaps it was foolish of her to walk alone at night, even though she had done it often.

"Did I alarm you, Melia?"

A slight laugh escaped Amelia's lips just as the moonlight washed over Nick's face.

"I thought perhaps I had been unwise for not walking with an escort for once. I always feel safe here, so never thought having someone come with me was necessary until a second ago."

"I think you are still perfectly safe," he said.

"What is Nathanial up to?" she asked.

"He is reading in the library. I was going over some numbers with Mother, then she turned in for the night. I picked out my own book, but caught you out here walking."

"And you thought you would interrupt my solitude?"

"Or perhaps keep you safe."

"Hm, but you mentioned that I am perfectly safe."

"Okay, you found me out. I wanted to come see you and make sure you were well."

"I am. I was just thinking about my time here the past couple of months and how quickly my stay has gone by."

"We will miss you," Nick said.

Amelia noticed a strange sound in Nick's voice. She wondered if it was sadness or nerves. The idea it could be the same longing Ivy had hinted at seeing at the beginning of the summer scared her. She didn't allow her mind to investigate it further.

"I should probably go in," Amelia said.

"It is getting late."

"Goodnight, sir," she said and started to walk past Nick.

Nick reached out, stopping her, and quickly let go. They were inches from each other. Amelia sucked in the air and took a step back.

"I'm sorry, Melia. I don't know why I did that."

"Perhaps if timing and things were different."

"Yes, perhaps if they were."

"But you are marrying my cousin, and I'm still getting my sea legs after a loss."

Nick smiled, and Amelia was sure it was because of her sea legs reference. But when he didn't say anything further, she turned and walked on.

"You will always have a friend in me," Nick said before she was out of earshot.

She kept walking toward the house without responding. She ignored the strange feelings welling up in her and pushed them as far down as she could. By the time she made it to her bedroom, she decided perhaps it was better she left soon, after all.

A knock at the door pulled her out of her reverie, and she said, "Come in."

"There you are," Ivy said, moving to sit in a chair by the fireplace.

"Is everything okay?" Amelia asked, crossing the room to sit opposite her friend.

"Yes, I'm just sad to share with you that we have finally heard from your dear mother. She has made all the final arrangements for our return home."

"You seemed apprehensive about sharing this with me."

"I was because I know you love it here and want to stay longer if possible."

"Yes, but perhaps it's best we return home."

"What's changed?" Ivy asked.

"Sometimes I think Mr. Nilsson might be having some, should I say, conflicting feelings about me," Amelia said.

"Which Mr. Nilsson would that be?" Ivy asked. "If you ask me, I can see both men are falling for you."

"It wouldn't be so bad if it were Nathanial," Amelia said.

"Then I'm going to wager a guess Nick has said or done something he shouldn't have."

"Not really. More hinting at something, and I won't be the woman who tore up her cousin's future."

"Smart woman, you are, but you are not the type of person that stands in anyone's way. You always give people all the room they need to feel and think for themselves, sometimes to your own detriment. You shouldn't always sacrifice yourself for everyone else, my friend. Besides, Madeline will have no trouble ruining any of her chances for her future all on her own."

"Maybe if I was at a different place in my life, but I'm not ready for another relationship. I want to enjoy my freedom for as long as I can."

"Do you think we will ever be back?" Ivy asked.

"Tuva has already hinted at future invitations for my return," Amelia said.

"That is wonderful news."

"I agree. I think it's good for us to go home for now, though."

"When do your cousins return?"

"They are arriving on Monday and will be here for the last couple weeks of our stay."

"That ought to be interesting. Especially if what you say is true about conflicting feelings."

"I'm going to stick close to Nathanial," Amelia said.

She was comforted by her plans to avoid Nick, but the thought of leaving still stung. She loved the bay, the water, and her friendship with Tuva, but she was terrified of falling in love if she stayed. She tried convincing herself she was happy to go home even as the pain in her heart grew.

Ivy said goodnight and left, and Amelia continued to wrestle with her mind long after she crawled into bed. Footsteps crunched on the path below, and she crossed to the window to peek out. Seeing Nick, she wondered if he was struggling with things, too.

Crawling back into bed, Amelia pushed her betraying thoughts aside. She tried focusing on her checklist for her departure home, but Nick and Nathanial danced across her mind as she drifted off to sleep.

Madeline walked into the house with such an air of confidence, Amelia took a step back. Guilt settled in the pit of her stomach at minimizing her cousin's concerns earlier in the summer. Henry walked in behind his sister and scanned the room. Once he caught Amelia's eye, he crossed to her.

"So wonderful to see you, Amelia," Henry said. "We wish we could have come sooner."

"Yes, it would have been wonderful, but our social calendars were kept quite full," Madeline said.

"I'm happy your summer was such a success," Amelia said.

Nick came out of nowhere and rushed to embrace his fiancé, and Amelia's guilt eased away. Perhaps she saw something that wasn't there, but she was still happy she was heading home. It would be better if she had some distance.

Henry asked Amelia all sorts of questions about her summer and linked arms with her while they walked further into the house. He remained by her side until Kathleen suggested he and Madeline get settled. Amelia offered to go up with Madeline, and she agreed. Madeline talked about the parties she attended while she settled into the same room she had stayed in before.

She was so engrossed in hearing all the details, she was caught off guard when Madeline asked, "So did you fall for a Nilsson brother this summer, cousin?"

"What?"

"Isn't that why you stayed?"

"Gracious, no!"

"Then why are your cheeks turning pink?"

"Maddy, I am not looking for, nor do I want a husband. At least not right now."

"Hm, I haven't made up my mind if I believe you or not," Madeline said.

"I can't believe we are discussing this again," Amelia said. "I don't want to find a husband right now. Or ever. I like my freedom, especially right now."

"Not ever?"

"Perhaps eventually, but I'm just not ready for that," Amelia said.

"Okay, fine. My apologies for reading into something that isn't there. I just have a hard time believing that any woman wouldn't be looking for a husband."

"Don't be sorry. I understand why you would feel that way."

"Perfectly normal to be jealous of my beautiful cousin staying in close proximity to my wonderful fiancé," Madeline said.

"He is ever your faithful servant. I assure you," Amelia said.

"When do you return home?" Madeline asked.

"I assumed you would have been told."

"I may have, but don't bother with other people's plans usually."

"Somehow, that doesn't surprise me," Amelia blurted out.

"Well, that was just rude."

"You're right. My apologies."

"I bought you a new dress," Madeline said, changing the subject.

Amelia couldn't believe how quickly Madeline could jump from one topic to the next with her primary focus on fashion and herself. None of it made sense to Amelia. But she was happy her cousin thought of her enough to buy her the gift of a new dress.

"That was so thoughtful of you," Amelia said. "Thank you."

"If I'm being perfectly honest. Mother suggested it and Henry encouraged us to do it. I just helped pick out the material and style."

"Thank you just the same. Do I get to see it?" Amelia asked.

"I gave instructions to the help to put it in your room."

Amelia's eyebrow lifted. "The help?"

"Yes, Izzy. I think that's her name."

"You mean Ivy?"

Amelia's annoyance returned, and she realized she would never be close to her cousin. She would always love her, but they would never be friends. Madeline's views on life would always bother her, and she was content in keeping her distance going forward.

"Do you mind terribly leaving now?" Madeline said.

"Oh, of course. My apologies," Amelia said and got up to leave.

"See you at dinner, cousin."

"See you at dinner," Amelia repeated and shut the door behind her.

She shook her head as she walked down the hallway toward her own bedroom. She would never understand her cousin's shallow thoughts and behaviors.

Chapter Twelve

Smoothing the front of her dress, Amelia stood in the corner, pretending to hide. The party had been equal to the one at the beginning of the summer, and she was tired. She had danced with several men but hadn't danced with either of the Nilsson brothers. Thinking they were avoiding her, she tried not to let it hurt.

"Trying to hide, are we?" Henry asked, handing Amelia a cocktail.

"You came out of nowhere," she said.

"Did I? Or did I perhaps just catch you lost in thought?" Henry asked.

"It's most likely the latter."

"I guessed as much. Do you want to talk about it?"

"Not really. I'm mostly just tired. And can't believe my time here is ending."

"Heading home after such an amazing summer will be hard. But you can always come visit me in New York if you get bored," Henry said.

"I would love that, even though New York isn't my favorite place."

"You would love what?" Nathanial asked, joining the conversation.

"Visiting my cousin, even though it would be in New York," Amelia said.

"Sounds stifling. No offense, Henry," Nathanial said with a gallant wave toward Henry. "It isn't the company as much as the city that would be challenging for me."

"I feel the same. But visiting my cousin might be a nice way to break things up," Amelia said.

"Yes, and one never knows who they might meet on such excursions," Henry said.

She knew her cousin was teasing her but still said, "I don't need to meet anyone."

"That comment gives hope to the rest of us," Nathanial said.

"I don't believe I have seen the two of you dance yet tonight," Henry said.

"You're reading my mind, my good man," Nathanial said. "I came over here just to ask Amelia to dance."

"I would be delighted," she said, handing her glass to Henry.

"Have fun, you two," Henry said.

Nathanial led Amelia to the dance floor just as the musicians started a new song. The two connected well on the dance floor, and by the time the second song started, she couldn't hide her enjoyment.

"Would you write to me when I go away?" she asked, surprising herself.

His grin widened. "I was going to ask if I could."

"That's just wonderful. I'm sorry I was so forward in asking, though."

"No need to apologize. You didn't come across as forward. I'm actually glad you asked, so I know you wouldn't have agreed out of pity if I had asked."

"Why would you think I would agree out of pity?"

"You seem to have a certain spark about you when my brother is around, and I thought perhaps you wouldn't want second best."

"You are not second best, Nathanial. You are one of a kind."

"Just like my brother is?"

"You are both equally wonderful in your own ways."

"And I'm the one who is not betrothed."

"That's not fair to say," she said, her excitement fading.

"I'm sorry. You're right, that wasn't fair. I must sound like a jealous schoolboy."

"No, just a silly one," Amelia said, teasing him.

Nathanial chuckled, and she joined him. They were still laughing when they walked off the dance floor in search of refreshments.

"What's so funny?" Madeline asked, coming to stand next to her.

"We are just teasing one another," Nathanial said.

Amelia knew Nathanial was irritated that Madeline interrupted their interlude. Thankfully, Nick rescued the situation and whisked Madeline away to get their own refreshments.

"You need to find peace with the match," Amelia said.

"I don't think I ever will."

"She is a bit silly, perhaps, but she seems to care for Nick."

"Or she cares for the family money."

"That's rather harsh. Especially since she comes from money herself."

"Perhaps, but it appears to be true sometimes. She doesn't seem to care at all about anything Nick wants. Nick has attempted to go along with whatever she wants ever since their engagement, even when she is being petty and childish—much to his detriment."

"Have you discussed your concerns with your brother?" Amelia asked.

"On several occasions, yes. But it doesn't seem to matter."

"Could he be stuck? That whole being honorable thing which both of you have."

"You know us well, Amelia."

"I did spend some wonderful times with you this summer."

"I can't believe the summer is ending. You will be missed."

"I will miss you and this wonderful place."

"We will invite you back. I'm sure Gram is already making plans."

"Yes. She and I discussed that yesterday actually. I think she is going to try and invite me again next summer."

"We'll only have to get through the winter, then."

"Nathanial, I want us to write, but I don't want you to get the wrong impression."

"Amelia, I know you are not ready for a new relationship. But I'm a very patient man and perfectly happy with letter writing for now."

"Am I interrupting things?" Nick asked.

Annoyance flashed on Nathanial's face.

"We were discussing plans for when we meet again," Amelia said.

"Sorry to disturb your plotting, but the evening is almost over, and I would like at least one dance with you, Melia," Nick said.

Nathanial took a step back and waved his hand like he was giving his blessing. Amelia followed Nick out onto the dance floor. She tried to ignore that they were one of only a handful of couples left dancing. She couldn't help but feel like she was a little on display.

The music started playing, and Nick led her into the One-Step. "Where is Maddy?"

"She had a headache, so went upstairs for the night," Nick said.

"She gets headaches often. I hope she is well."

"I believe she is. She just sometimes overindulges."

"I see," Amelia said.

Concern for Nick's future with her cousin washed over her, and she frowned slightly. She caught herself and forced a more cheerful expression.

"What is it?" Nick asked.

"Nothing."

"Don't tell me it's nothing. I caught the expression on your face before you tried to hide it."

"I just worry for your future with Maddy."

"You have been talking with Nathanial."

"No, well, yes, I have been, but it's not just that."

"I know she can be difficult, but she has a good heart. Or at least I used to see it in her."

"I used to see it in her, too. Perhaps it's still in there somewhere."

"One can hope, but it doesn't matter. I made a promise. And it's a promise I plan to keep. Even if it hurts to do so."

"I will never understand the sacrificial lamb mentality when it comes to honor and the code of a gentleman," Amelia said.

"That's a bit harsh," Nick said.

"Maybe, but it's how I feel. I cautioned my brother not to pick someone who he would one day regret marrying just for the furtherance of our family holdings and business. Thankfully, he married someone who is wonderful, and she is someone he absolutely adores."

"Not everyone can be so lucky. After my father died, Nathanial and I felt like we needed to make sure we always did what was best for the family business, so to speak."

"What does Tuva say about it?"

"Gram thinks I'm being ridiculous."

"Well, I agree with Tuva."

The song ended, and they stared at each other until Amelia heard a cough in the distance, breaking the trance. She reluctantly pulled away and started to walk off the dance floor. Nick grabbed her hand as she walked by him, stopping her progression. She looked back at him, waiting, but when he didn't say anything, she slipped her hand out of his and walked on.

"Write to me, please," Nick finally said.

Amelia glanced over her shoulder. "Only if you write me first."

Chapter Thirteen

The train whistled, announcing its arrival, and Amelia pulled her nose out of her book. She glanced at Ivy and realized she was still asleep. She nudged her gently, but Ivy jolted, frantically looking around.

"Sorry, I didn't mean to startle you," Amelia said.

Ivy squeezed Amelia's hand. "It's okay. I didn't mean to sleep so soundly."

"Home again," Amelia said with a sigh.

"Are you excited to see your mother?"

"I am. I missed her, if you can believe it."

"She is still your mother even when you don't agree with her on things."

The train rumbled to a stop while Amelia and Ivy gathered their things. Once it was safe to walk, they made their way to the exit.

"Who is picking us up?" Ivy asked.

"I think it's just going to be Charles," Amelia said. "I can't imagine my mother would meet us at the train."

Amelia found Charles quickly, confirming her assumptions. She wasn't bothered by her mother not being at the station. Charles loaded the car, and they were off toward home. Ivy chatted about returning to normal protocol when they arrived, and Amelia hated the idea that Ivy couldn't just be her companion or friend and said as much.

Ivy waved the idea away and changed the subject, but Amelia knew she would discuss it with her mother. Especially since she hoped to travel more on her own. The rest of the ride, they talked of simpler things until they pulled into her driveway. She was instantly claustrophobic, which surprised her.

She had always loved her home, but the summer in Willow Bay had changed her in ways she was still learning about. City life would never be something Amelia ever wanted again. She wouldn't mind visiting her Boston home, but the idea of living there was almost too much for her now.

She went in search of her mother and found her where expected—sitting on her favorite chair reading a book. Her mother didn't often read, but when she did, it was a book of poems from Amelia's father—a beloved wedding present.

"Oh, there you are," her mother said, closing the book. She sat it beside her and stood, allowing Amelia to hug her.

"It's wonderful to see you, Mother."

"Is it? I was beginning to wonder if I had lost you forever to that place, especially from what you wrote about in your letters."

"It's a grand place, Mother, if you would just give it a chance."

"The home was beautiful to be sure."

Knowing she wouldn't get her mother to say anything else, Amelia changed the subject. They talked briefly about the trip before her mother suggested Amelia go settle into her room. Amelia agreed and left. She would wait to discuss the situation with Ivy at dinner.

When the bedroom door was shut behind her, she allowed herself to think about what the brothers were doing. No doubt they were on their boat or going over financials or having tea with Tuva. Amelia wiped at the dampness she was surprised was on her cheek. She knew she would miss her friends and Willow Bay, but had no idea she would ache to return as much as she did.

Crossing to sit at her desk, she pulled out pen and paper and started a letter to Nathanial. Once done, she wrote one for Tuva and finally one for Kathleen. She summoned Charles and requested the letters be sent out that evening. He agreed and mentioned her mother was waiting for her whenever she was ready to go down for dinner.

Amelia realized she had been so caught up in her letters she had lost track of time. Seconds later, a flushed Ivy ran into her room.

"I fell asleep, Amelia. I never fall asleep. What is wrong with me?"

"You're just tired. And I'm fine. We will blame my tardiness on me, so please don't feel flustered," Amelia said.

Ivy helped her get ready and Amelia rushed downstairs.

"Forgive me, Mother. I was writing letters and lost track of time."

"Letters already. I can't believe how quickly you dove into that chore. Is one to a certain gentleman, I hope?" her mother asked.

"One is to Nathanial, but it isn't what you think. We are just friends."

"Well, that's how it can start. So, I will take it."

Amelia tried to hide her irritation and went to sit at the dining room table. Throughout dinner, her mother discussed the gossip of their friends and the happenings Amelia missed while she was away. Amelia followed along as best as she could, but her mind continued to wander to the realization she could no longer hear waves.

"Honestly, Amelia, I feel like you're not listening to me," her mother said.

"I am, Mother. I was just distracted for a second, but I'm listening. I promise."

"As I was saying, we are going to England for the holidays instead of George coming here," her mother said.

"Wait. What? Do I have to go?" Amelia asked.

"Of course you do. Don't be ridiculous. What would your brother say? Not to mention it would be a snub to your sister-in-law, who invited us."

"I suppose. Ivy is coming too, correct?"

"Yes, she is your companion, is she not?"

"Are you suggesting she no longer serve as a lady's maid?"

"She has always been somewhat of a companion for you since you grew up. And her staying in Minnesota with you solidified it."

"This is wonderful news. I thought I would have to convince you of this," Amelia said.

"I'm not as blind as you think, Amelia. But are you sure Ivy will want to do this? Her wages will be different. Her expenses will be paid for, of course, to match the role of a companion and she will be given an allowance of sorts, but she may prefer to keep her same wages as before."

"I didn't think of that. I will discuss it with her and let you know."

"No need," her mother said. "Charles, go and get Ivy, please."

"Yes, Mrs. Campbell."

"Mother, don't put Ivy on the spot," Amelia said.

"Why not? She needs to be prepared for this as a companion to someone of your stature."

Ivy walked into the dining room and looked at Amelia questioningly.

"Mother and I were talking," Amelia said.

"I will handle this, Amelia," her mother said. "Ivy, it has come to my attention that perhaps your role in this household should no longer be that of a housekeeper and more of a companion to my daughter. You already fill that role in some ways, but I want to make sure you will be okay with this before we solidify this change. Your expenses will be mostly paid by our estate of course, and you will receive an allowance. But you must travel with Amelia from now on."

"I would be delighted to assist in this way," Ivy said.

"Excellent, why don't you join us for dinner," Charlotte said. "Charles, grab another place setting for Ivy, please."

"Yes, Mrs. Campbell," Charles said as he winked at Ivy.

"What about you, Mother? Will you be okay not having someone with you as you travel since Maria can't always go?"

"I have you, my darling, and if not, Maria will just have to help more. But when we go to England, your brother will have a lady's maid for me. In the meantime, Ivy will assist both of us when necessary."

"Why do I get the feeling you have something up your sleeve?" Amelia said.

"I don't know what you are talking about, darling," her mother said and changed the subject.

The rest of dinner, they discussed preparations for their trip to England. They would be leaving in a few weeks and planned to stay at least through the new year. Amelia couldn't stop the sinking feeling that she was being pulled further away from Willow Bay.

Chapter Fourteen

Dear Nathanial,

The sway of the ship is so different from the sway of your boat on the lake. I hate that I'm being taken so far from Willow Bay, but I keep telling myself it is only temporary. Ivy has settled into her new role, which is no surprise, since she was already doing so well at it before it became official.

You asked about my paintings in your last letter. I did not bring all of them with me when I left Willow Bay. I left one for your gram and a few are in my room there. However, there is one I thought you might like, and I am having Charles send it to you as an early Christmas gift, which you will probably receive before you even get this letter.

I'm enclosing a card that has the information on where you can write to me while I'm staying at my brother's home, Strongwell Manor, in Yorkshire, England. I'm not sure yet if we will spend any time in London, but if my mother has a say, I'm sure we will find our way there eventually.

I miss the water where you are, and I miss the bay.

Amelia

Dear Amelia,

The painting is beautiful. It is hanging above my chair in the library, where I can see it often. Nick says the small figure you painted represents you, but I thought it might be Gram. Either way, you captured the scene perfectly and I love it. I won't bore you with the business side of things but know that all is well there.

I received several letters from you at once. Your crossing sounded uneventful, but I was glad to hear you arrived at your destination just the same. I'm envious of your trip to England, for I have never been. I've been to several places in the United States, but nowhere beyond her shores. Consider yourself fortunate to take such a trip, even if it means you are being taken further from us here.

Gram has been ill lately. We think she will rebound before the holidays, but I know Mother is worried about her. She is getting more fragile than we have ever seen her, so if she doesn't write to you often, it's because she doesn't have the strength and is resting. Nick and I plan to visit her every day, and we can help her write if she wants. But she may decline, as I know the two of you have your own secrets.

I know you will be busy on your trip, so I don't expect to hear from you as often, but I would love to know about your surroundings there whenever possible.

The water here and the bay miss you too. As do I.

Nathanial

Chapter Fifteen

AMELIA STUDIED THE POND before turning back to her canvas. Her hand was poised, and she tried to focus on painting, but her thoughts kept drifting. The weather was cool, but the air wasn't what bothered her.

Ivy leaned over her shoulder. "The pond won't paint itself, dear one."

Amelia flinched. "You startled me. For heaven's sake, where is my brain?"

"I would wager it's across the ocean."

"Perhaps it is."

"How was your letter from Nathanial?"

"It was lovely. He received my painting and loved it."

"But no letters from Nick yet."

"No letters from Nick."

Amelia put her paintbrush down and started to gather her supplies.

"This is a foolish activity so late in the day. I should probably return to the house so I can freshen up before dinner," she said.

"Leave your supplies. I will have someone fetch them for you. In the meantime, let's walk for a bit," Ivy said.

"I wish I could, but I promised Mother I would stop in to see her before I head to my room."

"Ah, yes. The weekly reminder of how you should act," Ivy said with a laugh.

"I have no doubt there will be more gentlemen guests joining us this evening."

"Why don't you tell your mother that Nathanial is pursuing a relationship with you, even if by correspondence?"

"I'm not ready for that conversation. Besides, we are only friends. I don't want to give my mother false hope."

"Maybe it's for the best, but it would be nice for you not to have such a stream of men being paraded in front of you."

"There is that, but no, I won't lie to my mother."

Amelia jumped as leaves crunched behind them. She turned as a man on horseback slipped out of the shadows of the trees. Something about him set warning bells off in her head.

"Is it a man you're looking for, miss?"

"I beg your pardon, sir, but were you eavesdropping?" Amelia asked.

The man halted his horse and glared down at her. "What's it to ya?"

"Listening to a lady's conversation is rude."

"You must be the American sister here to tantalize the men of this country so that you can gain a title."

"How dare you talk to me in such a way?" Amelia said.

"How dare I?"

The man jumped off his horse and shortened the distance between the two of them.

Smelling the alcohol on his breath, Amelia took a step back. "You need to leave, sir!"

"I think maybe you should be the one to leave."

"Amelia, perhaps we should just go," Ivy said.

"This is my brother's land, and he is the trespasser. He should go."

"I worked this land long before your brother showed up," the man said.

Amelia's chin jutted out and she stood taller. "That doesn't give you the right to treat me with such disrespect. Please leave. Now."

He raised his fist in the air and swung. She ducked before his hand could connect with her cheek. Ivy grabbed her hand, and they ran in the direction of the house.

"Come back here, you insolent peasant."

They didn't stop running until they were feet from the house. George ran out the side door as Amelia crossed the patio.

"Amelia, you look as though you are frightened. Are you okay?" George asked.

"A man attacked us, sir," Ivy said.

"Is this true, Amelia? Are you hurt?"

"I'm fine, but yes, Ivy speaks the truth. There was a man who came out of the shadows. He startled us, I confronted him, and he tried to strike me."

"I will take care of this. Go and tell Violet, and I will see you at dinner."

"But, George, I don't want you to get hurt," she said.

"I will not get hurt. Now go."

She obeyed and rushed into the house, with Ivy close behind. She followed her brother's instructions before finding her mother. She explained what happened, but while her mother showed a rare form of sympathy, she focused more on her weekly reminder about how to act in England. Amelia patiently endured the lecture but had to rush to get ready for dinner on time.

Ivy helped Amelia and escorted her downstairs. She made sure Amelia was okay before disappearing back upstairs with the excuse of a headache. George crossed to meet Amelia when she walked into the drawing room.

"Brother, I'm happy to find you well," Amelia said.

"I am. I discovered who made attempts at attacking you. He is a groundskeeper who we had to let go earlier this week," George explained.

"What was he doing here, then?" Amelia asked.

"I worry he may be a bit disgruntled," Violet said.

"He had been drinking, which is why his actions were a bit more violent," George said.

"Should we be worried?" Charlotte asked.

"No, Mother. All should be well going forward. He was detained and charged."

"You are not worried this might aggravate him further?" Amelia asked.

"No, I am not. I believe he just needs to sober up a bit, and he will come to his senses."

"To help cheer you up, I would love your assistance in preparing for our annual holiday ball," Violet said.

"I would like that very much," Amelia said, forcing a pleasant expression she didn't feel.

"That's settled then," Violet said as the butler appeared in the doorway to announce dinner was ready.

The family started to move toward the dining room when George paused, patting his coat and pants.

"In all the excitement, I almost forgot," George said.

"Forgot what?" Amelia asked.

"Another letter came for you."

Chapter Sixteen

Dear Melia,

My apologies for my flirtatious behavior while you were in our bay. I forgot my place for a moment. But I hope you know I am ever your friend and still plan to write. Nathanial shared you went to your brother's place in England and was kind enough to let me have your address there. I hope it doesn't cause your mother to chatter on too much about you receiving letters from not one gentleman, but two. I can see you roll your eyes as I write these words. And if I'm lucky, you are laughing instead of being angry at my teasing you. You told me you would only write if I wrote to you first. Well, it's your turn now.

Don't fall in love with an English aristocrat so that you can one day come home to us in Willow Bay.

Nick

Dear Nick

I'm still rolling my eyes at your remark. And yes, my mother is pestering me about the letters. But I would be lying if I was to say I wasn't pleased to hear from you.

No falling in love with any English gentleman here. But there have been plenty of dinner parties. And my sister-in-law has roped me into helping her with their annual holiday ball. I must admit it is a welcome distraction and it helps pass the time.

We had a scare recently when a disgruntled employee attempted to cause me some harm. I happened upon him another time when he was trying to steal supplies and he got into some trouble. For some reason, he is holding me responsible and has sent some threats against me. There was another attempt at harming me, but I was able to avoid it, and all seems to be well now. Please don't share that with anyone else. It is all quite embarrassing.

I liked the sound of calling Willow Bay home.

Melia

Dear Melia,

It will be difficult for me not to worry about you. I hate to think of you in harm's way. But I must trust your brother is keeping you safe. However, I will push to have Gram continue to send you invites with the hopes one will stick and you may return to us here soon.

And don't worry, your story is safe with me. I will not share it with anyone else as long as you promise to let me know if I can be of any other service.

I must mention that it made me happy when you wrote you were pleased to hear from me, and I laughed at your rolling eyes. Nathanial also shared about the parties and events you must endure, and I'm sorry you are no doubt being paraded around, but was surprised to hear you are joining in the planning of one of the balls.

Just remember, we have the one thing they don't. Willow Bay.

Come home to us as soon as you can. Maddy will want some help with the wedding, no doubt. Nope, that's not true. She will want to do it all by herself. Lord help me, what have I gotten myself into? Why couldn't I have met you sooner?

Counting the days until we get to see you again. Even though that is all I will ever be able to do.

Yours,
Nick

Dear Nick

You shouldn't say such things to me while betrothed to my cousin. But I understand wishing for something that can't happen. I wish for similar things, sometimes.

Sorry you believe yourself to be in an impossible position.

Being the main event in the parade of men at parties is a daunting task. Nothing will ever catch my eye like Willow Bay, though.

Counting the days too,

Melia

Chapter Seventeen

THE SHIMMER FROM THE new electric lights lit up the ballroom. George danced with Amelia and bragged about the accomplishment of being the first home in the area to have electricity in almost every room of the house.

"Was this your or Violet's idea?" she asked.

"It was both of us."

"I'm happy to hear that you include her in your planning and changes."

"She actually makes most of the decisions when it comes to our homes."

"I suppose that allows you to focus on the business side of things," Amelia said.

"Yes, but it's not like I have left her out of that altogether. I just try to handle the heaviest burden on my own."

Amelia rolled her eyes and started to say something to the effect of women aren't feeble-minded, but George cut her off.

"I know what you are about to say, sister. But you can climb down off your high horse. She chooses to be involved as much or as little as she wants. I have always kept that door open for her. Violet just chooses to let me take on most of the business side of things."

"I suppose running several houses keeps her busy enough. It does make my heart happy to hear you handle things as a partnership, though," she said.

"I learned that from you."

"So, you *were* listening."

"I suppose I was. I wish the same for you, Melia."

"I know you do."

"These gentlemen writing to you, are they suitors?"

"Not suitors. They are just friends."

"Then would you be open to finding a suitor here when you're ready to open your heart again?" George asked.

Amelia couldn't stop the laughter from bubbling out of her. "Absolutely not. I want to return to Willow Bay someday."

"What is it with you and that place?"

"I'm not sure I could explain it if I tried."

"Well, perhaps you should try if I'm to support you in any schemes for you to return."

The music stopped, and Amelia stepped away from her brother. "Perhaps another time. Now go dance with your beautiful wife so I can rest my feet for a bit."

"Don't wander too far, Melia."

"Of course not."

Amelia watched the dancers for the first half of the song but slipped outside when no one was looking in her direction. She needed some air, even if it was cold outside. She was frustrated with her mother for extending their stay until spring. She wanted to return home as several invitations to return to Willow Bay had already been received. Although the invitations were for the summer, she had the idea if she were closer, she could return earlier.

Thinking about Willow Bay prompted her to think of Nathanial's letters and was surprised at how happy she was to be in correspondence with him. She frowned at the thought of her last letter to him. She had written about the title her brother had received when he married her sister-in-law and all of their great properties, including the castle-like home she was currently staying in.

She was afraid she was coming across as superficial as Madeline was. It dawned on her she had a hard time discussing more serious matters with Nathanial. She contemplated what that might mean since she could discuss almost anything with Nick.

Brushing thoughts of letters and the brothers aside, Amelia looked up at the night sky. She shivered, realizing it was much colder than she had originally thought.

"Perhaps you shouldn't be out on such a cold night, miss," a voice sounded behind her.

Spinning around, a tingle slid up her spine. It was the same man from a month ago. George had assured her the matter was settled, so she hadn't thought about him until this moment. Not wanting to wait until he tried something new, Amelia rushed to the safety of indoors.

When she stumbled into the ballroom, she realized he was hot on her heels. His fingers snaked around her arm, and he jolted her into the shadows. She attempted to scream, but he clamped a hand over her mouth.

"You wouldn't want to embarrass your sister-in-law, now would ya?"

Amelia dug her heel into the man's foot and bit his fingers, allowing her to break free. His fingers reached to snag her again, but she yelled for George, forcing the man to pause. The whole room stilled, and all eyes turned in their direction. The man turned to flee, but several people blocked his escape.

"Mr. Donovan," George yelled. "How dare you return! Have you not learned your lesson? Perhaps I shouldn't have been so lenient last time. You will be locked up for a while this time."

"No, please, my lord," Mr. Donovan said, falling to his knees. "I didn't mean your sister no harm. I just wanted to talk, is all, to make sure she knew she misunderstood our last encounter."

"You attempted to strike me when I saw you last, and it wasn't the first time you tried to do that. How is that a misunderstanding?" Amelia asked.

"I wasn't in my right mind," Mr. Donovan said.

"And tonight, when you grabbed me and pulled me into the shadows, I suppose your excuse is you're not in your right mind still?"

"No, miss. I just wanted to talk, is all."

Murmurs from the crowd grew louder, and Amelia closed her eyes. She realized this whole scene was causing a spectacle during her brother's party, and she wanted to disappear.

She stepped closer to George. "Perhaps we should just let him go with a warning not to return."

George glanced at his sister. "Are you okay?"

"Yes, but we are causing a scene in front of all of your wife's friends."

"It isn't like you to worry so much about what others think, Melia," George said as his face softened.

"True, but it does bother me to create a scene so grand it could cause distress to you or your wife. Please, George. Just let him go."

"Very well, Melia," George said. He turned to the butler, who had gathered with several other men from his household staff. "Please see Mr. Donovan to the door, but before you let him go, remind him to never return."

Violet moved closer to Amelia. "Is this wise?"

Amelia turned to her sister-in-law. "I'm so sorry for the scene here tonight."

"Amelia, I don't care about that. Are you okay?"

"Yes, dear sister, but if it's okay with you, I would like to retire for the rest of the evening."

"Of course."

Her mother and Ivy offered to escort her upstairs, but she waved them off.

"Please go back to the party. I'm fine. I'm just so embarrassed. And I feel terrible for ruining the night," she said.

"You did not ruin the night, Amelia," her mother said.

"Thank you for your kindness, Mother. But, please return to the beautiful evening. I insist."

"You go ahead, Mrs. Campbell. I will go with her upstairs," Ivy said.

"Are you sure?" her mother asked.

"Yes, I'm sure. I will help her with a bath and get her settled for the night. Go have some fun," Ivy said.

"Alright then. But send for me if I'm needed," Charlotte said and returned to the ballroom.

Once Charlotte was out of earshot, Ivy turned to Amelia. "Are you sure you're okay?"

"Yes, Ivy. I'm not hurt. He just frightened me, and I was embarrassed. But I'm unharmed."

"Fine, then I will get some wine, request a bath, and help you get your nerves to settle at least."

"Thank you, Ivy. You always know what I need."

"Oh, I almost forgot. A letter came for you," Ivy said and handed it to Amelia.

"Is it from Nick?"

Ivy tilted her head. "No, it's from Nathanial."

Chapter Eighteen

Dear Amelia

Your brother's home sounds wonderful. What a trip you have had. Perhaps it's better that you did extend your stay as it may help pass the time quickly. Although, if you were on this side of the ocean, I could come to visit you. Gram is doing so much better these last few weeks. But I don't think she will ever be as strong as she was before she got ill. I still worry about her.

As I look out my window, I can almost see you walking along the shoreline. I can't wait for the time when it is more than an illusion and I get to walk with you there. Perhaps even hold your hand. Missing you so much.

Nathanial

Dear Nathanial

I wish I was in Boston too so that you could come visit or I could come sooner to Willow Bay. I find myself missing it more and more.

I find myself missing you, too.

Amelia

Dear Amelia

I know you don't want anything more from me just yet, but I find my heart longing for you. I hope I do not speak out of turn when I share my feelings.

Yours,
Nathanial

Dear Nathanial

Perhaps I am ready to think about something more.

Missing you,
Amelia

Dear Amelia

Is it too soon to write the words, I'm falling in love with you? I hope it doesn't scare you away.

Yours
Nathanial

Dear Nathanial

It doesn't scare me away. My feelings are growing, too, but I hope you understand that I can't profess love just yet. But I am quite fond of you and wish to know you more when I return.

Amelia

Chapter Nineteen

Dear Melia

Nathanial tells me things are progressing in your friendship with him. Having you in the family would be a gift. And there is no better man for you than Nathanial. Although I know things haven't moved that quickly, I love the idea of you possibly being a Nilsson one day.

We all miss you. I think even the lake longs for your return.

Yours,
Nick

Dear Nick

I'm happy you rejoice in what might eventually be between Nathanial and me. But let's not discuss being a part of the family quite yet.

I long for my return too.

Melia

—— *ele* ——

Melia

Come home. We worry about Gram's health, and I know you will want to be with her, especially if we are in her last days.

Yours,
Nick

Chapter Twenty

AMELIA REREAD THE LETTER and her fingers began to tremble. She had to go back. She wasn't sure how, but she had to convince her mother it was time to go home so she could return to Willow Bay.

"We should head down for dinner," Ivy said. She walked across the room to grab Amelia's gloves, but paused when she noticed Amelia's expression. "What is it?"

"I've had a letter from the bay. Tuva is ill. I must go back before it's too late."

"You know that will be a hard sell for your mother."

"I know. Do you remember before we left, I told you I thought Mother had something she was keeping from me? I think I've figured it out. I think she plans for us to stay here permanently since George has made this his permanent home."

"What would she do with your home in Boston?"

"I don't know, but I could see her selling it to remain here. I must convince her to let me return home. I would bring you with me, of course."

"Oh goodness, look at the time. Your mother is going to be cross with me that you are tardy again."

"Don't worry about her. I will take care of it," Amelia said.

She rushed to finish final preparations and went below to find her mother agitated. She was relieved when Violet came to her rescue.

Violet placed her hand on Amelia's arm. "You look flustered, Amelia. I know you received a letter from home. Was it bad news?"

"Yes, it was. The elder Mrs. Nilsson is ill again, and they worry she won't be with us much longer."

"Such awful news," Violet said.

"Yes, I'm quite distressed by it. Please forgive my tardiness to dinner."

"It is to be expected after receiving such a letter," Violet said.

"Thank you for your graciousness," Charlotte said.

"Of course, Mother," Violet said.

"Dinner is served," the butler called from the doorway.

"George, please escort your sister to dinner. She is worried about things at home," Violet said.

Following the instructions given by his wife, George led Amelia into the dining room. They discussed her letter and how she was worried about Tuva.

"You must help me convince Mother that I must return home. I promise to bring Ivy with me so I wouldn't be traveling alone."

"I take it Mother hasn't explained her plans to you," George said.

"What plans?"

"She and I inspected a cottage on the grounds today. She means to stay for good, Melia."

"I knew it."

"So, she did explain things to you?"

"No, she didn't, but I knew she was up to something, especially after postponing our return."

"What are you children discussing?" their mother asked.

"Mother, I thought you had mentioned to Melia your plans to move to England permanently. Unfortunately, I may have just let that secret slip," George said.

"It's not so much a secret. I just hadn't discussed it with Amelia as it has nothing to do with her."

"Nothing to do with me?" Amelia asked. "How could you say such a thing? This affects me too."

"Well, it affects you in that we must move your things here, I suppose."

"What you meant to say is, I don't have a choice in this, so I didn't deserve the information before you made the decision and started making plans."

"I suppose one could say it that way, but that sounds heartless, and I am not heartless."

"But this is all so hurtful still, Mother."

"How is that hurtful? Honestly, Amelia, please don't be so dramatic. What will Violet think?"

Amelia inhaled and let the air out slowly. "Mother, I want to return to Willow Bay."

"What? You can't be serious."

"I told you before, I was invited to return for the summer. I want to return now and remain there for the foreseeable future."

"Amelia, I won't let you travel alone, darling."

"I won't be alone. Ivy will be with me."

"That may be, but I don't like the idea of my daughter going off to such an untamed land."

"It isn't untamed, and you know it. Besides, with the harassment I continue to receive from Mr. Donovan, in some ways I would be safer there," Amelia said.

"Amelia has a point about Mr. Donovan. Perhaps I could offer a solution," George said.

"You can't seriously be supporting her," their mother said.

"It's not so much supporting her as much as I'm trying to keep the peace. I want to help us all come to a compromise," George said.

"Fine, then. What is your plan?" their mother asked.

"I must return to New York for a few weeks, and I need to go and prepare the Boston home to sell and have your things shipped here. I could just leave a few weeks early and take Amelia and Ivy to Willow Bay. Then, before I return to England, they can rendezvous with me in New York, and we can set sail to England together."

"That might work, dear. You were planning on being in New York for the summer anyway. What's an additional couple of weeks," Violet said.

"I hate for you to be away from your family for so long, George. Especially just to appease a whim of Amelia's."

"This isn't a whim, Mother. You knew I wanted to return there this summer."

"I was hoping after we had been here for a while, you would have changed your mind."

"Would it help if I told you one of the Nilsson brothers is all but courting me as much as one can do long distance and in letters? But I have reason to believe, upon my return, it could become more official."

"Does this mean I will be apart from you, Amelia? Or that I can't move here. I so wanted to remain in England, but if you marry and stay in Willow Bay, how can those plans come to fruition?"

"You can still stay, Mother. I wouldn't be living in Boston anyway. You might as well be where you want to be," she said.

Her mother played with her food, which Amelia knew was out of character for her unless she was contemplating giving in to what Amelia was requesting. Amelia getting her way was a rare occurrence, but she became jittery with anticipation and held her breath.

"If George doesn't mind taking you to Willow Bay, how can I stop him? But, Amelia, you only have permission to stay through the summer. If you are not betrothed by then, you must return."

"I can't guarantee anything beyond a courtship in that timeframe, Mother," she said.

"Fine, you may stay for a year. If things are not moving in the direction of a proposal by the end of it, you must return to England."

Amelia clapped her hands together. "Thank you, Mother."

During the rest of dinner, Amelia had a hard time concentrating on the conversation and eating her food. She wanted to run back to her room and start packing. She reminded herself it would be a bit premature as passage wasn't even secured yet, and she could be there another month. At the least, she wanted to write a note to let the Nilssons know she was returning.

When she finally made it to her room, she pulled out a piece of paper but paused. Instead of writing a letter to Nathanial or Nick, she wrote to Tuva and let her know to keep her return a secret so she could surprise the brothers. She provided a rough estimate of her return date and wrote, *Tuva, please hang on. I'm coming home.*

Chapter Twenty-One

Amelia tugged on her brother's sleeve. "George, you are going to miss it."

"Miss what?" George asked, lifting his head to look around.

"The view I was telling you about. There is a point on our journey right before we head down into Duluth where you can see Lake Superior in all her glory. You are going to miss it if you don't pull your head out of your papers."

"Yes, well, I need to have all of this finalized before I head on to Boston in a few days."

"I know, but at least take a small break. For me."

George set his papers on his lap just as Ivy clasped Amelia's hand.

"Look, there it is," Amelia said.

All three passengers looked out the car window to admire the beauty Amelia had referred to moments before.

"I must say, Amelia. I'm not sure what I was expecting, but this is quite pretty," George said.

"Isn't it? She calls to me," she said without thinking.

"Don't let Mother hear you talk like that. She will have you committed."

Laughing was the only way Amelia would allow herself to respond, and she turned to study the landscape out her window. The rest of the way into the heart of the city, she had to force herself to keep quiet. Ivy squeezed her hand, smiled a knowing smile, and looked out the window as well. Amelia appreciated Ivy's friendship, especially now.

The car slowed to a stop in front of the Holland Hotel. George gathered his papers as the door was opened and a hand reached in to help Amelia climb out. As Amelia got her bearings, she turned and squealed.

"Henry! What are you doing here?" Amelia asked. "I thought for sure you would be in New York."

"George wrote to me and asked for some assistance in getting boat passage up to Willow Bay. He knew that would be the only way you would want to travel, and I decided this was a great opportunity to come see our favorite place," Henry said.

"Are you staying at your house here in Duluth?" Amelia asked.

"I am, but the house isn't quite open for guests," Henry said.

"I wouldn't care about our accommodations, but I know Aunt Lucille would be upset if we stayed without the house being opened properly, and filled with the right staff for the occasion," Amelia said.

"You know my mother well," Henry said.

Ivy stepped closer to Amelia to ask a question just as George climbed out of the back seat of the car.

"Henry, what a pleasure to see you," he said.

"George, it certainly is. I'm happy to help with this adventure for Amelia."

"You didn't say anything to Maddy, did you?" Amelia asked.

"We both know there would be no surprise if I had done that," Henry said with a laugh.

"Thank you so much," Amelia said. "Henry, you remember Ivy, don't you? She was with me last summer."

"Absolutely, I do," Henry said, tipping his hat and bending slightly. "It's a pleasure to see you again, Ivy."

When he straightened, he winked at Ivy, causing her cheeks to turn pink.

"You're embarrassing my friend, Henry," Amelia said, grinning.

"Well then, I must rectify that," Henry said.

He reached out his arm, offering to escort Ivy. She winked at Amelia and allowed herself to be led into the hotel. Amelia followed with her brother in tow, and they checked in for the night. Once they settled into their rooms, the four met up for dinner in the hotel's café. The rest of the evening was filled with laughter and good food before they turned in for the night. She could hardly sleep, though, for the following day would bring her back to Willow Bay.

The boat sailed around the corner into the Bay, and Amelia could hear her brother gasp at the sight of it. She leaned over the railing and kept her eyes peeled for anyone who looked familiar as they floated into the marina. Panic gripped her at the thought of Tuva, and she worried she hadn't made it in time. She caught sight of the *Vide Fjärd,* the Nilsson brothers' main boat. It had just docked, and crewmen were moving about. Knowing they wouldn't have gone out if something had happened to Tuva, relief rushed through her, and she ran to disembark.

George caught her arm. "One must not seem too eager, little sis."

"I'm just excited to finally be home," she said.

"Home?" George asked. "You don't even know what truly awaits you here. Perhaps you shouldn't be calling this place home quite yet."

"It feels like it, though."

"I can understand that, but I must caution you not to get ahead of yourself. Come along, I will escort you," George said, offering his arm.

He looked over his shoulder, asked Henry to assist Ivy, and walked down the gangplank with Amelia. She started to share with George about the first time she had stepped on these docks, but hearing her name, she paused. She looked around and caught sight of a figure coming around the corner of the dock. She broke into a grin when he ran toward her, repeating her name. She let go of George as she was engulfed in a hug and swung about.

"Melia! I can't believe you're here!"

Amelia's heart skipped a beat as she steadied her feet.

Her racing thoughts were cut off by George asking, "Is this the one who is supposedly courting you?"

"This is Nick. He is one of the brothers," she said.

Nick glanced at George and asked, "Is this another cousin, Melia?"

"Melia? Wait, you call her Melia?" George asked.

"Yes, he does," Amelia said. "Ironic, isn't it?"

"Yes, Melia, it is," George said.

"Ah, this is your brother, George. The favored son," Nick said, winking at her.

"Did you ask him to call you that?" George asked. "And what does he mean by the favored son?"

"No, he just started calling me that himself. Why are you questioning it so much? And it's an inside joke. What's wrong with you, George?"

"It's just so familiar."

"Oh, stop it, George. Forgive him, Nick. He is just acting like a ridiculous big brother."

"It's quite alright. Did Nathanial know you were coming and didn't tell me?" Nick asked, his smile fading.

"No. I only told Tuva. How is she?" Amelia asked.

"She is still with us," Nick said, reaching over to squeeze her hand.

George cleared his throat and Nick let go.

"Nick, so great to see you," Henry said.

"Always a pleasure, my friend," Nick said. "It's wonderful to see you as well, Ivy."

Amelia and Ivy exchanged glances while the men discussed the plans for the next couple of days.

"I alerted your mother that I would be coming with guests so that she wouldn't be caught off guard," Henry said.

"We would have made accommodations no matter what," Nick said as he offered his arm to escort Amelia.

She willingly obliged, and George sent her a pointed look. Amelia ignored her brother and chatted with Nick about her trip to the bay, forcing George to follow behind. Henry walked with Ivy and the group wound their way through the docks to the car that had arrived to pick up Nick.

Nick nestled in beside Amelia and discussed a few of the latest developments with the Nilsson business. She asked several questions, wondering what her brother was thinking based on his dumbfounded expression.

"You must consider yourself fortunate to have such a sister, George. She is quite intelligent and a great conversationalist," Nick said.

"Of course, I am fortunate. Melia is the best of us," George said.

"That's so kind of you to say, George," Amelia said.

Nick asked George several questions about his business. George returned the inquiry in kind, leading to a more in-depth conversation between the two of them. This allowed her to focus on what she was seeing outside the car as they drove along.

When they pulled under the carport of the Nilsson home, Nick didn't waste any time helping Amelia out of the car. When she started to walk away, he held firm to her hand, whispering for her to hang back a moment. He instructed Johnston to lead the guests inside.

"I'm right behind you, George. I think I dropped something in the car," Amelia said.

"Very well," George said after a few seconds of studying her.

When the rest of the party disappeared into the house, Nick turned to her. "I know you're here for Nathanial, and I am betrothed, but I must say, my heart exploded with joy seeing you on the docks today."

"I was equally joyous," Amelia said.

Nick studied her, and she wondered what he must be thinking since he appeared to be warring with something internally. She started to ask, but he cut her off.

"We should get inside. Nathanial will be so pleased you're here."

"What is it, Nick?"

"Nothing worth being said out loud."

"That's fine. But just know this, I'm not here for Nathanial. I came here for myself."

Nick's eyes sparkled and his lips curved up, but he didn't say anything else.

"I suppose we should go in," Amelia said.

"Yes, my mother and brother will be waiting," Nick said.

They took a few steps toward the side entrance when Nathanial burst through the door.

"Amelia!"

"Nathanial. It is so wonderful to see you," Amelia said as she hurried over to him.

They hugged but with less exuberance than with Nick earlier. She filed the information away for her to study later, but for now, she couldn't wait to get inside and get settled.

"You will be staying in your old rooms," Nathanial said, escorting her inside. "It's so wonderful to have you back in our bay."

"Yes, it's so good to have you home," Nick said.

Chapter Twenty-Two

Caressing Tuva's hand, Amelia couldn't stop the fear from welling up inside her.

"I look a bit worn, don't I?" Tuva asked.

"Maybe just a little."

"And tell me, how are you faring?"

"I'm better now that I'm here."

"And your mother?"

"She has stayed in England. She gave me a year."

"A year? And what happens when that year is up?"

Amelia giggled. "Your guess is as good as mine."

"We must figure out a way for you to stay once and for all."

"I would love that. But I'm happy to just be here for now and that I don't have to leave at the end of the summer."

"Will I get to meet your brother while he is here?" Tuva asked.

"I would love for you to meet him. He is one of my favorite people. Just as you are."

"Well then, we must make it happen. Perhaps come to tea tomorrow since it's his last day with us. It would be a joy to meet him."

"We will be here."

The conversation turned to Amelia's trip to England, the homes her brother lives in, and the endless parties and parade of men trying to catch her eye. Tuva laughed often but would be cut off by bouts of coughing. Each fit would last longer until Amelia finally said it was probably best if she left and let Tuva rest.

"I think I will come early tomorrow and help prepare for the tea," she explained.

Amelia hugged Tuva and left. She let the tears trickle down her cheeks as she walked. She rounded a bend and ran into Nick.

"Goodness me. I need to watch where I'm going. My apologies," Nick said.

"It's fine," she said.

"What's this? Oh, Melia, please don't cry," he said, pulling her to him.

"She looks dreadful."

"I know. We're all scared for her."

"I'm so glad I returned in time."

"I am too," Nick said, stroking her hair.

Once Amelia regained her composure, she stepped back. "Thank you for always being here and for being such a great friend."

"Always," Nick said with affection. He nervously cleared his throat. "I would offer to walk you back to the house, but I'm off to see Gram myself. Will you be okay?"

"I will be fine."

Nick hugged her once more and left in the direction of Tuva's. Amelia walked on, feeling better. A memory of her being held by Daniel another time when she had been crying flitted through her mind and she frowned. It had been a while since she had thought of him, and she wondered what he would think of her in Willow Bay instead of in Boston or even England.

Her time with Daniel seemed so long ago, and she was thankful her heart was healing. For the first time, she was ready to open it up to another. Nick's face danced across her mind. She frowned and pushed thoughts of him aside. He was not free. She thought of Nathanial, smiled, and decided to go search for him.

When Amelia couldn't find him, she went to her room and wrote a letter to Mrs. Thompson. She started to write the date and realized it had been exactly one year since she had come to Willow Bay the first time. A lot had changed.

She missed Daniel but was thankful she had come this far after death had stolen him and her future from her.

George sat comfortably across from Amelia. He had an amused look as he studied the room. Amelia didn't understand why she was so nervous at their meeting.

Perhaps it's because they are two of the people I admire most, outside the brothers.

Amelia offered to serve tea, and George nodded his thanks. Tuva agreed it was better a steadier hand took control. A comfortable silence fell over the room as sips of tea drained away and bites of cookie disappeared.

"George, please tell me more about this Strongwell Manor of yours in England and your wonderful family," Tuva said.

"My life there is like a dream. I took Melia's advice and found a woman who I love and married her. Thankfully, her father and I were amiable business partners as well. We have one small child, a little boy named Albert, and I just received word that my Violet is expecting another."

"Oh, George, you didn't tell me," Amelia said.

"I hadn't found the time, I guess."

"This is a cause worth celebrating. Melia, please fetch us some champagne. There is a small bottle in the kitchen," Tuva said.

"That sounds splendid," Amelia said and followed the instructions she had been given.

When she returned to the back porch, she found Tuva and George discussing business, and had to hide her grin. She would love this arrangement to bring about another opportunity for her to stay in the bay instead of having to marry right away. Although she was ready to start exploring another relationship, she didn't want to rush it. She hated the idea of her staying, hinging on getting married at all.

Amelia handed the bottle of champagne to her brother, who obligingly opened it. Small cheers rang out from the three, and they toasted to new life. The rest of the afternoon, they discussed Amelia's plans while she stayed in Willow Bay and George's upcoming travel. When it was time to leave, Tuva stood and held George's hand firmly.

"You must come and see us again, George. And you must consider my offer on the business side of things. Just send word when you are ready to proceed, and I will have Nick reach out to you."

"Yes, Mrs. Nilsson," he said.

"Tuva, dear boy. As I said before, my name is Tuva."

"Yes, Tuva, I will be in touch."

Amelia hugged Tuva with promises to return the following day once George had departed. As she walked, she peered at George out of the corner of her eye, wondering what he was thinking.

"I see why you love it here. And Tuva is just wonderful, Melia."

"Isn't she, though?"

"Her strength and determination remind me of you."

"Nick says the same thing. I don't see it. I see a woman who I aspire to be, though."

"You have an ally in me now. Mother would most likely prefer this idea of yours not to work. Which I hope you know is just because she wants to be near her children. But going forward, I will be rooting for you."

"She wants you close so she can sing your praises. She wants me close, only to keep an eye on me. She can't control me from England," Amelia said.

"Don't be so hard on her. She is doing the best she can. She didn't have a father who nurtured her brain. She is just as intelligent as the rest of us, but was only ever able to learn about being the proper wife and mother."

"She could have broken the cycle."

"As you are no doubt trying to do," he said.

"Perhaps, but the thought of sitting in a circle with a bunch of women to discuss the latest gossip makes me want to vomit."

"Melia, don't be so vulgar."

Amelia couldn't keep from laughing, and George joined her.

"You sound just like Mother when you talk that way, George."

"Ha. That part isn't funny."

"I'm sorry," she said.

"I'm going to miss you, little sister," he said tenderly.

Amelia sobered. "And I will miss you, big brother."

The siblings walked arm in arm, and their teasing and laughter echoed across the bay. Once they reached the main house, her chest tightened, and she wanted to keep walking. They wouldn't have time to freshen up before dinner, but she may never have time like this with her brother again. George obliged her, and they continued on to the shoreline. Amelia tucked the memories being made deep into her heart. She would bring them out later when she missed George the most.

Chapter
Twenty-Three

GEORGE DROVE AWAY, AND Amelia was surprised at the tears forming in the corners of her eyes. She pulled out a handkerchief and realized it was one he had bought for her when she turned twenty, and the tears came on stronger.

Nathanial moved closer to her. "Are you okay?"

"I will be," Amelia said.

"Goodbyes are always difficult, especially when they are to the ones we love the most."

"Yes, he and I are very close. And it's strange not knowing when I will see him next."

"That would be a strange feeling. I can't imagine having to say such a goodbye to my brother."

"Perhaps ask her for a walk, Nathanial," Nick suggested.

"That sounds like a lovely idea," Amelia said.

"It does. I suppose I should have thought of it first," Nathanial said, giving his brother an annoyed look.

"Nonsense, Nathanial. I appreciate you being willing to join me," she said.

He offered his arm to her, and they walked down toward the lake. It was a sunny day and Amelia enjoyed the rays of light warming her face. They walked in silence for some time, and she wondered if it was because Nathanial wanted to respect her need for serenity or if he didn't know how to talk to her. He answered her musings by interjecting into her thoughts.

"I sometimes struggle with what I should say next. You are so confident and know your mind, and I'm unsure at times if I'm reading you clearly."

"That makes me a little sad. I thought you knew me better. You never hesitated to share your thoughts in your letters," she said.

"I guess I had more confidence in letter writing. With letters, one can contemplate the words on paper. Whereas in person I feel like I must think swiftly and respond accordingly, and I worry I won't get it right."

"I just want you to be yourself, Nathanial. You were so much more at ease with me when we first met. What's changed?"

"Perhaps it's because my feelings have changed, and I don't want to mess it up. One would be a fool not to see how incredible you are and the kind of partner in life you would be."

Amelia's heart beat faster, and she looked out at the sparkles on the water.

"Nathanial, I love the idea of being someone's partner. That is the type of relationship I'm looking for. One where we care for each other but also work together to build a life."

"You don't care that we don't love one another as some may?" Nathanial asked.

"What we could have would be more than some relationships. Plus, I believe the fondness we have for one another could perhaps grow to love."

"It warms my heart that you are open to growing a relationship with me. I will not speak of engagement quite yet, but perhaps someday soon we can talk of such things as well."

"I'm open to seeing where things lead."

Nick's face dashed through her thoughts, and she paused. Her lips tightened together, and she smoothed the front of her dress.

"What is it?" Nathanial asked.

"Nothing really," Amelia said, forcing a smile.

"You are thinking of my brother, perhaps?" Nathanial asked.

"Why would you think that?

"I see the connection the two of you have. If he hadn't committed himself to someone else, I wouldn't stand a chance, but his rash decision is my gain."

Amelia tried not to let Nathanial's statement bother her, but his remarks hit close. She told herself it was best to put any thoughts of Nick out of her mind for all their sakes, but her mind didn't always cooperate.

She squeezed Nathanial's arms. "You do know me more than you think. You must trust yourself."

"You are so good for me, Amelia. You give me that boost of confidence I sometimes need."

She only smiled, and the conversation changed to lighter things. They finished their walk and Nathanial left to head to the marina, while Amelia went to freshen up to go visit Tuva.

The rest of the summer went by much the same way. Nathanial and Amelia took morning walks and Amelia would head to Tuva's after. The evenings consisted of dinners with some or all of the family. Nick came and went to visit Madeline or to conduct business out of town. Nathanial would travel with Nick at times, but mostly wanted to stay in the bay to handle things at home.

She kept her promise to herself. She stayed away from Nick and dove into the budding relationship with Nathanial. Toward the end of the summer, Kathleen announced she wanted to have an end-of-summer dinner party and Amelia grew excited at the prospect. She offered to help with planning it and Kathleen agreed.

Amelia was assisting Kathleen with the guest list when a letter arrived from George. He was supposed to leave for England several weeks prior, but was delayed and asked if he could visit once more before he started his voyage home. Kathleen agreed to his visit, and he arrived in the same vehicle that brought Madeline and Henry to the party.

Rushing to greet her brother, Amelia slowed just shy of jumping into his arms.

"Melia!"

"Brother!"

"It is such a delight to see you, even if it means a delay home," George said.

"I never thought I would see you so soon."

"Yes, well, perhaps we shouldn't be so rude and share greetings with everyone else around us," George said.

Amelia obliged and said hellos to Madeline and Henry, while George greeted his hosts. As she helped escort everyone indoors, she could tell something was troubling George. She worried she might have to leave Willow Bay after all.

The siblings sat huddled together on the couch, and Amelia asked, "George, is something the matter?"

"Ever the perceptive one," George said.

"I'm right, aren't I? Something is wrong," Amelia said.

"Yes, Melia. I came not just to say goodbye. My delay wasn't due to business, but rather, I needed to investigate further information that pertains to your safety," George said.

Nick moved closer. "What's this about, George?"

"Come now, Nick. It can't be all that bad," Maddy said, her eyes shooting daggers in Amelia's direction.

Nathanial stood and asked, "George, perhaps you and I should walk a bit and discuss this situation further?"

"As thoughtful as you are, Nathanial, in trying to protect me and keep me from worry, I have a right to know what is going on, especially if I'm in danger," Amelia said.

"Let's all just sit and calm ourselves, and let George here explain," Henry said.

Nick and Nathanial followed Henry's instruction, and George cleared his throat. "I've received a letter from Violet. Mr. Donovan—"

"Mr. Donovan?" Amelia blurted out. "Please don't tell me—"

"Surely this isn't the same man who caused you harm in England?" Nick asked.

"How do you know about someone causing Amelia harm and I don't?" Nathanial asked.

"I didn't want to worry you, Nathanial," Amelia said.

"Please, everyone, let us allow Mr. Campbell to explain," Kathleen said.

George tried to start his explanation once more, but was interrupted again.

"You wrote to my cousin while she was away?" Madeline asked Nick.

"Maddy, you know I did," Nick said with a hint of irritation in his voice.

"I can't believe this," Madeline said, dabbing at her eyes.

"For heaven's sake, Madeline. The two of them are friends," Henry said. "Don't act like the jealous fiancé, sis."

"Besides, this moment isn't about you," Nathanial said.

"It never is about me, is it?" Madeline said.

"Would everyone please stop this nonsense?" Kathleen blurted out.

The room stilled, and Amelia sent Kathleen a look of gratitude.

"Please, George, explain to us what is going on," Kathleen said.

"As I mentioned, Violet sent me a letter. Mr. Donovan broke into our home not long after we left. No one worried that much about it because he was taken into custody.

Upon his release, he broke into our home a second time. Only this time, he escaped, and he left England for New York."

Amelia walked across the room to look out at the water. She stared at the waves rolling gently toward the shoreline.

"Should I worry that he is after me?" she asked.

"But why would he be after you, Amelia?" Nathanial asked, moving to stand next to her.

"He believes she's the reason for his recent bad luck," George said.

"I don't understand," Nick said.

"Mr. Donovan worked for my brother at his estate," Amelia said, turning to face the room. "He was let go from his job and had become quite drunk. I provoked him unintentionally. He attacked me and was jailed for a short time."

"When he got out, he disrupted one of our parties," George said, interrupting Amelia's attempt to continue with the explanation. "Melia felt sorry for him and pleaded for him to be given a pardon. We gave it to him, but what Melia doesn't know is, his wife left him shortly after. And then he lost his home."

"And I suppose he blames everything on Melia," Nick said.

"That's correct," George said.

"Should we be worried he might come here?" Kathleen asked.

"I have some men looking for him as we speak," George said. "The last we found anything, he was headed to Boston. Thankfully, he will find a dead-end since I sold our home there. And he shouldn't be able to locate the apartments I purchased for when I must return to Boston for business."

"If any attempt at finding me would grow cold in Boston, let's not worry. Besides, he may just be in America to start over. Let's give him the benefit of the doubt," Amelia said.

"Such a brave one," Nathanial said.

Nick started to say something, but Amelia gave him a look and he kept quiet. She knew Nick could tell her bravery was a front. She was actually shaken by the news but didn't want to worry Nathanial or the rest of the family until they found out more information.

"Goodness me, look at the time. We should all freshen up for dinner," Kathleen said.

"Yes, we must all freshen up and put all of this nonsense out of our minds," Amelia said.

Everyone went their separate ways and Amelia managed to keep it together long enough to reach the confines of her room. Ivy stopped in to see if she needed assistance and found her in a puddle of emotions on the floor. Ivy sat next to her, holding her close until Amelia exhausted her tears.

Chapter Twenty-Four

THE LAKE BREEZE HAD a hint of coolness as it blew gently against Amelia's face. She closed her eyes and breathed it in. Strands of hair slipped from the confines of her updo as the warmth of the summer evening settled around her. She opened her eyes just in time to take in the beauty of the sunset.

"There you are," George said from behind.

"Isn't it just wonderful, George?"

"You sound so content, so at peace here, sis, considering the bad news recently."

"Perhaps it's because I am," Amelia said.

"This place suits you. I think I mentioned that on my last stay, but it truly does."

"Thank you for recognizing that."

"I hate to bring it up, but I received word that Mr. Donovan turned up in Boston. Unfortunately, we have lost track of him again, but we know he didn't go to our home there."

"Let's not worry about him tonight."

"The final summer party is not a time to talk about worrisome things, I suppose."

"Do you think you could ever convince Violet to visit me here? Or even Mother, for that matter."

"I suppose if there was a wedding someday—will there be a wedding, one day?"

Amelia grinned. "A woman never bares her soul to her big brother.

"I will take that as a maybe. It gives me hope to see you might have found a place to truly be happy. You've been so restless over the years, but that seems not to be the case here."

"Yes, I suppose I was born for this place."

"Always the deep thinker."

"Excuse me, Mr. Campbell," Ivy said, interrupting the siblings.

"Why, Ivy, you look lovely this evening," George said.

"Thank you, sir."

"Ivy, what is it?" Amelia asked.

"It's probably nothing, and I hate to accuse anyone of anything."

"Come now. We know you wouldn't say something unless you had reason to believe there's truth to it," George said.

"I overheard Miss Madeline discussing the Mr. Donovan situation with her housemaid, and it worried me a little," Ivy said.

"What do you mean? What did they say?" Amelia asked.

"I couldn't make out everything they were saying, so I don't want to repeat anything in case I'm wrong, but her tone was off, and I felt compelled to warn you just the same."

"Do you have reason to believe she would cause harm to her own cousin?" George asked.

"I would hope she wouldn't, but jealousy can make someone do things they wouldn't normally do," Ivy said.

"Thank you for sharing your concerns, Ivy," George said.

"Yes, thank you, my sweet friend." A chill went up Amelia's spine and she shivered. "Come, let's go inside. Guests will be arriving for the party any moment."

They walked inside together, but Amelia had to fight hard to keep her worried thoughts at bay. As the party wore on, she thought she was hiding her concerns well, until Nick asked her to dance. She quickly realized he saw right through her.

"Finally, a moment alone with you," Nick said.

Amelia chuckled. "Alone? We are surrounded by so many people."

"Perhaps, but we are out of earshot from them while we dance."

"True. But if you wanted to talk with me alone, why not just ask?"

"You know as well as I do that isn't a good idea since Maddy wouldn't understand."

"The dance won't last long, so if you wish to discuss something with me, you should hurry up."

"I see the shadows behind your eyes. What's wrong? Have you heard something more about this Mr. Donovan?" Nick asked.

"How is it that we are in a room filled with people, including the one I am close to becoming engaged to, and you seem to be the only person who sees right through my cheery façade?"

"Nathanial sees your struggle, I'm sure, even if he doesn't say anything about it."

Amelia tilted her head. "But why are you the only one to ask about my welfare?"

"Do you love my brother, Amelia?"

"Gracious, Nick. Such a question, and completely out of nowhere."

"If you don't, please let him down gently, for he is in love with you."

"Do you know something I don't? Does he mean to ask me soon?"

"Yes. And do you know something I don't? Is that why you are worried? Should we be worried about this Mr. Donovan?"

"I'm not ready for such a commitment quite yet, but I don't know what the future holds. And as for the other question, I can't share it with you yet."

"So, you are keeping secrets from me."

"Nick, it's for the good of all those involved. Trust me, if I believed I was in imminent danger, I would share it with you."

Nick glanced around the room as the song ended and the dancers applauded the musicians.

"Please put it out of your mind," Amelia said.

"Put what out of his mind?" Nathanial asked.

"Nothing. He was just asking about Mr. Donovan," Amelia said.

"Has there been a new development?" Nathanial asked.

"None that I wish to discuss right now. Come dance with me, Nathanial. After all, it is a party," Amelia said.

"Happy to oblige you. Excuse us, Nick."

Nick bowed and went to stand next to their mother. Amelia tried not to think about Mr. Donovan and focused on figuring out how to start the needed conversation with Nathanial.

"You don't wish to become engaged right away, do you?" Nathanial asked.

"How did you know that I was going to say anything about it?"

"Sometimes I can't read you very well and I wonder what you are really thinking. And then there are times I can read you like a book," Nathanial said.

"Are you upset with me?"

"Why would I be upset? We have all the time in the world." Nathanial paused. "Amelia, you know that over this past summer, I have grown to love you. But I haven't forgotten that you wanted to take things slow. I am a patient man."

"I don't deserve such devotion from you," she said.

"On the contrary, you deserve all good and wonderful things in this life."

"I do care for you. I hope you know that."

"I do know."

"Nathanial, I need to share something with you, but you must promise me to keep it to yourself until we find out more details."

"What is it?"

"Ivy overheard Maddy discussing the Mr. Donovan situation with her maid. Which, in and of itself, isn't a bad thing, but Ivy heard bits and pieces of things that have given her cause for concern," Amelia said.

"You don't think Madeline would do something stupid, do you? Never mind, I just answered my own question. Of course she would. Such a petty creature. I honestly don't understand the hold she has over Nick."

"Do you suppose it has something to do with business?" Amelia asked.

"I have often thought this very thing," Nathanial said. "He has such a need to go the extra mile to make sure the family is okay. Often at his expense."

"He does it for love of his family."

"You're right, you know."

"Of course, I'm right."

Nathanial laughed. "I do love you, Amelia."

She giggled, leaned in closer to Nathanial, and let herself be swept away by the dance.

Chapter Twenty-Five

Walking along the shore with her brother one last time was all Amelia wanted to do on his final morning in Willow Bay. No new information on the Mr. Donovan situation had turned up. She knew that as much as George wanted to protect her, he missed his family and needed to return to England.

"I will be okay, you know that, George," Amelia said.

"I hope so. It pains me to leave you during such a vulnerable time."

"The brothers will keep me safe. This bay will keep me safe. Besides, we have no proof he is even in the country for me. It's a big land and a place where so many start over."

"True. It just seems too coincidental that he went to Boston."

"Or he went there because that is a city he heard of from his old employer. We shouldn't read more into it without having more facts. It's a ridiculous idea that he would come all this way just to come after me," Amelia said.

"You may be right. Still, I will have my men continue to look for a few more months just to be safe," George said.

"That's fine with me. We should probably head back to the house. Henry will want to head out soon."

"Isn't Maddy coming along with us?" George asked.

"No, she has some wedding plans she wants to finalize with Nick."

"When is the wedding?" George asked.

"They have agreed on next spring. They are getting married in Saint Paul with a large reception there, but will have a small reception here in the bay, too."

"That sounds like it will be a grand affair. Perhaps Violet, Mother, and I can come to one of the events. I will discuss it with them when I return."

"It gives me joy knowing that we have the beginnings of a plan to see one another again."

"It makes me happy too. I hate leaving my little sister behind. But perhaps we'll be celebrating another wedding next year, too, and we can have one long visit."

"As much as you would love that, I'm not sure about it being next year. Perhaps the following, and you will have excuses to come for two years in a row."

"I never need an excuse to see you," George said.

"I know."

Amelia leaned her head against her brother's shoulder for a second and then walked into the house. A short time later, and after a round of goodbyes, Henry and George piled into the car and were off. This time, she wasn't overcome by the same emotions as the last time he'd left. Perhaps it was because she had an idea of when she might see him again.

Once the car was out of sight, Amelia said she was going to visit Tuva. She enjoyed the short walk to the elder's home and quickly found Tuva in her favorite spot on the rear enclosed porch. She had her eyes closed, and Amelia didn't want to disturb her if she was resting, so turned to leave.

"Come sit, Melia," Tuva said.

"I hope I didn't wake you."

"No. I was just resting my eyes. Your brother is off then, is he?"

"He is. As much as he hated to leave me, I think he was also excited to start his journey home."

"Both things can be true. One can feel two emotions."

"Wise as ever, Tuva."

"These are things you already know, though."

"Perhaps." Changing the subject, Amelia asked, "Did you have a nice visit with my brother yesterday?"

"Yes, we did. He didn't tell you about it?"

"No."

"He and I, and Nick, signed the paperwork for our future business venture together."

"That's exciting news. I suppose that solidifies me always being able to come back here no matter what happens between Nathanial and me."

"You could do far worse than Nathanial, but I understand your need to go slow in marrying. When I married my Isak, I didn't know him at all. We had so many wonderful times together over the years, but we also had difficult struggles to overcome. I sometimes wish we would have known each other better in the beginning. It would have saved so much hurt, I think."

"It's refreshing having someone who understands me and what I need."

"I would wager more people understand what you need, including your mother."

"You think so?" Amelia asked.

"I do. I think she understands, but her fear of not securing a proper future for you is what is driving her push to have you married."

"I can hope that's true. That would mean she may just let me take my time after all."

The conversation shifted after that, and Amelia went to make coffee. She spent the rest of the day with Tuva talking about the past and the future as they often did until Tuva encouraged her to head back to the main house for dinner.

Amelia walked along the path, content in her solitude until a branch snapped in the shadows of the trees. She spun around, hoping to find Nathanial or Nick walking around the corner, but seeing no one, she quickened her pace. Footsteps padded behind her. She twisted around, found nothing, and ran the rest of the way.

Once in the safety of the house, she leaned against the door. She tried to steady her pounding heart and slow her breathing. More in control, she went upstairs to her bedroom to freshen up for dinner. She was unnerved and couldn't put it out of her mind while she changed dresses.

"Stop being so silly," Amelia said to her reflection in the mirror.

A few seconds later, Ivy entered the room to escort Amelia down to dinner.

"Are you okay?" Ivy asked. "You look frazzled."

"I'm fine. I just thought someone was following me earlier on the way back to the house, but it was nothing."

"Are you sure? I can have someone go check the grounds and the rest of the point."

Amelia waved the idea away. "No. I'm sure it's nothing. Let's head to dinner, shall we?"

Ivy didn't press further and Amelia plastered a smile on her face, but it would be long into the night before she felt the calm she pretended to have.

Madeline motioned for Amelia to follow her off the path. They had been visiting Tuva, and Madeline suggested a walk before lunch. Amelia's original plan was to head to the house, but she took the opportunity to walk by the water instead.

They went in the direction of the rocky edges of the point when Madeline broke the silence. "Have you heard from George?"

"Yes, he made it home safely."

"It's hard to believe it's been a month since he left."

"Time goes by swiftly here. I'm so glad you decided to lengthen your stay with us," Amelia said.

"You say that like I'm a guest in your home," Madeline said with a huff.

"I didn't mean anything by it, Maddy. Why is it you always twist everything I say and do as an affront toward you?" Amelia asked.

"Because it appears to me like you are trying to steal the life I'm trying to capture for myself."

"How is that even true?" Amelia asked. "You don't even like being here. Plus, I'm in a courtship with Nathanial. I don't understand why you would be so threatened by any of that."

"I know you love Nick," Madeline said.

"That is something you have conjured in your own mind, cousin."

"Is it true, though?" Madeline said, stopping to face Amelia.

"I would be lying to say I didn't care for Nick, but he is Nathanial's brother. Besides, I would never act on any feelings I may or may not have due to my love for you and the respect I have for your relationship with him. He isn't free. And neither am I, for that matter."

"Nick respects and cares for you in ways he will never feel about me."

"Maddy, perhaps if you weren't so prickly all the time it would provide the opportunity for those types of feelings to grow."

"I am not prickly. How dare you say that."

Amelia threw up her arms. "The course you take is all in your control, Maddy. But it will never matter what I say, you will always find a way to be contrary. It saddens me as I had hoped our time together would have allowed our relationship to grow. Especially since we may become sisters-in-law someday."

"I will only change how I feel about things if you would just keep your hands off this family and leave."

Amelia took a step back and placed a hand over her heart. "Maddy, they are not possessions to be had. They are a wonderful family with hearts so big we both can fit within their confines. Will we never get past this?"

"Maybe if you would just admit your part in all of this."

"Part in all of what?" Amelia asked.

"That you are after Nick."

Amelia started laughing, but instead of saying anything more, she walked past Madeline.

"How dare you laugh at me," Madeline said.

"I'm not laughing at you, Maddy. I am laughing at your absurdity. I'm not after Nick. It's up to you to deal with whatever you have going on in your head and move past it. I'll continue to care for you as my cousin, but will keep my distance. And I'm not going anywhere. This is my home now."

Madeline stomped her foot, mumbled something about having too much fresh air, and left.

Amelia continued walking along the point. She rounded a bend, so the town was no longer in sight, and stared out at the beauty of the water. This was her favorite spot in the whole bay, and she stopped to take it in as she always did.

A rustling behind her caught her attention but instead of turning around, she just said, "Maddy, please tell me you have come to your senses."

When no one answered, she breathed in deeply. "Fine, suit yourself. But can you at least pretend to have made peace with me?"

"You sure do know how to mess up people's lives."

A chill ran through her body, and she slowly turned around. A fist connected with her cheek, and she tumbled backward. Her ears started ringing and pain radiated through her head. Amelia opened her mouth to scream, but everything went black.

⸻ ₰ₑₑ ⸻

At the sound of her name from far away, Amelia tried opening her eyes. Ivy's face blurred into view. "Wha...wha..."

"Don't try to speak. Oh, Amelia, who did this to you?"

"Mist..."

"It's okay. Just hush now and we will gather details later. I have sent for help," Ivy said, cradling Amelia's hand.

Amelia's eyes drooped closed as frantic voices rushed around her. She winced when something bumped against her side, and her body lifted in the air.

"Oh, Melia. Hang on, love," Nick's voice whispered against her ear, and she drifted away once more.

A shriek brought Amelia back to the surface, and she tried opening her eyes, but the pain rushing through her head forced her to close them again.

"What happened?" she asked.

"You were attacked, Amelia. The doctor is here, and he is going to fix you right up. You will be right as rain in no time," Nathanial said.

Everything flooded back to her, and she tried sitting up. "Mr. Donovan."

"Mr. Donovan? You saw him?" Nick asked.

"Yes, just before everything went black."

A cool cloth pressed against the sting on Amelia's face, and she sighed.

"It doesn't appear that anything is broken," the doctor said. "It looks like he just knocked her about a few times. Her ribs are bruised, so she might have pain in her right side for a while. It looks like he kicked her there. I will clean the gash on the back of her head from where she fell. I will be back in a few days to clean and re-bandage it. In the meantime, I recommend rest and isolation. She will most likely experience headaches for a few days, and her side will be in pain for a bit longer. But I suspect a full recovery."

"That is good news, at least," Ivy said.

Amelia tried to sit up once more, but Ivy forced her to lie back down. Nick asked a few questions, and she tried to open her eyes to help make sense of the rest of the conversation, but the pain kept forcing them to close. Giving in, she drifted off to sleep.

Chapter Twenty-Six

THE SUN FILTERED THROUGH the curtains, casting a line of light across the bedroom floor. Amelia looked around her room and noticed she was alone for the first time in days. She sat up slowly and stretched. She closed her eyes and breathed in deeply before releasing the air out of her mouth. It was the first time her bruised ribs didn't scream at her, and she flung her covers aside.

She walked to the window, pushed open her curtains, and blinked. She allowed her eyes to adjust to the brightness of the sun and looked out at the blue waves and sighed.

I think I'm going to be just fine.

"What are you doing out of bed?" Ivy asked, walking into the room with a tray filled with bread, coffee, and a bowl of fruit.

"I couldn't lay there another moment. You have to let me up. The swelling and bruises are gone, and my cuts have all scabbed over. I no longer need the bandage around my head. And I can breathe in deeply without my ribs yelling at me."

"We're all just trying to help you heal and keep you safe."

"I'm aware of that, but I feel like a prisoner, not a patient."

Ivy set the tray of food on the table next to the chair by the fireplace.

"Fine, sit here while you eat, then I will help you bathe and get dressed. Perhaps a walk outside will do you some good."

Amelia hugged Ivy. "Thank you!"

Ivy sat across from Amelia while she ate all her food and drank her coffee.

"You're not eating?" Amelia asked.

"I ate a while ago."

"What time is it?"

"It's midmorning."

"This is the last time I will allow myself to sleep so late. There are things I should be doing."

"Like what?" Ivy asked. "The only thing you should be focusing on is getting well."

"I am getting well," Amelia said, playing with the last bite of bread.

"I know you are," Ivy said and reached to squeeze Amelia's hand. "Perhaps a walk to visit Tuva would do you good. I will come with you if you like."

"Where is Nathanial?"

"He is at the marina with Nick. They had a shipment come in."

Silence fell over the room while Amelia tried to conjure the right words to ask about her attacker.

"He hasn't been found yet, but he isn't in the bay," Ivy said.

"It's just like you to read my mind, Ivy. I guess I was wrong about Mr. Donovan coming to this country to start anew, but I'm surprised he would put so much time and energy into finding me."

"Amelia, I wonder about that."

"What do you mean?"

"Remember the night of the party while your brother was here, and I shared that I was concerned about a conversation I overheard."

"You can't suggest Maddy would have something to do with this?"

"Jealousy clouds one's judgment. I'm not accusing her of plotting an attack. But I could see her doing something to scare you off."

"Like sharing my whereabouts with someone who wants to cause me harm."

"It's a theory I have, nothing more," Ivy said.

"Let's not say anything until we find out more information. Where is Maddy anyway? I've only seen her one time since the attack."

"She's in Saint Paul. She said the attack shook her up so much she could no longer stay in such a barbaric place."

Amelia started laughing, but grabbed her side at the sharpness in her ribs. "I can breathe better, but laughing isn't a hundred percent normal, apparently."

"I will call for a bath and let's get you dressed for the day. But are you sure a walk outside will be okay since you have some soreness left?"

"The outside is exactly what I need, Ivy."

"Very well. I'll be right back."

Ivy left and Amelia walked to the window a second time. The warmth of the sun radiated through the glass, and she closed her eyes. It would be chilly out, but she couldn't wait to feel the lake breeze and sunlight on her skin.

Ivy poured coffee into three separate cups and passed them out as the conversation lulled. Gratitude flooded over Amelia at her friendship with these two women. Ivy had never left her side while she was forced to stay in bed, and Tuva had come to visit, even though it was difficult for her.

As dappled sunlight filtered in through the open window on Tuva's porch, Tuva shared her own history of being attacked. Although Amelia's attack was different from Tuva's, she took comfort in knowing she wasn't alone while working to get over it.

The front door opened and closed, and Amelia stood to go see who it might be. Surprise registered on Nick's face when he saw her.

"You're looking so much better, Melia," Nick said.

"I feel better," she said, settling into her chair. She reached for her coffee and took a sip.

"I came to discuss that contract we wanted to possibly forgo, but it can wait," Nick said to Tuva.

"We can head out if you need to discuss business," Amelia said.

"Nonsense," Nick said. "Enjoy your visit. It's been a while since you were able to come. My matter can wait. There's no rush."

"Nick has decided not to pursue the contract he has been working on for several years now," Tuva said. "He discovered that his contract with the Campbell business has been much more profitable for all parties involved. His other pursuit wouldn't compare, so there is no need to move forward with it, especially since it isn't a foregone conclusion."

"You are not referring to the contract with Maddy's father, are you?" Amelia asked. "It's a shame you must drop it after all your hard work."

Nick ran his fingers through his hair. "Yes, I put in many hours on it, but we could never quite come to an agreement. Once Maddy and I became betrothed, her father wanted to pursue a new business venture together. However, he struggled to give us the data we needed to make a solid decision on that as well."

"Nick never felt right about the details," Tuva said. "And I've had my reservations as well. So, we have decided not to pursue any business with them at all."

"Henry mentioned in his letters that his father hasn't done such a great job with several aspects of their family business, and he is having to clean up several messes," Ivy said.

Amelia turned to Ivy. Surprise quickly changed to happiness at the idea of her favorite cousin and best friend becoming close enough to be corresponding.

"I suppose it's best you don't continue after all. I hope this doesn't damper your continued wedding plans," Amelia said.

Nick shrugged and handed Tuva a stack of papers along with a pen.

"If we are in agreement, please read, then sign, and I will take the paperwork to Saint Paul myself," Nick said.

"Just tell me where to sign, dear boy. I don't need to read anything," Tuva said.

She scrawled her name at the designated spots and Nick made ready to leave.

"It's wonderful to see you looking so well, Melia," Nick said.

He said his goodbyes and slipped out.

"I don't see him being tied to a certain woman much longer," Tuva said.

Amelia glanced at Ivy but asked Tuva, "You don't think she would break things off just because of business, do you?"

"She won't. He will," Tuva said. "I believe he realized his mistake of offering to marry her quite some time ago, but he was trying to remain the committed gentleman. Plus, he didn't want to negatively impact our family business. Mr. Granger may not handle business well, but the Grangers do have a name for themselves in certain circles, and I believe he feared repercussions that could set us back."

"But the business with my brother offsets any of that, doesn't it?" Amelia said.

"It does, but setting that aside, I told him months ago not to pursue the marriage if he didn't love her," Tuva said.

Amelia wouldn't allow herself to think about Nick being free. She was still in a courtship with Nathanial and cared for him even if she did not love him. She glanced at Ivy and could tell her friend was studying her intently. Growing tired, Amelia yawned.

"Perhaps we should head back to the house, Ivy," she said.

"Healing one's body, mind, and soul after an attack takes time, and it's exhausting. You must rest, my dear," Tuva said. "Besides, I need to go lay down myself. This old body has a hard time keeping up these days. It isn't long for this world."

"I hate the sound of that," Amelia said, gathering her shawl.

"One cannot stop the end of life," Tuva said.

Ivy took the dishes to the kitchen and grabbed her own wrap.

Linking arms with Amelia, she said, "Come, friend, let's get you back to the main house for a lie-down."

"Until next time, Tuva," Amelia said.

Tuva slowly moved to Amelia and wrapped her frail arms around her. "Until next time, my dear." She shuffled into the main part of her house and called for her house-keeper to help her to her room.

"I can help," Amelia said.

Tuva waved her off. "No, go rest. I have all the help I need."

Amelia and Ivy left Tuva's once they confirmed the housekeeper was assisting. They walked in silence until the wind picked up.

Shivering, Amelia said, "It won't be long before the first snow falls."

"How do you know that?" Ivy asked, laughing. "Your perception of this place always amazes me, and you always end up being right."

"I don't know, but right now I'm going to enjoy the beauty of the changing leaves on the trees."

"I believe Mrs. Nilsson mentioned they always like to have a harvest party or something."

"She told me she thought about canceling it, but I told her not to," Amelia said.

"What are your thoughts around Maddy and Nick no longer being engaged?" Ivy asked.

"I won't think about it until it actually happens. For now, let's focus on resting for the remainder of the afternoon. I plan to join everyone for dinner this evening."

"I love that idea. Just please don't overdo it."

"Would I ever do such a thing?"

Ivy's laughter echoed along the point.

"Are you going to tell me what is going on with you and a certain cousin of mine?" Amelia asked.

Ivy sobered and glanced at her. "I wasn't sure what you would think. I wasn't sure what I thought about it, really. I didn't believe he was sincere at first, but he seems to enjoy my company and he writes me several times a week."

"I love the idea of the two of you being together," Amelia said.

"You don't care that I don't have the right background?"

"I would never care about that. I have only ever cared about who you are on the inside. You are amazing, and if the person you are with matches that, I say go for it. The rest of his family may have an issue with it. But I never will."

"If I have your support, that is all that matters," Ivy said, squeezing Amelia's arm.

The wind picked up, causing red and yellow leaves to dance around them. Ivy and Amelia giggled as they hopped about. Amelia stopped and held her side. She was enjoying her time outside too much to let the pain in her ribs stop her, but the chill in the air made her shiver again. Ivy put an arm around Amelia, and they rushed into the warmth of the indoors while their laughter continued to echo across the bay.

Chapter Twenty-Seven

AMELIA LEANED CLOSER TO get a better study of Tuva's appearance. "Perhaps I shouldn't go to the party tonight."

"Nonsense, I will tell you as I told Kathleen and the boys. I may be going soon, but my passing will not be during the Harvest Ball."

"But, Tuva, I want to be here to help care for you."

"I have plenty to assist me, my dear," Tuva said. "Now go. Have fun. Dance to your heart's content. You are finally well enough to do just that."

"Okay, but only if you insist."

Ivy peeked in as Amelia stood to leave.

"Is everything okay?" Amelia asked.

"Yes, it's only a letter from George that just arrived. I thought you would want to read it right away, though," Ivy said.

"Go read your letter, have fun at the party, and come visit me tomorrow to tell me all about it," Tuva said.

Amelia kissed Tuva's forehead and followed Ivy out of the house. Ivy pulled the letter out of her pocket, handing it to Amelia. Amelia paused long enough to read it in its entirety and shared its contents with Ivy.

"Apparently, George and Mother made their way to America. They docked in New York just a few days ago. They are heading to Boston, and if weather permits, they are coming to Willow Bay."

"Because of what happened to you?" Ivy asked.

"Yes, but that's not all. Mother is so upset about the whole thing that she is taking me back to England with her as soon as possible. Ivy, I can't bear it. How could they steal me away? Mother promised I would at least have a year."

She couldn't hold back her tears.

"She is just worried about you. Maybe once they arrive, they will see you are okay, and she will let you stay," Ivy said.

"Perhaps I should have married Nathanial as soon as he mentioned his love for me."

"Amelia, you can't be serious. Don't rush things just because your future looks bleak right now. You never know what could happen."

"You're right, of course. I just can't stand the thought of leaving here again."

"I know, but let's push all sadness and all unknown futures aside and focus on the party tonight."

Ivy walked Amelia to her room, called for a bath for her, and disappeared to get ready herself. Amelia focused on bathing and dressing for the night and was about to start her hair when Ivy returned.

"Here, let me help you," Ivy said.

Amelia let Ivy take over and her friend quickly put together a beautiful updo.

"You are so good at doing my hair, my friend," Amelia said.

Ivy nodded.

"You look beautiful tonight. Are you excited to see Henry?" Amelia asked.

"I am. Now hush, I'm trying to concentrate."

Amelia chuckled. Ivy finished pinning the last strand of Amelia's hair when Maddy barged into the room.

"Have you forgotten your manners, Miss Madeline?" Ivy asked.

"How dare you speak to me in such a way? You're just a servant," Madeline said.

"Don't talk to Ivy like that," Amelia said. "You know she's right. Barging into my room was rather rude."

"Perhaps, but I had to see you," Madeline said.

"Why? You were so ready to leave after I was attacked," Amelia said.

"I couldn't bear the idea that you were hurt. I should have continued to walk with you. I blame myself for what happened."

"You shouldn't blame yourself," Amelia said.

"Unless you actually did have something to do with it," Ivy said.

"How dare you imply that I could ever have anything to do with an attack on my cousin. I will have you fired," Madeline said.

"I wasn't implying anything, but you're sure acting like maybe you did," Ivy said.

"Stop goading her. It isn't worth it," Amelia said.

"That's it. I'm going to have Ivy thrown out of this house at once," Madeline said.

Amelia stood. "Who do you think you are, Maddy? You have no say when it comes to Ivy. Besides that, Ivy is no more an employee of this house than I am. She is my friend."

Madeline mumbled a few protests, but stomped out of the room.

"Has she always been this mean and I never saw it?" Amelia asked, sitting back in her chair.

"She has never been kind to any of the staff," Ivy said. "I believe she's very good at pretending, but she's struggling to keep her façade with you. You're so good at reading people, you can discern people's true character when given the opportunity, and it unnerves her so much that it's causing her mask to slip."

"I just feel foolish that she tricked me for so long," Amelia said.

"But did she? I mean, she kept rubbing you the wrong way, right? Perhaps you just didn't want to see what you saw there all along, since she is your cousin. Especially since you were so close as children. But time and different up-bringings can allow people to change and move in opposite directions."

"I suppose. I hate to say it, but you're going to run into issues with her when you and Henry are finally honest with everyone about your relationship."

"She doesn't scare me," Ivy said.

"Good. What will Henry say, though?"

"He doesn't care one bit what she thinks. He believes her to be shallow and is frustrated by her most of the time."

Amelia slid her gloves over her fingers and stood. "Enough about her before it spoils our mood for the party. Escort me, my friend."

"I would be delighted to," Ivy said.

They linked arms and went downstairs. The brothers and Henry were huddled together, discussing something serious, but hushed their conversation when they noticed Amelia.

"Don't stop talking on my account, gentleman," Amelia said.

"We were just discussing news that I heard of Mr. Donovan," Henry said.

Amelia tried to hide her shock and was thankful when she managed to recover quickly.

"Henry, now is not the time," Nathanial said.

"No. It's okay. I want to know the details. It's my safety after all," Amelia said.

"George and I have been working together to find Mr. Donovan and have him arrested. Unfortunately, he escaped again and the last we heard, he was seen in Duluth," Henry said.

"How long ago was that?" Ivy asked.

"A week," Nick said, studying Amelia.

"He could be anywhere," Amelia said.

"Yes, but we won't worry about that tonight," Nick said with such tenderness, Amelia had to keep from looking at him so no one would read her betraying thoughts.

Henry complimented Ivy, asked if she would like a drink and offered his arm. Ivy made sure Amelia was okay before she and Henry disappeared around the corner, and Amelia turned back to the brothers.

"Perhaps Amelia would like a drink or to dance, Nathanial," Nick said as a pained expression crossed his face. He excused himself to go and greet Madeline.

"Shall we move closer to the dance floor?" Nathanial asked.

"What's wrong, Nathanial? There seems to be something besides Mr. Donovan's whereabouts that is bothering you."

"We had a letter from George. We know your mother is determined to come and take you away from us."

"I was hoping to share that news myself. He isn't for that idea. I hope you know that."

"We must persuade your mother to let you stay then," Nathanial said.

"Is that all?" Amelia asked.

"We have reason to believe Mr. Donovan is on his way here."

A sinking feeling settled in the pit of Amelia's stomach, and her throat became dry. "I think I need some water and to sit down for a moment, Nathanial."

"I hope my judgment in telling you wasn't an oversight on my part."

"On the contrary, I'm glad you told me. This helps me know I need to be that much more vigilant when doing anything by myself."

"Or perhaps you shouldn't do anything by yourself."

"You're most likely correct in that way of thinking," Amelia said. She realized there was something else troubling Nathanial and asked him about it.

"Nick will be breaking his engagement off when he goes back with the Granger family to Saint Paul a few days after the party," Nathanial said.

"I see. I would think you would be happy about this."

"I am. However, I can't help but wonder what will become of me and you. Nick, of course, won't stand in our way, but I also know my brother and how he feels about you. And I love both of you so much I wouldn't want to stand in your way either."

"Nathanial, I wish..."

Nathanial squeezed her hand. "It's okay. Truly it is. We can't stop what the heart longs for. Can we?"

"I don't even know what my heart longs for."

Nathanial tilted his head to the side. "I wonder if perhaps you just haven't allowed your heart to do what it wants in this matter. One's heart can't truly be broken if you keep it from feeling what it wants to feel, correct?"

"I don't know much about that," Amelia said, as a lump formed in the back of her throat. "I do know that you're a good man and deserve all of life's wonderful things. I would be a lucky woman to have you."

"I feel like I have brought the gloom to what should be a fun party," Henry said, interrupting the conversation. He stuck his hand out toward Amelia. "Dance with me, cousin."

Amelia squeezed Nathaniel's hand, winked at him, and joined her cousin on the dance floor.

"All the buzz in the room is around Mr. Donovan, you healing, and my dancing with Ivy. But all I see is the dance of heartbreak between my closest friends and my dearest cousin," Henry said, leading her into a slow waltz.

"You're seeing things, Henry."

"Come now. You never were a good liar," Henry said.

"Perhaps it's best I do leave Willow Bay."

"Maybe it's best for your safety, but I don't believe you are meant to be gone for long. This place calls to you as it does me."

"Tell me, Henry, do I need to protect my friend Ivy against my cousin?"

Henry's face lit up and a grin spread across his face. "I will be asking her to marry me at Christmas. And if you try to take her with you when you leave, I will just follow you and steal her back. I love her, Amelia."

"That makes my heart happy to hear. You better not hurt her."

"I will spend the rest of my life making sure I don't."

"Should I tell you what is about to happen to Maddy?" she asked.

"No need. I saw the writing on the wall as soon as her true nature started seeping out, even before you showed up. She would have eventually run him off. And if she hadn't, I would have intervened. Nick is too good a man and friend to be bound to such a creature."

"I'm surprised to hear you say that."

"Why? Because she's my sister?" Henry asked. "She's too much like my aunt on my father's side. They've spent a lot of time together over the years, and I'm afraid my aunt's ruthlessness has rubbed off on her."

"I almost feel sorry for Maddy."

"Please don't. Now let's focus on finishing the last part of this dance and then get a drink. I'm thirsty. And from now on, we will only focus on having fun."

"Sounds like a wonderful idea."

Amelia focused on Henry's plan of having a great time the rest of the night. She danced with Nathanial, but kept her distance from Nick and Madeline. She munched on delicious food and sipped glasses of champagne.

When most of the partygoers had left, Kathleen announced the annual bonfire had been lit for those remaining and more intimate guests. Grabbing her coat, Amelia went outside and watched the flames dance against the backdrop of the night sky. Waves rushed to meet the shore in the distance, and the sound of it pulled her away from everyone else.

An uneasy feeling settled into Amelia's stomach when she realized how far she was from the crowd, but she tried to push it aside. She refused to let Mr. Donovan ruin her sense of safety in her favorite place. She stepped closer to the edge of the point to get a better view when there was a rustling behind her. Amelia spun about but quickly relaxed.

"Oh, it's you," she said when she saw Madeline stumble into view.

"Who else would it be?" Madeline asked, her words slurring.

"You've been drinking quite a bit tonight, I see. Perhaps we should get you inside." Amelia wrapped her arms around her cousin to help guide her inside, but Madeline shoved her hard, knocking them both off balance.

"What is wrong with you?" Amelia asked as she steadied herself.

"I hate you, Amelia."

"Maddy, I am so heartbroken that you would say that to me, but I refuse to believe that it's true. I'm going to ignore your words and choose to believe it's the alcohol talking and not your heart."

"You are so stupid," Madeline said, stumbling against Amelia.

"That's it. Come on now, let's get you inside," Amelia said.

Amelia helped direct a swerving Madeline toward the house.

"You know what? I have a secret," Madeline said, leaning into Amelia's help.

"You do. What is that?"

"I'm the one who found Mr. Donovan and told him to come here."

The blood drained from Amelia's cheeks. "Madeline, what are you saying?"

"He didn't come to America to find you. You're not as important as you think. But I thought it might be a good idea to have him help me get rid of you."

Amelia pulled away from Madeline to examine her, but her cousin had a hard time standing on her own. Amelia wanted to hate her, but Madeline had allowed anger and bitterness to consume her. She had turned into a miserable creature who was no longer recognizable, and Amelia could only feel sorry for her.

"Perhaps you should sit down. I will fetch Nick or Henry to help you inside," Amelia said and turned to walk away.

"Watch your back, bitch."

Amelia flinched but kept walking in the direction of the bonfire. A loud crack sounded, and her arm stung. Blood seeped from the rip in her sleeve, and she realized a bullet had grazed her. Shock rushed through her body as another shot fired just missing her head. The gun fired again, and she ran toward Madeline. She hoped to reach her cousin in time, as another slug whistled past her ear.

Diving on top of her cousin, Amelia was surprised Madeline was laughing. There were shouts in the distance and Amelia rolled with Madeline toward the closest bushes. Dirt flew up around them where shells slammed into the ground. Madeline pushed against her, screaming for her to let go. Amelia slapped her, stunning her long enough to pull them to safety.

"Why are you trying to save me?" Madeline asked.

"Because you don't deserve to die," Amelia said.

"That's funny."

"What's funny?" Amelia asked.

"You're trying to save me, but I'm the one who keeps trying to have you hurt."

Amelia stopped struggling to hold her cousin, stood, and looked down at her. Madeline was in a drunken stupor, sprawled out against the grass with her eyes half closed.

Another blast pealed through the air, and someone shouted, "Stay down, Amelia."

Realizing she didn't have time to take cover, Amelia spread her arms, palms open, and closed her eyes. She waited to feel the bite of another bullet.

"I got him," Henry shouted.

The breeze blew through Amelia's hair, and she could only hear waves crashing against the rocks. Opening her eyes, she noticed the brothers running toward her from different directions. She breathed in one big gulp of air and collapsed into a heap on the ground. Madeline's laughter turned to sobs, but Amelia couldn't turn to comfort her cousin.

She buried her face in her hands and wept.

Chapter Twenty-Eight

Ivy's arm draped around Amelia's shoulders as everyone huddled in the drawing room. The shock of what had happened had worn off, and Amelia didn't want to leave. She had to know what was going to happen next.

"After questioning Mr. Donovan, the sheriff discovered that the man had been paid for his services and bribed to keep quiet if he was caught," Henry said.

"By whom?" Kathleen asked.

"Madeline," Ivy said.

"What's that?" Nick asked.

"I would wager anything it was Madeline," Ivy said.

All eyes turned toward Ivy, then to Madeline.

"Say this isn't true, Maddy," Henry said, moving closer to his sister.

"I'm afraid it might be," Amelia said.

She stood, trying to figure out how to explain things. Nick and Nathanial jumped to their feet, but neither moved toward her.

Madeline started laughing and attempted to get off the couch. She wobbled before steadying herself against its arm.

"Look at you all jumping to your feet over poor Amelia," Madeline said. "What about me? She came here to steal my life. I couldn't allow that to happen. Mr. Donovan came to this country, but his history with her would have destroyed him too, so two birds, one stone."

Mumbles of confusion trickled around the room. Amelia started to say something, but Madeline cut her off, though no one could understand her slurring words. She stumbled forward, regained her footing, mumbled a few more unintelligible words, and crumbled to the ground unconscious.

"Maddy," Henry said, rushing to his sister's side. He checked her pulse. "I don't think I have ever seen anyone so intoxicated."

"Amelia, do you know what's going on?" Nick asked.

"Madeline all but confessed she hired Mr. Donovan."

"Why didn't you tell anyone?" Henry asked.

"She just told me when we were out walking tonight."

"Amelia, are you hurt?" Nathanial asked, stepping forward.

Ivy looked at the blood coming from Amelia's arm.

"It's just a graze," Amelia said. "It's not so bad that I couldn't be here with the rest of you to find out what happened."

"That may be, but we are going to go clean you up," Ivy said. "No arguments."

Amelia couldn't protest when Ivy used that tone, so complied with her friend. They went to her bedroom where Ivy cleaned the wound, wrapped it, and helped Amelia change into her nightdress. Ivy was wrapping Amelia's dressing gown over her shoulders when there was a knock on the door.

"Come in," Amelia said, after slipping her arms into the sleeves.

Kathleen walked in with a tray holding a pitcher of water, a bottle of wine, and several glasses. "I wasn't sure what we would want to drink while we discuss things."

"A glass of water will work for my parched lips, but a glass of wine will help with my frayed nerves," Amelia said.

"I thought as much," Kathleen said and poured three glasses of water and three glasses of cabernet.

Ivy tidied up the mess from cleaning Amelia's wound and joined Amelia and Kathleen by the fire. When Ivy was settled, Amelia allowed the water and wine to rejuvenate her.

"Are you okay, Amelia?" Kathleen asked.

"I'm fine, truly I am," she said.

"Very well," Kathleen said. "I will go ahead and share what was discussed after you left."

"Thank you for not keeping things from me," Amelia said.

"Of course," Kathleen said. "Nick had the sheriff come in, and Henry explained what you and Madeline said. He has requested that we keep Madeline here until morning because of her intoxication. I don't think we need to worry about her trying to flee under the circumstances. He is taking Mr. Donovan to be held at the sheriff's office, and he will be tried here for attempted murder, instead of being sent back to England. The sheriff said it didn't take much for Mr. Donovan to share all that had occurred once the sheriff indicated he already knew Madeline was involved. Apparently, she told him the Campbells were looking for him, to send him back to England where he would go to prison, but that if he helped her, she would see to it he got a fresh start out west somewhere."

"It's hard for me to believe that Maddy planned this whole thing," Amelia said.

"I know," Kathleen said. "I'm so thankful Nick saw through her before all of this. The guilt would have been too much for him. I suppose we never thought she was capable of something this awful, though."

"Is Henry okay?" Ivy asked.

"He is pretty shaken up, but my boys are comforting him," Kathleen said. "On a side note, I'm happy he has found you, Ivy."

"You don't think it's wrong for me to be with him or someday marry him?" Ivy asked.

"We are just bay people here," Kathleen said. "Most of society's rules come into play only when we are doing business or leave Willow Bay. But our normal practice is to just love and accept one another based on their character, not their financial status or who their family is. I'm not sure what will happen with the Grangers now that their daughter will be charged with a crime, but Henry will always be accepted here. Just as you are, Ivy."

A knock sounded at the door, and Ivy went to answer it.

"Nick, is everything okay?" Ivy asked, letting the door swing open.

"Yes. I just wanted to make sure Amelia was okay."

"We are all okay, my sweet boy," Kathleen said. She rose and gathered the glasses.

"Mamma, I didn't realize you were here," he said.

"I was just checking on our girl and explaining to her what she missed," Kathleen said.

Amelia yawned. "We should all head to bed. Sleep will do us all good after the night we have had."

Kathleen and Ivy agreed. Amelia could tell Nick wanted a moment to chat with her, but she just wanted to collapse into bed. Goodnights were said, and Amelia encouraged Nick to talk with her the next day. When she was finally alone, she let the pain of being betrayed by her cousin ease in and she cried herself to sleep.

Amelia sat across the table from Madeline, waiting for her cousin to respond. They were alone in the dining room with Madeline tied loosely to her chair. Amelia wanted a chance to talk with her cousin privately before the sheriff arrived to pick her up, but she no longer trusted her. She had just told Madeline she wished no ill will toward her, but instead of responding, Madeline turned away and stared out the window. Growing impatient, Amelia moved away from the table to leave.

"Sit down," Madeline snapped. "I mean, please sit."

Even though Amelia complied, she was poised to leave if Madeline snapped at her again.

"I have nothing to say for myself, Amelia. I want to apologize, but there's still some part of me that feels like you deserved everything that happened to you."

"But why? I didn't do anything against you."

"Shortly before you arrived in Saint Paul over a year ago, I was contemplating breaking things off with Nick. Daddy came to me and told me that I needed to make sure I went through with my marriage. He had made some investments that didn't work out, and we were going to lose almost everything if the deal with the Nilssons didn't go through."

"Henry says your family is in some financial trouble, but nothing that can't be fixed."

. "Nothing that can't be fixed to some degree by Henry, but we would still lose some of our holdings. We would have to sell our home in Duluth and downsize our home in St. Paul. The embarrassment alone would kill me. It is of utmost importance for me to marry Nick, Amelia. Or at least it was."

"There is so much more to life than wealth."

"Easy to say, coming from someone who has a lot of it."

"I see how that could be your viewpoint. But, Maddy, what do your father's financial dealings have to do with me?"

A rumble of laughter started low in Madeline until she was laughing almost hysterically. She stopped suddenly and said, "You are such a fool, Amelia. Don't you see it? Nick is absolutely in love with you. He has been since that first conversation with you in my dining room."

"I have nothing to say about his feelings. But I never encouraged him, and I tried desperately to make my courtship with Nathanial work. You must know that. I never wanted to hurt you. Ever."

"The funny thing is, I don't even like Nick. And I hate Willow Bay. I always wanted to marry a wealthy man in Saint Paul, but the business dealings with Nick were the only ones that would work to save my father."

"And you wonder why I hate being a pawn in the game of marriage," Amelia said.

"I think I get it now. Perhaps I should have asked you for help instead of turning against you."

"Sadly, it's too late for that now. I will never trust you, but I hope the courts go lenient on you. After all, you are my cousin, and I care for you still."

"How is Henry?" Madeline asked.

"He hasn't come to see you?"

"No. Nick did. Just long enough to officially break things off with me and to tell me he hopes he never has to lay eyes on me ever again."

"Did you really think you would get away with this?"

"Honestly, Amelia? I believed you would get scared and either run to your mother or she would come to get you. Either way, I thought I would be rid of you after Mr. Donovan attacked you the first time. I obviously under-estimated you."

"How could you let him beat me that way?"

"I didn't think he would beat you like that. He was supposed to just scare you. But you are so tough and refused to leave, so I had to up the game and have him come back. He wasn't supposed to actually shoot you."

"Maddy, my mother is on her way here to take me away from Willow Bay. She was already doing that before you had Mr. Donovan return."

"What?" Her face grew red as veins bulged from her forehead. "I could have gotten away with it. I could have won. You bitch! Why didn't you tell me your mother was coming to get you?"

Amelia crossed to stand over Madeline. "Perhaps your last statement is a good indication as to why I didn't tell you."

"You better watch your back, Amelia."

Amelia walked to the door. "I won't watch my back. Do you know why? I don't have to. All the people that I love will be doing it for me."

"I hope you have nightmares about me," Madeline screeched as she struggled against her restraints.

"On the contrary, Maddy. Once I leave this room, I will never think of you again except to feel sorry for you. Goodbye, cousin."

"Come back here. Amelia! Come back here!"

In the hallway, Amelia linked arms with Ivy and told her friend she needed some fresh air. Madeline's scream could be heard until she shut the front door behind her.

Once on the lawn, and Ivy was sure Amelia was okay, they decided to go visit Tuva. When they arrived, they discovered Tuva was sleeping, so Ivy went back to the main house. Amelia wanted to wait to make sure Tuva was doing okay so wandered about looking at pictures on the walls.

Enjoying the quiet, she went to sit on the front porch and watch the water. She wasn't sure how much time had passed, but when Tuva woke up, Amelia moved to her room. She sat next to her bed and shared everything that had happened. Amelia tried not to let the hurt come to the surface.

"This isn't your fault," Tuva said.

"It's hard not to blame myself," Amelia said.

"You can't control other people's actions."

"I suppose not, but perhaps I led Nick on. Did I flaunt that in front of Maddy?"

"So what if you did? It doesn't give anyone the right to cause harm. And besides that, it isn't like you to flaunt anything in front of anyone."

Amelia started to respond when the front door slammed open. She jumped out of her seat, ready to protect Tuva, but relaxed slightly as a breathless Ivy rushed into the bedroom. Seeing the alarm on her friend's face, she frowned.

"Ivy, what is it?" Amelia asked.

Ivy took a couple of deep breaths. "Madeline got loose and slipped out of the house."

Amelia's hand flew to her mouth. "Is she?"

"She's gone."

Chapter Twenty-Nine

Wringing her hands together, Amelia paced back and forth. "I should have gone. Perhaps I should have gone."

"I think you made the right decision in not going," Ivy said.

"Have you heard from Henry?"

"He will be arriving sometime later this evening, I think."

"What about Nick?"

"He is coming tomorrow by water on the *Vide Fjärd*. But you already knew that," Ivy said. "Amelia, you must calm down."

"I can't. My cousin is still missing. The trial starts today for Mr. Donovan, and I feel like I'm not where I'm supposed to be for the first time since coming to Willow Bay."

"It's best that I came to take you away from here then," her mother said, entering the room.

"Mother," Amelia squealed and ran into her mother's arms.

George was right behind her and took his turn to hug Amelia close. They settled in the drawing room to visit, and Ivy excused herself, saying she was going to find Henry. Amelia updated them on the latest, and George shared how Violet was faring. Their reunion was cut short when Nathanial walked in requesting to speak with Amelia alone.

Receiving permission from her mother, Amelia grabbed his arm and allowed him to lead her to the front porch. The sun was trying to peek through the clouds, but she shivered at the cold.

Nathanial wrapped her coat around her. "Come, let's walk a little."

"That's the best idea I've heard all day."

"I've been thinking. The weather is going to be changing soon to the point we can't get out on the water much, and I know your mother will be taking you away from Willow Bay again. What would you say to joining us when we go out on the boats tomorrow?"

"Really? Are you sure that's such a good idea?"

"It will be fine. Besides, if we run into any trouble, Nick will be coming up on the *Vide Fjärd* and will rescue us."

Amelia chuckled. "I love that idea. Maybe we should bring George along."

"I was actually hoping we could go alone. As alone as one can be with our other fishing boat casting off with us and the crewmen on board our boat. I know it isn't proper, but I want a few last moments alone with you to make some memories before you go."

"I'm not dying, Nathanial. I'm just going to England. Don't think for a minute I won't find a way to return. But a boat ride sounds lovely before I sail away for a while."

"So, it's settled?"

"I'm looking forward to it."

Leaning as far over the railing as she could, Amelia studied the water closely. She noticed the swells of the waves were growing and wondered what the lake was trying to tell her.

"One of these times you're going to fall overboard doing that," Nathanial said.

Straightening, she said, "Perhaps, but today is not that day."

"Captain Nathanial, a word please," a crewman said, nodding his head in the direction of Amelia.

"Go on. I will be fine here. I promise to keep my body on this side of the railing."

"Very well."

Nathanial followed the crewman, and Amelia looked out over the water. The other fishing boat, the *Bay Minnow*, was further away from them than she expected. Her boat listed in a strange way and she knew immediately something was wrong. She studied her surroundings and realized the winds had picked up.

Maybe it wasn't such a good idea for me to come out today after all.

A few minutes later, Nathanial joined her, interrupting her worried thoughts.

"Everything okay?" Amelia asked.

"A couple of things broke, which isn't surprising for this old rust bucket. I should have brought the *Sailor Anne*. But no need to fret, Amelia. The men are diligently working, and if things aren't repaired before Nick passes by, I will send you home with him on the *Vide Fjärd.*

"How was Nick the last time you talked with him?" she asked.

"He is blaming himself for not seeing what type of person Madeline really was and for bringing her into your life. To which I reminded him she is your cousin, and Madeline was the one that brought you into our lives. He's hurting."

"Is he angry with me?"

"Why would he be angry with you? This isn't your fault. He just has to work things out in his head and heart. He will be fine and will go back to the same ol' Nick we all love."

Amelia accepted his explanation for now, and Nathanial went back to work on the repairs. Trying to keep herself preoccupied, she wandered around the boat, talking with different crewmen and enjoying the sway of the boat on water. Time went by quickly, and she was surprised when the sun dipping into the horizon turned to night. It had grown colder, so she added a sweater over her dress and put pants on. She decided to leave her dress on for added layers and was finishing buttoning her coat when Nathanial found her.

"I was beginning to think you had fallen overboard," Nathanial said.

"No, just adding some layers so I don't get cold. Do you think Nick changed his mind since he isn't here yet?" Amelia asked.

"I think he just got a later start than intended. He will be along soon. Don't worry."

"Okay, but should I worry that we are still out here? It's getting so late, and the weather isn't cooperating. I'm sure my mother is frantic."

"We will be fine, and I sent word to the marina to pass along a message to our families," Nathanial said. "Did you eat something?"

"I did," Amelia said.

"Speaking of your mother, she will really want to take you away after being detained by this piece of junk," he said with a chuckle.

"Will you write to me when I leave?" Amelia asked.

"Is that such a good idea going forward?"

"Why not?"

"I'm okay with writing you, but I believe it's time for us to break off our courtship."

A wave of hurt rushed over her, which surprised Amelia. "I'm not sure what to say."

"I see you're troubled by me breaking things off with you. That helps me feel better knowing that this wasn't just me caring for you," he said, leaning against the rail.

"Of course I care about you, Nathanial."

"I'm not sure if that helps or makes this harder."

"Nothing has changed for me," Amelia said, touching his elbow.

"Nothing has changed yet," Nathanial said, squeezing her hand.

He let go and moved to create space between them.

"We don't know what the future holds," Amelia said, inching closer.

"You're right. I just know my future doesn't have you in it as my wife."

Amelia paused and took a step back. "Nathanial, I will be returning to Willow Bay. I promise you that."

"It's not about that, and you know it."

"Excuse me, sir, I hate to interrupt, but we have a situation brewing. Plus, I believe I see the *Vide Fjärd* coming toward us."

Amelia realized the waves had become stronger, the wind had picked up, and it had begun to snow. She had been so focused on the conversation with Nathanial, she hadn't been paying attention to the worsening seas.

A storm's coming, and it's going to be bad.

The *Vide Fjärd* came up on them quickly. Amelia wondered if it was the approaching storm pushing Nick's determination to get to them so fast or if the growing intensity of the waves shoved him along. Nick climbed aboard along with another one of his crewmen, and the brothers had a meeting in the wheelhouse to discuss what to do next.

Amelia walked around on deck, feeling the sting of Nick ignoring her. When the boat dipped with a swell of the lake, she went inside. She inched closer to hear what the brothers were discussing. She tried not to let her disappointment show when Nick still hadn't acknowledged her presence.

"You can take Amelia back to shore, Nathanial," Nick said.

"No. It's my fault we are out here on this rickety piece of garbage. You take her on the *Vide Fjärd,* and I will help our crewmen limp this thing back to shore."

"We almost have it fixed if you want to just wait, and we can all go in together just in case something else breaks," a crewman said.

"That's not a bad idea," Nick said.

"Well, I suppose so," Nathanial said.

"Whatever we are going to do, might I suggest we do it swiftly? Lady Superior is about to raise her pretty little head against us," Amelia said.

All eyes turned to her.

"Have none of you been paying attention to what is going on? Not only are we further out, but the storm is all but on top of us," Amelia said.

Nick scrambled outside, jumped onto the railing, and scanned the horizon. "Nathanial, we may need to just abandon this boat and all head back on the *Vide Fjärd.*"

"But this is the *Kathleen.* It was Father's favorite boat. I hate to lose her."

"You're right. Let's hurry and maybe we can outrun the worst of this storm," Nick said. "Amelia, please go inside out of the weather."

"I would rather not. But I promise to stay out of your way, and if it gets worse, I promise I will go inside."

Nick huffed, but didn't say anything further. The men scuttled about making repairs, and Amelia kept an eye on the weather. The waves grew stronger, and she went in search of a blanket.

When she came back on deck, she had a hard time hearing the men's shouts over the howling wind and the lake crashing against the boat. She wrapped the blanket around her arms and held on to a ladder next to her. She fell to her knees as the boat was tossed about and sea spray mixed with snow flew all around her.

Nick suddenly appeared, and she studied him closely.

"This is bad, isn't it?" Amelia shouted above the wind.

"It isn't good," Nick shouted back.

"Is this a time I should be afraid of her?" Amelia asked.

"You have been talking with Gram," Nick said with amusement, despite the seriousness of the situation. "Yes, this is one of those times, but don't worry, Nathanial and I will make sure you get home safely."

"Nick, I need your help over here," Nathanial hollered.

"I know you won't go inside, but please, at least crouch down here. And don't move, so I don't have to worry about you."

"I promise."

Nick rushed to help Nathanial, and Amelia tried to keep her promise of staying where she was, but she noticed a crewman who needed assistance. She jumped up to help hold a line for him, then bounded from task to task, aiding wherever needed until she slammed into Nathanial.

"I thought Nick told you to stay put," Nathanial yelled.

"I have a hard time just standing by when everyone else is trying to get us home safely."

"Fine, hand me that wrench."

"We are finally headed toward the bay," Amelia said, following his instructions.

"Yes, these last repairs are holding. But how did you know we are headed toward the bay?"

"I can feel it."

"The *Bay Minnow* has lost their bearings," a crewman shouted from behind Nathanial.

"Damn it," shouted Nathanial. "Where's Nick?"

"He is preparing to head back over to the *Vide Fjärd*."

Nathanial stumbled to the other side of the boat, with Amelia on his heels. He grabbed his brother just as Nick pulled on the line connecting them to the *Vide Fjärd*.

"What are you doing?" Nathanial shouted.

"I'm going to go after the men on the *Bay Minnow*."

"I can't let you do that. You are the better sailor to get the *Kathleen* home. I will head out to see what I can do to help the *Bay Minnow*."

Dread coursed through Amelia, and she reached out to touch both brothers' arms. "Can't we send one of your other crewmen?"

"You know we can't do that," Nathanial shouted.

"I suppose I do know, but I hate the idea of it."

"I will go, Nathanial," Nick yelled.

"Come on, Nick. I've been the captain of the *Vide Fjärd* for the past couple of years when you haven't been home. Plus, I would feel better knowing you were here taking care of Melia."

Amelia studied Nathanial, and realization slowly dawned on her. Nathanial had never called her Melia, and he was using it now to win the argument. He knew whoever went may not make it home, and he was sacrificing himself.

"No, Nathanial. I can't let you do this," she said.

"She's right," Nick said.

"No. I'm right and you know it. It makes more sense for me to go. I have been the one sailing her the most, and you are better at making sure Amelia gets home."

Nick nodded and handed the line to Nathanial. The brothers hugged, and Amelia started crying.

Nathanial turned to Amelia and pulled her close. "You will be safe with Nick. Promise me you will stop fighting against your true feelings and allow yourself to love him."

"Nathanial, please, there must be another way."

"I love you, Amelia," Nathanial said against her ear before letting her go.

Nathanial jumped onto the railing and balanced himself against the blowing winds and raging waves. The *Vide Fjärd* rocked into them, and he was knocked back onto the deck, the line slipping from his hand. He grabbed the rope and bounded back up.

"We have to disconnect the boats before we all go down," Nick shouted. "Perhaps we should just have Carl on the *Vide Fjärd* go after the *Bay Minnow.*"

"We could never live with ourselves, Nick."

"Then let me go. You're hurt after falling."

"I'm fine. And besides, we already decided."

"Nathanial, listen to reason. You can't make it across," Amelia shouted.

"I will make it. I love you, Nick. Take care of her and love her for the both of us," Nathanial shouted.

He took one last look at Amelia, jumped onto the rail, and swung across to the *Vide Fjärd.* He landed safely, cut the lines between the two boats, and the *Vide Fjärd* drifted away from them.

Amelia screamed and lunged toward the rope. Nick caught her around the waist, holding tight.

"Nathanial, no! Please come back," she cried, arms outstretched. "Nathanial! Come back! No! Nathanial!"

Nick folded himself around her while the wind howled against them. The waves grew higher, and the *Kathleen* tilted, knocking them off their feet. She scrambled to stand just as the *Vide Fjärd* veered into the belly of the storm and disappeared.

"Will he make it?" Amelia asked.

Tears streamed down Nick's face. "He is at the mercy of the lake now."

Chapter Thirty

THE *KATHLEEN* HAD BEEN battling against the waves for several hours. Every time Amelia believed they were making progress, the lake pushed them further back. She pulled the blanket tighter around her arms as she huddled between a cabinet bolted to the floor and the wall.

Nick fought to maintain course, but the lake continued to toss them in different directions. The crewmen stumbled about helping keep the boat afloat. The wind howled. The snow mixed with the waves had drenched them all.

"This storm came out of nowhere, cap," a crewman hollered.

"I don't think we were expecting things to be so severe," Nick yelled back.

"We can't hold out much longer against this beating. We need to change course or start thinking about what we're going to do if she falls apart."

Nick glanced at her. "No. We will make it. We have to make it."

"Cap, you know as well as I, the *Kathleen* isn't the vessel she once was."

"We have to make it," Nick said, glancing at Amelia a second time.

"Having Miss Amelia on board doesn't change how the *Kathleen* is going to operate in this mess. She's falling apart around us."

Nick focused on the next swell as it crashed across the bow and splintered more deck railing.

"Cap, she's falling apart around us!"

More waves pounded. The wind shrieked.

"Cap—"

"I heard you!"

Amelia stumbled from her spot in the corner and rested a hand on Nick's arm. "You don't have to keep fighting a losing battle to try and save me. Do what you would if I wasn't here."

Nick looked into her eyes, and she flinched at the pain she saw there. "I may have lost my brother. I can't lose you too."

"You can't think about that right now. I believe you know what needs to be done, so why aren't you doing it?" she asked.

"I'm not sure that I do," he said.

"I don't believe that for a second. I think you do know, but for some reason, you're fighting against it. Is it because I'm here? Is it because of Nathanial? Either way, you must fight the Lady the only way you know how."

Nick studied Amelia, and she knew the second he stopped resisting his thoughts. Confidence replaced the pain, and amusement twinkled in his eyes.

"You always do know what to say, Melia."

She squeezed his arm. "Get us home."

Nick stopped fighting to maintain the course he had been clinging to and started shouting orders. He sailed the *Kathleen* into the wind, down the coastline beyond Willow Bay.

"There we go, cap," the crewman hollered and stumbled about, following the directions he had just been given.

"We will ride this out yet," Nick shouted.

"Surely the storm will pass over us before we get swept too far away from home," Amelia yelled.

"I don't know. I've never seen anything like this before."

"What does that mean?"

"I feel like I'm on the ocean right now, Melia. I've never experienced swells this high and wind this ferocious."

The lake swept over the bow, cracked another section of railing, and snapped a line. Crewmen struggled to repair anything necessary while Nick fought against another wave.

"Nick, they need help, so I'll go," she shouted.

"No. Damn it." Nick warred with himself until his shoulders slumped forward in resignation. "Okay, let me show you how to do this and I will go. Hold the wheel steady, like this."

Amelia grabbed on as Nick instructed. "Like this?"

"Yes, now when you see another wave coming at us, turn the wheel just so."

"I got it," she said.

"I have no doubt you do. But let's have you give it a go while I'm still here."

After following Nick's instructions through the next round of wind and water, she yelled, "Go. Help your crew. I got this."

Nick ran out, battling against the elements to help his men, while Amelia was left alone to guide the boat through the raging storm. She successfully navigated several large waves, but her arms were growing tired. She threw the blanket off her shoulders and steadied her feet. She maneuvered through one embankment after another until Nick and another crewman appeared.

"Take the wheel from her," Nick hollered, pulling Amelia away.

"Everything okay out there?" she asked.

Nick hugged Amelia and kissed the top of her head. "You are the bravest, most amazing woman I know."

"Uh, cap. I don't like the looks of this next one."

Nick swung his head in the direction the crewman was pointing. "Damn it. Brace yourselves!"

The lake engulfed the boat and tossed it around. Amelia was knocked off her feet and tumbled across the floor. Nick tried to catch her, but fell alongside her. The crewman toppled backward, leaving the wheel to spin out of control.

Amelia realized what was happening and scrambled to reach it. She forced herself to stand, clinging tightly to the wheel. She fought against the next swell, but held the boat steady. Nick crawled toward her as an identical wave rose up against them. She held fast during the impact, never letting go.

Nick fell against the wall but yelled, "Do you have a hold of her still?"

"I do."

"As the next one hits, turn the wheel to the left. We must keep the *Kathleen* from rolling."

"Got it."

Nick crawled across the floor to check the crewman.

"Is he okay?" Amelia shouted.

"Focus on the boat and water!"

"I am! Is he okay?"

"He is unconscious, but still breathing."

"Here we go again. Hang on," Amelia shouted. She followed Nick's instructions, and the boat sailed over the surge and stayed upright.

"Great job, Melia!"

"I think we are getting pushed further out toward the middle of the lake again."

"I agree," Nick said.

Nick scrambled to take the wheel, and Amelia maneuvered over to do her own assessment of the crewman. She tore the hem of her undergarment and wrapped it around the laceration across his forehead.

"What's his name?" she asked.

"Lars," Nick said. "He's been sailing with us for several years."

"I think he's coming back to us." Amelia leaned closer to the crewman's face. "Lars, can you hear me? Are you okay? Does it hurt anywhere?"

Lars opened his eyes and tried to sit up.

"Take it easy," she said, forcing him to lie back down. "You were knocked unconscious."

"I'm fine. Just a headache. I need to go see if the men still need my help outside."

"No, you can't. You're hurt and need to stay here."

"But they were trying to tie down the last line and were struggling to hold it steady. I told them I would be right back before these last waves."

"You need to rest. I'll go."

"Like hell you will," Nick shouted.

Amelia didn't listen to Nick's protests and stumbled out the door. The wind took her breath away, and she struggled to see through the snow and sea spray. She walked with the rhythm of the boat and held on to whatever she could cling to.

When she reached the men, the line was flying loose, and they were trying to capture it. It flew in front of her, and she let go of the railing and lunged for the rope. She captured it but was knocked off her feet as it tried to rip away from her.

A crewman landed on top of her seconds later. "Well done, Miss Amelia."

He grabbed the line from her and handed it off to another man before helping her get to her feet.

"Help hold it steady," someone shouted.

Amelia joined the men and held the rope until it was secure. Water poured all around her, knocking her off her feet, and she slid across the deck. Her body went sailing through the broken railing over the side of the boat.

This is the end.

A hand caught her arm, and she slammed into the side of the boat. Swells leapt up to capture her, but she was pulled back into safety before she was taken. Amelia rolled to a sitting position and slammed into Nick.

"You saved me," she said.

"Don't you ever do that again!" he yelled.

"I'm sorry. I wasn't thinking. I just wanted to help."

"Yes, but I almost lost you. I can't live in a world without you in it, Melia."

"Cap, the mainsail's about to go!" someone yelled from behind.

Nick clambered up, pulling Amelia with him. They dove into the wheelhouse just as the mast broke in two, crashing down. Wood splintered and broken glass flew all around them, bringing the outside elements in.

"Are you okay, Melia?" Nick yelled.

"I'm fine. What about Lars?"

"He appears to be okay."

"What do we do now?" Amelia asked.

"Gather everyone and hang on for dear life."

"That's it?"

"Too much is broken now."

"So, we ride it out and hope she doesn't take us."

Nick folded Amelia into his arms and kissed her passionately. She was breathless as they separated and couldn't keep her eyes off him. The crewman staggered to sit around them, encompassing the pair.

"We've been through worse," Lars said.

"Name it," Nick said.

"Okay, we haven't, but we will survive."

"I love your positivity, Lars," Nick said.

Amelia leaned against Nick's chest and listened to his pounding heart. She closed her eyes and swallowed her tears. With each crash of water, the men huddled closer.

Please have mercy on us, Lady Superior.

"The crash of her waves in the cold dark night," Amelia started to sing. "Oh, lady, relent. Oh, lady of might. Be calm, be still, so we can survive until light."

"Where did you learn that?" Nick asked.

Amelia straightened to look into Nick's eyes. "Tuva. She sang it for me before I left the first time. She told me her brother-in-law, I think his name was Adam, wrote it and used to play it on his violin. She sent me the words in a letter once when I was missing Willow Bay the most."

Nick hugged her to him and started to sing the words softly against her ear. She sighed and joined in. One by one, the men followed, and the melody rose up to be swept away by the wind.

Chapter Thirty-One

A HUMMING SOUND WOKE Amelia with a start. She was leaning against Nick with several crewmen huddled around them. They were shivering with their eyes closed, the smokiness of their breath pooling just outside their mouths.

She tried to sit up but was stiff from the cold and lack of movement. She stretched her arms as best as she could and realized there was light shining through the mass of snowflakes. She moved to a standing position, and although the lake was bouncing them around, the waves had softened from their rage the night before.

"Nick, wake up," Amelia said. "I think the worst of it is over."

Several crewmen opened their eyes, and Nick bounded up to stand next to her. "Snow's still coming down, but I think we might be able to limp back to the bay if we can fix the mast and main sail."

"Let's get started," Amelia said.

"Are we able to notify the marina that we are still here?" Lars asked.

"I don't think so. Everything was damaged when the mast fell on the wheelhouse," Nick said.

"We can't worry about people at home right now. They will know we're okay once we sail into the cove," Amelia said.

"Melia's right," Nick said. "Let's get to work."

The crewmen were slow to start, but as Nick started calling out orders, they snapped to attention and dove into their duties. Amelia kept asking to help with various things, but Nick told her to go rest.

Bristling after his latest brush-off, she straightened her shoulders and said, "I am not a weak thing who needs to sit by while everyone else is working to get us home. Let me help, Nicholas."

Surprise registered on Nick's face before he burst into laughter. Sobering enough to talk, Nick said, "Fine, Melia. Go help Lars."

"Why are you laughing at me?"

"I'm not laughing at you. I'm laughing because of the joy you bring to my heart. Your strength and determination are always such a breath of fresh air."

"Fine, then," she said, her tone softening.

"Now, go help Lars," Nick barked at her playfully.

"Watch yourself," she said, but grinned as she walked away.

Amelia dove into helping Lars and was amazed at his knowledge of everything about the boat and how to fix it. He worked patiently with her, and she appreciated that he didn't talk down to her. They worked for several hours before it was time to raise the pole.

Lines were wrapped around the large mast pulley style, and all the crewmen held tight, waiting for their cue from Nick.

"Steady men, on three, let's heave her on up," Nick said.

Amelia held tightly to the line next to Lars and waited for the countdown. Her heart raced with anticipation. On the mark, she started pulling, and her lips parted into a wide grin. Once the mast was in place, they held tight while several men secured the pole.

"She should be secure, cap."

"Okay, men," Nick shouted, "let her go."

Everyone released their ropes, and Amelia held her breath. When the mast held strong, a cheer rose up across the boat. Lars grabbed her into a bear hug and released her enough to dance a jig with her.

"Best not to get too excited," Nick said from behind.

Amelia and Lars stopped twirling and stifled their laughter.

"It's always good to celebrate each success along the way of one's accomplishments," Amelia said.

Nick nodded at Lars, dismissing him. When the crewman was far enough away, Nick pulled Amelia into his own dance with her, and laughter echoed across the boat. She stumbled on a piece of stray wood, and Nick caught her before she fell to the deck.

As Amelia righted, their eyes met, and everything seemed to stop. She struggled to calm her racing heart and knew it wasn't beating out of her chest from the dancing. She tried to take a step back as yearning tingled through her body, but Nick pulled her closer and leaned in for a kiss.

"Cap!"

Nick released her and Amelia sprang back, but their eyes remained locked on each other.

"I think I see the *Bay Minnow,*" Lars said.

Breaking out of their trance, Amelia and Nick rushed to the rail to get a better look at where Lars was pointing. The faint yellows and blues of a boat broke through the gray and white of the snow, and tears slid down Amelia's cheeks.

Surely the Vide Fjärd is right behind them.

She leaned over the railing, hoping to see the blue of a second boat, with Nathanial smiling and waving on its bow. When nothing appeared behind the *Bay Minnow*, she glanced over at Nick. She saw him fighting to keep his expression neutral, but could tell he was worried what this might mean.

"Surely, it's just slow to come along," Amelia said.

"One can hope," Nick said. Turning to Lars, he said, "Make ready for the *Bay Minnow* to come alongside."

"Nick, are you—"

"We just have to wait and see, Melia."

Nick walked to what was left of the bridge before turning to face the direction of the *Bay Minnow*. Amelia scanned the horizon past the vessel once more and tamped down any fears trying to seep in.

The *Bay Minnow* pulled alongside the *Kathleen* and the captain climbed aboard. Nick came out to meet him a short distance away from Amelia. She struggled to hear what they were saying, and Nick avoided her gaze. He pulled his cap off his head, ran his fingers through his hair, secured it, glanced at her, and shook his head.

"No," Amelia said, rushing toward Nick.

The captain stepped away, and Nick struggled to talk.

She placed her hand on his arm and asked, "What do we know?"

"Captain Marks explained that Nathanial got to the *Bay Minnow*. He was obviously able to help them. There was a mayday from another boat close by, so Nathanial took a skeleton crew and went after it. As it sailed further into the storm, it was swallowed by a massive wave and disappeared. It was the last they saw of the *Vide Fjärd*. One can assume that it's gone."

"That can't be. Surely it was just clouds and the storm that prevented anyone from seeing it."

"No, Melia."

"Surely, we should be able to find them. Find him."

"The lake never gives up her dead."

"Oh, god. Nathanial!" Amelia wailed.

Nick hugged her to him, and she wept. The captain cleared his throat, bringing Amelia back to the circumstances of their situation. They separated, and Amelia took several steps back to allow the captain to talk.

"Right," Nick said. "We must carry on. We still have to get home, and the storm isn't quite over."

"What can we do?" Captain Marks asked.

"If you weren't already full, I would say we could abandon ship, but you're already over capacity as it is. Instead, I will have you take Amelia with you, along with anyone else that can fit," Nick said.

"I'm not going anywhere without you," she said.

Nick gathered her hand in his. "I want nothing more than to remain with you, to see that you get home. But since we are sitting ducks in the water at the moment, I must send you on to Willow Bay."

"Nick, please, let me stay with you," Amelia said.

"It is safer for you to go on, Melia," Nick said. "We will carry on with the repairs and be right behind you. I promise."

She flung herself into Nick's arms and let her tears fall. "You had better keep your promise. I couldn't bear it if I lost someone else to her."

Nick kissed her with desperation, and Amelia clung to him. When they broke apart, they stared into each other's eyes until Nick nodded at the captain.

"Come, Miss Amelia, we should get along while we still can," Captain Marks said.

Amelia hugged Nick once more, kissed him on the cheek, then grabbed Captain Marks' outstretched hand. She followed him over to the *Bay Minnow* with ease.

Once she was steady on deck, she yelled. "You made a promise, Nick. You better come home to me. I can't live in a world without you in it, either."

"I promise, my love!" Nick hollered.

The *Bay Minnow* disconnected from the *Kathleen* and sailed on toward Willow Bay. Amelia stood on deck until the *Kathleen* was no longer in sight. Captain Marks came to stand by her.

"Captain Nilsson is the best there is, Miss Amelia. I have no doubt they will be along shortly."

Amelia mumbled a thank you and found a quiet corner. She leaned against the wall as tears rained down her cheeks. Her body slid into a ball as all her pain and fears poured out.

Chapter Thirty-Two

The *Bay Minnow* slowed into its spot along the docks in the marina. Amelia stood on deck patiently waiting to disembark. The snow was still falling, and the winds were picking up again. She glanced across the water, willing the *Kathleen* to appear. She sighed when it didn't and allowed the captain to lead her off the boat.

She pulled her blanket tighter as she walked off the dock onto land. The snow was several feet deep, and it was hard to maneuver. She dredged through and climbed into a waiting sleigh. The wind howled, and the horses whinnied as the captain settled beside her.

"Best get a move on," Captain Marks said.

The man driving the sleigh spurred the horses on, and they moved slowly toward the Nilsson's home. The sun had disappeared for the night, and Amelia wondered what time it was. She closed her eyes and rested her head against the captain's shoulder.

She wasn't sure how long it took to get her home, but was thankful when the door opened to the house and she was ushered inside. She stood in the drawing room while someone went to wake her brother and mother.

Commotion in the doorway alerted her that the entire household had woken up. Exhaustion rushed over her, and she reached out to the captain to steady herself. George ran to her side and gave her a warm hug.

"Oh, George," Amelia cried.

"Where are Nick and Nathanial?" Ivy asked.

"I don't know," Amelia said.

"She is exhausted," Captain Marks said.

"You're all exhausted, are you not?" Kathleen said.

"Yes, Mrs. Nilsson."

"Perhaps you should reside here, Captain Marks, until the snow stops. I will have a room readied for you."

"Thank you, Mrs. Nilsson."

"Kathleen, um, Mrs. Nilsson—"

"We shall wait until the morning before learning all the details," Kathleen said, interrupting Amelia.

"Ivy, please take Amelia upstairs and help her get into bed. A bath will wait until morning, I think," her mother said.

"George, can you help me get her upstairs?" Ivy asked.

"I will assist, Miss Ivy," Captain Marks said. "I made a promise to Nick to see to it that she is safely home and doing well."

"You've done enough, captain," George said. "You need to rest as well. As her brother, I can assure you that you fulfilled that promise and then some."

Amelia hugged Captain Marks. "Thank you, sir, for keeping your promise to Nick. Thank you for bringing me home safely."

"It was my pleasure, Miss Amelia. Now go, you're dead on your feet. And if I may be so bold, you are the strongest woman I have ever had the privilege to know."

Ivy and George led Amelia out of the room, with her mother following behind. Amelia stumbled a few times on the stairs and had a difficult time keeping her eyes open.

"I don't think I've ever been this tired," she said.

"Well, as soon as you have rested enough, we will be out of this place so that you never have to worry about that again," her mother said.

"Mother, now is not the time," George said.

"That may be, but mark my words, this will not ever be a place I will allow my daughter to live."

"Please, Mrs. Campbell, can't you see you're upsetting Amelia?" Ivy said.

"She's upset? What about the upset I have endured the past couple of days?" Charlotte asked.

"Mother, you're seriously thinking only of yourself right now. Amelia has just been through hell and back. Let it be," George said.

"Fine, we will discuss it further after she has rested," Charlotte said and stormed off to her room.

"Are you okay, Melia?" George asked, leading Amelia to sit by the fire in her room.

"I just want to close my eyes."

"Please keep them open for a few more minutes until we can get you out of your clothes," Ivy said. "George, perhaps you could send a housekeeper or even your mother to help with this part?"

"I'm here," Kathleen said before crossing the room. "Go on, George."

George hugged his sister and slipped out of the room. Kathleen and Ivy helped take off the layers of clothes Amelia wore and into a warm nightgown. They helped her cross the room, and she murmured a thank you. She thought she heard someone say, "You're welcome," but she collapsed on the bed and let sleep take over before she could figure out who it was.

Blinking, Amelia put a hand over her eyes, sat up, and looked around. She was no longer on the boat but neatly tucked in her bed.

Nick!

She shoved her covers aside and bounded out of bed. She grabbed a robe and flew downstairs. She stopped short when she entered the drawing room.

"For heaven's sake, Amelia. Have you lost all sense of propriety?" her mother asked.

"I don't care about that." Amelia turned to Captain Marks. "Have we heard anything?"

"Nothing yet, but don't worry, I'm sure Nick will turn up soon, especially since the storm has passed on and the snow has stopped," Captain Marks said.

"Perhaps I could help you to your room and assist with getting you dressed," Ivy said.

"Yes, thank you, Ivy," Charlotte said.

"I will help as well," Kathleen said.

They went back to Amelia's room, helped her bathe and get dressed for the day.

"You must still be so tired," Kathleen said.

"I'm fine. Besides, I couldn't sleep another moment even if I wanted to. Not until I know…"

"Perhaps some food then," Ivy said. She excused herself and left the room.

"My apologies for barging into the drawing room without being properly dressed," Amelia said.

"Nonsense. You were just worried about my sons. It just shows me how much you care."

"Did the captain tell you anything further?"

"He did. He explained things very well."

"I'm so sorry, Kathleen. I can't help but feel like this is partly my fault."

"How on earth is this your fault? You couldn't have predicted the weather, and you certainly had no control over how sound the boats were or the stubbornness of my sons. No, you mustn't blame yourself."

"My hope is that we will see Nick and Nathanial come sailing into the bay together," Amelia said.

"I also have that hope, but I'm also realistic," Kathleen said as tears welled up in her eyes.

"Your sons are heroes."

"Yes. I suppose they are."

"But it doesn't lessen the pain."

Ivy returned with a tray filled with bacon, eggs, toast, and fruit. She quietly set the food on the table next to

Amelia, hugged her, and sat across from her. Amelia dove into her plate, forcing herself to slow down.

"Careful, you don't want to make yourself sick," Kathleen said.

"Yes, please slow down, Amelia," Ivy said.

Silence fell over the room while Amelia ate. Kathleen wiped tears away occasionally but didn't say another word about it. Ivy sat stoically, and Amelia had a hard time swallowing her food past the lump in her throat.

"Please have hope," Ivy said, breaking into the silence.

"I do," Amelia said, after swallowing her last bite of food. Her eyes grew heavy from a full belly, and she struggled to keep them open.

"Go back to bed," Kathleen said, standing to assist.

"I can't. I have to be awake. To keep watch," Amelia said.

"Your dedication is a joy to see. You have such a big heart, so full of love, but you must take care of yourself. Please go to bed and rest so that you can help when he returns," Kathleen said.

"Okay, perhaps for a few moments," Amelia said.

She allowed herself to be led back to bed and curled up in a ball. She could hear Ivy and Kathleen whispering about something. She wanted to figure out what they were saying but fell asleep instead.

Amelia slept the rest of the afternoon and on into the night. She woke up briefly and wandered to the kitchen to fill her empty belly. Once full, she went back to bed and slept until morning. The following day dawned with clear skies and the sun shining brightly. She dressed in warm clothes and went in search of breakfast. She was just finishing her juice when Kathleen walked in.

"Goodness, you look so much more refreshed, Amelia."

"Thank you, I feel it."

Kathleen ate her breakfast, and the two talked of unimportant things until the rest of the household joined them. After everyone finished eating, they moved into the drawing room. Amelia paced back and forth, wringing her hands.

"Gracious child," her mother said. "You must calm yourself."

"I'm fine, Mother."

"You're making me nervous."

"I don't mean to. I just can't keep my mind on anything else and it's making me restless."

"It's okay, Mrs. Campbell," Kathleen said. "She isn't bothering anyone."

"I appreciate your candor and your graciousness," her mother said, but gave Amelia a pointed look before dropping the subject.

A knock at the door reverberated through the house, and Amelia ran to see who it was with Kathleen on her heels. Her mother protested Amelia's rudeness, but she didn't stop.

When the butler flung open the door, Captain Marks rushed in. "I believe we might be seeing the *Kathleen* limping into the bay."

"I'm coming with you to check," Amelia said.

"So am I," Kathleen said.

The butler grabbed their coats, and they flew out the door into the waiting sleigh. Amelia kept looking out at the water to see if she could catch a glimpse, but couldn't get a clear enough view. Kathleen reached over and squeezed Amelia's hand.

"I'm so sorry. Am I making you nervous?" Amelia asked.

"On the contrary, your excitement is infectious. I hope we can convince your mother that it isn't going to hurt if you were to stay."

Surprised, Amelia said, "I don't know why she's having such a hard time with this."

"I do," Kathleen said. "This is a hard place to live. And only the right ones can make a go of it."

"You think I'm a right one?"

"I know you are," Kathleen said.

"My mother is set on us leaving. I'm not sure I can do anything about that."

"Perhaps, but maybe we can soften her heart to the idea. I will talk with her."

"We're here, Miss Amelia, Mrs. Nilsson," Captain Marks said.

Captain Marks assisted the women out of the sleigh, and they all trudged down to the docks just as a battered and broken boat sailed slowly to a stop. Amelia hurried her footsteps and noticed Lars securing the boat along with one of the other crewmen, but there was no sign of Nick.

Dread coursed through her until she caught sight of the top of another man's head. She hopped in the air just as Nick's face came into view. Their eyes met for only a second before she landed on her feet.

She turned to Kathleen. "I think I saw him."

"I think I did too."

Amelia turned as Nick bounded across the dock toward them. Unable to stop herself, Amelia ran toward him and flew into his arms. He kissed her soundly. Overcome with emotion, Amelia held him tight but couldn't stop her tears.

"Don't cry, Melia. Please don't cry," Nick said, pulling away slightly.

She rested her head against his chest and closed her eyes. When Kathleen reached the pair, Nick held out his arm and included her in their embrace. The trio hugged until Nick stumbled.

"Oh, Nick, you're just exhausted. Lean on me," Amelia said.

"Come along, my son. Let's get you home," Kathleen said.

The women helped him to the sled, and they rode home with little talking. Amelia looked across Nick to Kathleen and read the look of pain. Only one son returned. She was no doubt rejoicing at Nick's arrival but heartbroken at the reality of Nathaniel's fate.

"Kathleen, would you like me to help you assist Nick to his room when we arrive?" Amelia asked.

"Thank you, that would be most helpful," Kathleen said.

Amelia nodded and looked out toward the approaching house. Several people huddled in the window and her mother's face came into view. Thoughts of leaving Willow Bay flitted through her mind, and she frowned.

"Are you okay, Melia?" Nick asked.

"You shouldn't be thinking about me at a time like this."

"It was thoughts of you that brought me home," Nick said.

Amelia looked over at Kathleen and saw the flicker of joy mixed with grief.

What must she think of me now? I left on the boat courting Nathanial and came home loving Nick.

Thoughts of love surprised Amelia, and she moved away slightly. She hadn't allowed herself to analyze her feelings for Nick for so long, the idea of jumping straight to love scared her.

Nick pulled her closer and kissed the top of her head. "It's okay, Melia."

She always wondered at Nick's ability to read her. She looked over at Kathleen again and caught the woman studying her.

"We're here," the driver said.

Forcing her troubled thoughts and feelings aside, Amelia assisted Kathleen with helping Nick into the house. Amelia's family attempted to approach and greet Nick, but she brushed them away. She caught her mother's disapproval but ignored it and carried on. When they reached Nick's room, Amelia realized this was the first time she had been in this part of the house. She tamped down the sudden butterflies in her stomach and helped Nick to a chair by his fireplace.

"Nick, perhaps you would like something to eat?" Kathleen asked.

"Something to fill my stomach sounds wonderful before I collapse into bed."

"I'll go," Amelia said.

"No, Amelia, you stay," Kathleen said.

Amelia followed her to the door. "But don't you think perhaps this isn't proper?"

"I don't care about proper right now. I need a minute," Kathleen said.

Hugging Kathleen, Amelia whispered, "Take all the time you need."

When the door closed, Amelia walked over to Nick. He was staring into the fire, and she didn't want to disturb him, so kept her distance.

He glanced in her direction and smiled sadly. "What are you doing?"

"I wanted to give you space if you needed it," she said.

"Of course you did, for you are always thinking of others."

"How are you really doing?"

"I'm so tired that I'm not sure."

"That's understandable."

"Melia," Nick started, stopped, and took a big deep breath in. "Melia," he repeated and buried his face in his hands.

She rushed to his side and held him while he let out his sorrow. She kissed the top of his head several times, and he pulled her into his lap.

"You've lost a brother. A best friend. I can't imagine all that you are feeling right now," Amelia said.

"And you have lost another person whom you were going to marry," Nick said.

"You're right. I was planning on marrying Nathanial. I did care for him."

"And here I am, holding you in my arms. What a disgrace I am."

"No," Amelia said, gathering his face in her hands. "You are not a disgrace. You are a wonderful brother and friend. Nathanial was not blind."

"You may be right. I'm just not sure how things can be in the future, but for now, I have to hold you."

"I feel the same way, but we shouldn't talk now. We are both so tired and hurting. You need food and sleep and then we can talk."

Kathleen walked into the room, and Amelia got up from Nick's lap and helped her arrange the tray. Once Nick was finished eating, he stumbled to his bed, collapsing onto it.

"Sleep well, my sweet boy," Kathleen said while covering him with a blanket.

After following Kathleen out of the room, Amelia started in the direction of her own room.

"Amelia, wait," Kathleen called.

"I'm sorry. I thought you might want some more time alone," Amelia said.

"I will take the time I need, but are you okay?"

"I'm not sure. It's been a difficult couple of weeks."

"Yes. And what of you and my son?"

"My fear is that too much has happened for there to ever be a me and your son. Maybe my mother is right, and as much as it breaks my heart, perhaps I should leave this place at least for a time. Although I fear once I leave again, I may never return."

"You can't mean that," Kathleen said.

"As hard as I have tried to find reasons to stay in Willow Bay other than marriage or courtships, I would find it be beyond difficult to remain here if he can't love me."

Chapter Thirty-Three

Shifting nervously under Tuva's gaze, Amelia stood and walked across the room to stand in front of the window.

"Your attempts at avoiding what I'm trying to say will not keep you from hearing it," Tuva said.

"But, Tuva, how can I stay here with all that has happened?" Amelia said.

"When we first came to this place, it tried to break us so many times I lost count. And yet we remained. Why? Because our love for this land and our love for each other was stronger than anything it threw at us. I have a hard time believing your love for Willow Bay and for my grandson isn't just as strong, Melia."

"Love. You speak of love as though it is something that I have. I don't have a great love like you had with Isak."

"You have love, my dear. From me, your family, from Ivy, from Kathleen. You had it from Nathanial, and you most especially have it from Nick. He just needs time to heal his broken heart after losing his twin."

Amelia rubbed her hands across her face and walked back to sit next to Tuva. "But what if he can't overcome his pain?"

"Oh, Melia. You and I have often talked about the early days, but I don't think I ever shared the greatest division between Isak and me and how incredibly difficult it was to overcome. It almost broke our marriage. But I refused to give in to this great hurt and confusion and misunderstanding between us. I refused to give up. I knew we could survive it. You must decide for yourself if you can do the same. And you may have to be the one to fight for both of you until he can start fighting for you as well."

"Mother is taking me away. We leave in just a couple of days. My heart breaks not knowing if I will return, and yet I almost feel a relief at leaving so I don't have to face what may come next."

"I will write to you and send you an invitation every week if I must, so you will always have a reason to return. But me extending that invitation isn't going to matter if you're not willing to lean into the strength that I know you possess to help you face things."

Ivy popped her head into the room and said, "I hate to interrupt, Amelia, but I promised your mother I would have you stop by before we go to dinner, and if we stay much longer, I fear we won't keep that promise."

"You must go, Melia," Tuva said.

"Let me help with the coffee dishes," Amelia said.

"Nonsense, my housekeeper can help. You mustn't leave your mother waiting. Come by before you leave to say goodbye."

"I will," Amelia said.

She hugged Tuva and followed Ivy out of the house. They walked arm in arm along the path and Amelia breathed in the cold air. Tears formed at the corner of her eyes, and she slowed her pace.

"I know we must rush to see Mother, but somehow I can't face the conversation with her," Amelia said.

"Then let's not worry about the time and when you're ready, we will go see her, even if that means we're late for dinner. Your heart is worth more than any protocols right now."

"And this is why I love you and our friendship so much," Amelia said.

The friends walked past the house and made it to the edge of the point. Amelia looked out at the water. It lay calm today, but flashes of being out in the storm rushed through her mind. She flinched, and Ivy put her arm around Amelia's shoulders.

"I can't imagine the pain and difficulty of all you have been through," Ivy said.

"I was terrified for a moment or two at times, but somehow, as long as Nathanial or Nick was with me, I felt safe. Even when the lake rose up to take us down, I found continuous strength in the fight and determination we all had to survive."

Ivy started laughing.

"What are you laughing about? This isn't funny."

"You were telling Tuva you weren't sure you could handle what was to come and yet you fought against the worst storm this area has ever seen with bravery. Your fear about being afraid seems a little silly."

"Stop making fun of me."

"I'm not. I just think you're scared of your own heart."

Amelia considered Ivy, but instead of continuing the conversation, she walked toward the house.

"Where are you going, Amelia? Please don't walk away mad," Ivy said, trying to keep up.

"I'm not. I just have to go see my mother."

"Yes, but I feel like you're mad at me."

"I don't know how I feel right now. I feel so confused, so I would rather go face my mother than all the other thoughts and feelings swirling around."

Ivy followed Amelia into the house, but once they reached her mother's room, Ivy walked on down the hallway. Amelia knocked on her mother's door and waited for her to answer.

"Is that you finally, Amelia?" her mother said, flinging open the door. "What have I told you about keeping me waiting?"

"My apologies, Mother. I was visiting with Tuva," she said, walking into her mother's room.

The door closed, and silence fell over the room. Amelia waited for the barrage of anger, which was sure to come at her tardiness, constant lack of propriety, and forcing her mother to be in such a harsh place. Instead, her mother motioned for her to sit by the fireplace.

"You're making me uncomfortable. What is it?" Amelia asked.

"Funny that it's my silence you find uncomfortable. But no matter. I know these past few weeks have been so difficult for you. I can't honestly imagine how hard this has been. I'm sorry you are suffering. You know I want you to come to England with me. That has not changed. But I wanted you to know I'm sorry this place hasn't worked out for you as hoped."

"Thank you for your kind words."

"You're welcome, my darling. Now I know I originally said we would be leaving in a couple of days, but we had to move up our travel date due to the possibility of more bad weather. I will not get stuck here."

"When are we leaving?"

"Tomorrow."

"Tomorrow? You can't be serious. How can I leave so soon? I'm still barely getting my head around the fact that Nathanial is gone and the storm. And what about this stuff with Maddy? I can't leave just yet."

"George will stay in contact with the Nilssons to keep us all in the loop. After all, we are in business with them. But we must go, darling. It's time."

"But what if Nathanial shows up and I'm gone?"

"Honey," her mother squeezed Amelia's hand, a gesture of comfort rarely given, and said, "You know as well as I, he is most likely not returning to us. Most have already accepted that he is gone from this earth."

Amelia flinched and jerked her hand away. "How dare you?"

"Amelia, I'm sorry, but tiptoeing around this isn't doing you any good."

"I can't believe you."

"I'm only trying to be honest with you. I cannot imagine what your heart must be feeling at the loss of not one, but two, you would have hoped to marry. But perhaps this is a sign for you to start listening to me and let me help you find someone."

"And what about love and partnership? What about that?"

"Those things can always be found, but they often come later. You just need to start trusting me on this."

"It goes against all that I believe in."

"Maybe, but what you believe in has only hurt you."

Rushing to leave the room, Amelia paused at the door and said, "Very well, Mother. I will come with you. I will even allow you to parade me about. But I will always refuse to be sold to the highest bidder. You may end up having an old maid as a daughter."

"You can't be ser—"

Amelia slammed the door, cutting off her mother's words. She inhaled deeply and looked about. The silence in the hallway was almost comforting, but she hurried to find Ivy. She would have Ivy make excuses for her regarding dinner. She told herself it was because she had so much to do to prepare to leave the next day. Deep down, she couldn't face seeing Nick, knowing it would be her last dinner with him. There was so much still left unsaid between them. She feared what he must think after all that happened.

She couldn't bear the idea that whenever he looked at her, he was reminded of his dead brother.

Chapter Thirty-Four

THE LEAVES RUSTLED IN the breeze as Amelia walked toward her brother's home in Yorkshire. They had been in England for several months, and she mostly took long walks to pass the time. She had no drive or purpose other than to make it through one day at a time.

George rode up to her and steadied his horse. She pretended to ignore him and walked past.

"Come on, Melia," George said. "You have to stop punishing everyone for being here."

Amelia continued to walk on, so George jumped off his horse and caught up to walk alongside her, pulling his horse behind them.

"I have nothing to say," she said.

"I doubt that," George said.

"Nothing to say that anyone will listen to anyway."

"You sound so dejected and sad. I hurt for you. What can I do?"

"I don't even know, George."

"Do you want to return to Willow Bay?"

"What life would I have there? The situations with Maddy and Nick and Nathanial and the storm. How can I go back?"

"Have you had any letters?" George asked.

"You know I haven't. At least not recently."

"Not even from Ivy?"

"She is preparing for her wedding with Henry. He has set up his own business in Willow Bay outside of our uncle's business. And the last I heard, no one from that side of the family will be attending. But they are not deterred and plan to be married in the fall."

"Do you want to attend? She is your closest friend."

"How could I show my face there after how I left things?"

"Surely it wasn't that bad, Melia."

Amelia stopped walking and turned to George. "It was awful. We argued about things. He said he couldn't see how his brother would forgive him for stealing me away from him. I, of course, told him we both knew the truth, that what we felt for one another grew because of the storm, which was after he had broken things off with Maddy and after Nathanial had broken things off with me. He told me I wasn't being honest with myself, and our feelings started long before anything happened, we just weren't willing to own up to them. He said he wished he'd never met me so he wouldn't feel so conflicted. And perhaps his brother wouldn't have sacrificed himself. I couldn't say anything to that because he was right. So, I told him it was best I was leaving, and left slamming the door behind me. Then, when Mother told me we were leaving even sooner, I just avoided him. I didn't even say goodbye."

"He was hurting," George said.

"So was I, George," Amelia said and started walking again.

"But men can be quite stupid when we are in pain. He says he feels guilty. For what? Loving you? One can't fault a man for loving you, sister. No matter the circumstances."

"You are being overly kind."

"No, I am being truthful."

"Your words do soothe the ache in my heart a little."

"The way I see it, there just wasn't a lot of time for you to talk, work through this or reconcile things. The two of you would make a beautiful couple, especially if you can get past this."

"He hasn't written at all, so I don't see how we could. Besides, Mother is determined for me to find a suitable English Lord and remain here."

"What do you want?"

Amelia paused and studied her hands. "I want to go home."

"If that is what your heart desires, you must go."

"And what about Mother? No, what I want just isn't an option for me. Not anymore."

Dropping the matter, Amelia left to go take a nap, and George went to put away his horse. She was on her way upstairs when the butler handed her a letter. She studied it closely and realized it was from Kathleen. She bounded upstairs, worried that something had happened to Nick or Tuva.

Before she could open it, she was called away by her mother to have tea with the family and more special visitors. Amelia tucked the letter away on her desk and followed her mother downstairs. It would be hours before she would be able to return to it.

Dear Amelia,

I hesitated in writing to you because I always promised myself I would not interfere with matters of the heart with my sons. I raised them to know their own minds and to trust themselves. But I never imagined we would face such sorrows and that Nick's confidence would be so shaken.

Before I continue with the topic of Nick, I want to share about Nathanial. Although the wreckage of his boat has not been found, and no signs of his passing were presented, it has officially been determined that he died, along with so many others, during that storm. I suppose in this case, it is as the saying goes, the lake will not give up her dead. It pains me to write these words. But I take comfort in knowing he died doing the things he loved the most—sailing on the lake and helping others.

Nick shared with me how he had to hold you down when you and Nathanial parted, and I want to thank you for caring for my son. I knew he was going to break his courtship with you. He knew where your heart was, and he knew he could never live with himself if he stood in the way of your true love and happiness. It is ironic for me to see that his death has brought about the very thing he feared he would take away from you in life.

Now I must write a few words about the son who survived—my son who is living and is so in love with you. He is in so much pain, missing his brother and missing you. It's not for me to say, but I can't help but think that your leaving in such a way has hurt in reconciling things between you. I know your mother was very determined you leave, but I wish a few moments could have been spared to discuss things further. Nick is stubborn, I know, and that may be playing some part in you not hearing from him, even now. The truth is, though, he is so afraid of not having your love returned, he can't bring himself to send you even the smallest of notes. He has lost hope that you could ever love him.

Perhaps I read things wrong while you were here, and please forgive me if I shouldn't have written about such things after all, but my heart breaks for you both, and I am desperate to help, even if it's not my place.

Ivy's wedding preparations are coming along beautifully. I know she would love for you to attend but understands your hesitation. Consider this an urging on my part to at least consider returning to Willow Bay for her wedding.

Tuva's health continues to decline, but she is determined to remain with us until she sees Ivy married. I can't help but wonder if she is hanging on with hopes that she may see you one last time.

We all miss you, our sweet Melia.

Yours affectionately,
Kathleen

As the sun set in the distance, the wind blew, causing the waves of grass in the field to mimic the waves on the lake. Homesickness flooded Amelia as she looked out the window and wiped a tear away. The letter in her lap was frayed at the edges, as she had read it so many times. She pulled out a new sheet of paper and scrawled four words across it. She tucked it into the waiting envelope, called for a servant to make sure it was mailed immediately, and turned in for the night.

As she lay in bed, all she could think of was her small letter and whether it would matter at all. When she finally drifted off to sleep, she dreamed of Nick reading the mail from her, but could never quite see his face.

The next morning, Amelia woke with a start and chided herself for not writing more, but she hoped the words *Missing you desperately, Nick,* would be enough.

Chapter Thirty-Five

THE FIRST SUMMER PARTY was well underway, and Amelia put on a show of having fun. She had just finished dancing with one suitor when another asked her to dance the next song. She turned him down graciously, excused herself, and hurried off the dance floor.

Her mother tried to admonish her, but Amelia flew past her to avoid another lecture on how she needed to get over things and move on already. She snuck outside and breathed in the night air. She leaned against the cool stone of the house and closed her eyes.

Footsteps clicked across the patio, and Amelia's eyes flew open. Desperate to be alone, she slipped into the shadows and ran to the garden. She loved walking there. Beautifully groomed flowers and bushes lined multiple pathways where benches allowed for rest or conversation. All the paths met in the middle at a large fountain that flowed almost year round.

Amelia strolled along and dreamed that the sounds and voices from the party were really the sounds and voices from a party in Willow Bay. She was so lost in her memories, she thought she heard a familiar voice calling her name. When she brought herself back to the present, she didn't hear anyone and admonished herself, deciding it was best to go back inside.

She walked toward the house, rounded the fountain, and slammed into a man. Amelia stumbled, mumbled an apology, and tried to run off. But the man caught her hand, stopping her.

She swung around with words on the tip of her tongue, cursing anyone who manhandles women, but stopped short at the shadowy figure.

"Nick?"

The man moved so his face was in the light. "It's me, Melia."

Amelia flew into Nick's arms and burst into tears. He whispered her name and begged her not to cry.

Gaining control, she pulled away and asked, "But how are you here?"

"I got your note and had to come. Mother came with me, as did Ivy and Henry. They are inside. My apologies for crashing your party. It was later in the day when we got to the hotel. We discussed waiting to come by in the morning, but being so close to you, I had to come immediately."

"I just can't believe that you're here. In England. At my brother's house."

"You mean castle?"

"Oh, come now, your home is just as grand."

They both started laughing nervously but were cut off when Nick pulled her into a passionate kiss. When they parted, they were both breathing deeply and staring into each other's eyes. Amelia leaned in for a softer kiss, searing her heart. Fear gripped her at the thought of losing him.

She took a few steps back. "I don't know if I can do this."

"Please don't say that," Nick said. "I mean, I understand why, but please don't doubt me or us."

"You said some hurtful things to me."

"I said things out of fear and confusion."

"I will admit that it was a confusing time."

"Look, I know we have a lot to talk about, but can it be enough for now that I came here to see you."

"Is that all you want? Just to see me?"

"For right this moment, seeing you and holding you in my arms will do. But tomorrow, perhaps we can discuss other things."

Amelia hugged Nick one more time, linked her arm with his, and they walked back to the party. Once inside, she scanned the room for Ivy. She rushed to her friend, and they laughed at seeing each other again. Hugs for Henry and Kathleen were next before her mother joined the commotion.

"It's truly wonderful you all came to visit. We're just sorry we didn't know you were coming, or we could have made room for you," Charlotte said.

"We always have room for close friends and family," Violet said.

"Thank you for inviting them to stay here at Strongwell Manor, Violet," Amelia said.

"Of course. This is the most joy I have seen on your face in months. It is well worth it."

"Always the best hostess," Charlotte said, but sent Amelia a warning look before excusing herself to get a refreshment.

George had their belongings brought from the hotel in town and told the housekeeper to find rooms for everyone. The party continued with the new guests being introduced, and Amelia held Nick's arm, beaming with delight. She couldn't help but notice that her previous dance partners looked on with envy as she danced with Nick the rest of the evening.

Once the party was over and the last of the guests had left, everyone turned in for the night. Amelia found it difficult to sleep. She worried about what the following day would bring and if her conversation with Nick would be in her favor.

Her mother walked across the room to sit next to Amelia. Not everyone had arrived for lunch, and Amelia knew her mother would take the opportunity to talk with her.

"You need to be careful about what plans you make," her mother said.

"I haven't made any plans yet."

"Don't be coy, darling. You and I both know what the arrival of our guests could mean. You should know that I will never agree to you returning to Willow Bay on a permanent basis."

"Does my happiness mean nothing to you at all?"

"Not if it means it could threaten your safety."

"You know that the storm was a fluke, right? They were talking about it for months. And may talk about it for years to come. The storm that developed wasn't a normal type of storm. That's why they are calling it the white hurricane."

"I don't care about that. Your safety is what I do care about. Besides, you need to settle down soon, and so far, an actual proposal of marriage has not been presented by the Nilssons."

"What is it that worries you so much about my marrying or not marrying? I don't understand this obsession you have."

"We will not discuss this anymore right now, Amelia. I will not cause a scene as everyone else is finding their way here."

Amelia tried to continue the conversation but was cut off by her mother, who walked away to talk with George. Nick waved at Amelia when he entered the room, but Henry stopped him. Kathleen wound her way to Amelia and hugged her closely. It was the first time they had a moment to say more than a greeting.

"I must apologize if my letter was too forward," Kathleen said.

"No, not at all. I read it several times. It's what gave me the courage to send my note to Nick," Amelia said.

"I feel compelled to tell you. When it was handed to him, he had been having a rough day. When he saw it was from England, his face went white, and he ripped it open. He must have read it five times before he looked at me and said we had to leave for England immediately. I don't know what his thoughts were. He still hasn't shared anything with me. I just know your letter gave him hope."

"We haven't talked about anything yet and there is the obstacle of having my mother agree to my leaving, but for the first time in a while I have a little hope," Amelia said. Changing the subject, she asked, "How is Tuva?"

"She was doing as okay as one would expect at this point. It is my fear, though, that this will be the year we must say goodbye," Kathleen said.

The butler announced lunch was ready, and everyone started to make their way to the dining room.

"Mother, Amelia," Nick said as he approached. "May I escort both of you in to eat?"

"It would be a pleasure, son," Kathleen said.

Amelia only nodded, but grabbed his arm and walked into the dining room. She found her place at the table and avoided her mother's gaze as she settled in her chair. She ate her lunch quietly while everyone else discussed the weather and their different plans for the afternoon. When lunch was over, she and Ivy went for a walk on the grounds.

"It's such a delight to see you so happy, my friend," Amelia said as they walked among the trees.

"You could be this happy, too," Ivy said.

"One can hope anyway," Amelia said.

"What do you think we are doing here? He came all the way here to get you and bring you home."

"He may have that thought, but we have so much to talk about. Plus, my mother won't just let me leave."

"George can handle your mother if we can get him on our side," Ivy said.

"What side is that?" Nick asked.

He walked around to stand in front of Amelia. "Please forgive me if I startled you. That was not my intention. And don't worry, I wasn't eavesdropping. I can see that question on your face, Melia."

"I should probably go find Henry," Ivy said. "We were going to discuss a few things regarding the wedding. Excuse me."

Amelia grew nervous at having the conversation with Nick already, so she protested Ivy leaving, but her friend ignored her and kept walking.

"Afraid to be alone with me?" Nick asked, tilting his head to the side.

"No, I am not," Amelia said with a huff.

Nick's grin was infectious, and she couldn't stay irritated with him. He held out his arm to escort her, and she willingly obliged. They walked for a while, talking about the beauty of the landscape until Nick cleared his throat, signaling the conversation was about to get deeper. Amelia tried not to panic.

"We must talk about things, Melia. As much as you and I can be stubborn, we have to at least try to come to terms with things. Make peace if you will," Nick said.

"Where do we start?" Amelia asked.

"Let's start at the beginning," Nick said. "I will never forget sitting next to you that first day in your cousin's home. You fascinated me, which I must admit scared me a little, but I just had to know what you were always thinking. I often found myself studying you even when you may not have known I was there. I wanted to be near you as much as I could."

"I always knew you were there. I just never allowed myself to analyze what that might mean and pushed it aside."

"Do you think Maddy could see my feelings for you?" Nick asked.

"Yes, she saw them that first day. She told me that she knew you loved me from the first time you saw me," Amelia said.

"Which is why she was jealous of you," Nick said.

"She wasn't necessarily jealous as much as she was worried that she couldn't fulfill her father's wish for her to marry you."

"Maddy never loved me, you know," Nick said.

"Yes, she said as much to me."

"But Nathanial loved you. I know he did."

"Yes," Amelia said.

"Which adds another layer to this whole situation."

"I thought it did too. But let me ask you, do you not remember that he had broken things off with me before the storm?"

"He what?" Nick asked.

"I thought I shared this with you. He knew you never loved Maddy, and when things ended between the two of you, he told me he had to step aside so you and I could be together. As much as he cared for me, he believed you and I had a stronger connection and could not live with himself if he stood in our way."

"Did you love him?"

"I loved the idea of having a life with him. It was much the same situation as with Daniel. I cared about him. I was even starting to become excited again about the prospect of building a life with someone. He treated me fairly, and I knew he wouldn't look at me as just his wife but as a partner."

"Are you sure he knew how you felt?" Nick asked.

"Yes, we talked about it several times. But he didn't seem to care. He was content to make a life with me anyway. He believed that with time and once you had left Willow Bay, I might learn to love him, too."

"In the end, you were so heartbroken."

"I cared about him, Nick. Maybe I did have feelings for him I didn't realize I had, but never in the same way he loved me. He and I courted, and I was planning to marry him, so yes, I was heartbroken. And even though our relationship hadn't worked out, he didn't deserve to die."

Amelia had to stop and catch her breath as her emotions threatened to spill over. Nick wrapped his arms around her and held her while she regained her composure. When she looked up at him, his tears matched her own. They turned back to their walk and she began to wonder if Nick was done talking about things, at least for now.

"Can you ever love me?" Nick asked.

Amelia stopped and turned to him. "When we were on the boat, Nathanial told me that I needed to let myself love you and to stop fighting it. I denied having love for you because I refused to have feelings for you. The very idea of loving anyone terrified me, but he read me better than I thought he did. He saw what I couldn't see in myself."

"Which is what?"

"How very much in love with you I am. I think I loved you from the start, too."

"Oh, Melia." Nick's lips hovered above hers, his arms tightened around her. "I think I could die without you. I am so in love with you."

Nick kissed her with the same passion as the night before. When Amelia came up for air, her mother's words flitted through her mind. Her eyebrows drew together, her body tensed, and she bit her lip.

"What is it?" Nick asked.

"My mother insists I will never leave England to return to Willow Bay."

"Even if we are betrothed?"

The idea of being engaged to Nick made her heart soar, but the match would be a hard sell for her mother.

"She is fearful of what my life would be like in Willow Bay. She wants me to remain here and marry an English aristocrat."

"Can I steal you away in the night?"

Laughing, Amelia said, "As delightful as that sounds. No, I don't think that will help win her over."

"I'm not leaving here without you, Melia."

Amelia's heart flip-flopped, and heat coursed through her body. She had never felt anything like this before, and as much as it excited her, she was still fearful things wouldn't work out.

"Can I ask you something?" Amelia asked.

"Anything."

"That time on the boat. You kissed me. You danced with me. You knew your brother's leaving was a risk. Why the sudden change when we got home?"

"I was terrified of my love for you," Nick said. He ran his fingers through his hair and looked down at the ground. "We were finally free to have feelings for each other, but I worried I had willed the circumstances to happen so that my brother would be out of the way. Perhaps I didn't fight harder to be the one to go instead of him because I wanted you so bad."

"Do you still believe these things?"

"No, especially not since finding out he had already broken things off with you. Besides that, he was determined to make sure I was the one left to take care of you. He made me promise to love you enough for the both of us."

"I remember him saying that. You promised me that you would return to Willow Bay. And you kept that promise," Amelia said, kissing Nick.

Nick lifted his head slightly and looked into Amelia's eyes. "And I will spend the rest of my life keeping my promise to my brother."

Chapter Thirty-Six

George poured another glass of brandy and drank it down. He topped off his glass and turned back to his family.

"Mother, why won't you budge on this?" George asked.

"I will not have her so far away and in danger," their mother said.

"I am not in danger in Willow Bay," Amelia said.

"And yet you were almost killed there on three separate occasions," their mother said.

"Two of the occasions had to do with something that started here and was tied to our family," Amelia said.

"That may be, but I won't have you living so far away. I am not getting any younger, and traveling back and forth will become increasingly more difficult."

"You're not the only one who can travel," Violet said.

"When George married you, which I was thrilled he did, he stopped coming home as much. I saw him less and less.

I was okay with that, though. He was my son. The son is supposed to leave the nest and fly far away."

"But the daughter is not. She is to marry the one her mother wants so that she can stay close to home," Amelia said.

"Don't make it sound so controlling and sinister, Amelia."

"I would have been closer to home if you had stayed in Boston. It isn't my fault you decided to move to a different country without talking to me first," Amelia said.

"I get the feeling it isn't just about Amelia's safety, though. Am I right?" George asked.

"Fine," Charlotte said. "I received a letter from Mrs. Thompson. There are rumors floating around that Amelia went a bit mad after Daniel's death since she stayed so long in Minnesota. They also are questioning the fact that she was on a boat with men without a chaperone."

Laughter bubbled up inside Amelia.

"This is no laughing matter," her mother said.

"The absurdity of that last statement is beyond laughable. If they had any idea of what they were talking about, they wouldn't have brought it up at all," Amelia said.

"Is it so far-fetched that some may wonder why you were on the boat for so long? What really happened? Why couldn't you really get back?"

"You know why, Mother. You were there. Hurricane-force winds. The boat shattered into pieces. Trust me, there was no time for a romantic tryst in the middle of such a storm. I could have died."

"Yes, but others were not there. And I couldn't help but question it myself at times the more I heard about the rumors."

"You can't be serious."

"I'm able to stop my questioning thoughts, but our friends don't understand, so they do question."

"So, you want me to stay in England because some of your friends can't stop gossiping about me? And you wonder why I hate society so much," Amelia said.

"Amelia, you can't say that in front of Violet."

"It's okay, Charlotte," Violet said. "I am not offended."

"Always so gracious, darling," Charlotte said. "I know it doesn't make sense to you, Amelia, but it makes perfect sense to me. If you stay here, you get to start over. You're a novelty of sorts, being the American sister with lots of money and the sister-in-law to a Lady. You could have your pick of men, get married, and the rumors back home would stop."

"For heaven's sake, Mother."

"Okay, okay," George said. "Let's all just take a minute here."

Amelia walked to the window. It was a warm night, the moon and stars were shining, and she wanted to go outside to walk under their light.

"What of Madeline?" her mother asked. "Have we not forgotten Amelia's role in that whole mess?"

"You can't believe I had any fault in that," Amelia said, spinning around to face her mother.

"I just know how distraught my sister was. She said Madeline was driven to this by a fiancé who loved you instead. The same fiancé, I might add, who is here now and was with you on that boat."

"We can't hold Amelia responsible for the actions Madeline took," George said.

"She told me she did it because of pressure from her father, not from anything I did per se, and speaking of him, look at the mess he has made," Amelia said.

"It doesn't matter. My sister is telling her society friends that you played a part, and those rumors are getting back to our friends."

"Are they truly your friends?" Amelia asked.

"What type of question is that? Of course, they are."

"I can't help but think, real friends, true friends, wouldn't listen to gossip, especially when they have no idea what they are talking about. And why is it you worry more about what they think than you do about my own happiness? It's rather hurtful," Amelia said.

"We don't mean to hurt you," George said.

"Right, you just want to do what is fair for all. Which usually means I must sacrifice what I really and truly want."

"Is staying here that much of a sacrifice?" her mother asked.

"I love him," Amelia said.

"Amelia, you should have said that upfront. That changes everything, of course," George said.

"It changes nothing, George," their mother said. "It will only add fuel to the gossip, and I won't have our family name dragged through the mud. Your father worked too hard to build up our family. I won't have his spoiled daughter ruin it with her selfishness."

Gasping, Amelia's hand flew to her mouth. The sting of her mother's words couldn't have hurt worse if she had been slapped. She ran out and up to her room. Once she was inside, she slid to her knees and sobbed.

A knock sounded, and Amelia calmed herself. She answered the door, ready to continue the fight, but softened her countenance when she saw it was Ivy.

"May I come in?"

Amelia held open the door wider, shutting it once Ivy walked through.

"Are you okay?" Ivy asked.

"Did you hear?"

"It was hard not to hear. Nick wanted to run up here, but I told him it was probably better if he didn't."

"Why does she hate me so much?" Amelia asked.

"I'm sure she doesn't hate you," Ivy said.

Another knock at the door interrupted them, and Ivy went to answer it.

"I don't think she feels like talking about anything else tonight," Ivy said.

"We won't take long," George said.

"It's fine, Ivy. Let them in."

After George and her mother walked in, George said, "Perhaps give us a minute, Ivy."

"No, she can stay. Everyone might as well know," her mother said.

"What do you mean, Mother?" George asked.

"We should all sit down," her mother said.

Once everyone was comfortable, she said, "My deepest apologies for hurting your feelings, Amelia."

"Thank you for apologizing, Mother."

"And that's the issue, isn't it? All of this comes back to one thing," her mother said.

"What's that?" Amelia asked.

"I'm not your real mother, Amelia."

George gasped, and Ivy's hand flew to her mouth. The room started spinning, and Amelia placed a hand over her pounding heart. She asked her mother to repeat herself, but had a hard time hearing over the ringing in her ears.

"Amelia, are you okay?" Ivy asked. "You look like you're going to be sick."

Shaking her head, Amelia put a hand on her stomach and said, "I don't understand."

"We should have Mother explain more," George said.

Amelia jumped to her feet, swayed, steadied herself, and asked, "George, did you know about this? Are we even siblings?"

"I know as much as you," George said.

"You and George are still siblings. Your father was your father. But George is the only child I gave birth to," her mother said.

"I don't understand," Amelia said, sitting back in her chair.

Her mother stared at the fireplace, and just as Amelia thought she wasn't going to explain further, she said, "I cared for your father, and he cared for me, in the end especially. But it wasn't always like that. We had to marry. He may have had a little bit of a choice in who he married, but

I never had a choice. It was good business for his family, and my family needed the prestige of being tied to the Campbell name. Once I had George, your father never again slept in my bed. Then one day he came to me and said we were going to have a child. He had fallen in love with one of our housemaids, she was pregnant, and he meant to keep the baby. To raise it publicly. I told him he could keep the baby, that I would even raise the child as my own, but only if he sent the maid away. He agreed. The maid and I went away for a while, and I came back with a new maid and a baby girl."

"Is this why you hate me?" Amelia asked.

"I don't hate you, Melia," her mother said. "I never have. The truth is the first time I held you in my arms, I loved you. I didn't care that you weren't my own flesh and blood. I had always wanted a little girl and out of my broken heart I got my gift of you."

"Is this why you are so hard on me? Do I remind you of her?"

"No, you remind me of your father," her mother said. "He was always so passionate. So incredibly brilliant. A helper. And very kind. He never meant to hurt me. But he couldn't give you up. You children were his greatest accomplishments. His greatest gifts. When he died, I made a promise that I would always keep you from scandal and pain, because once one scandal occurs, people start digging around for other pieces of dirt. As things started to snowball, I realized I needed to have you married before it was too late."

Heat radiated through Amelia, and she had a hard time catching her breath. She pressed a trembling hand against her stomach and tried to stave off a wave of nausea.

She went to open a window, inhaled slowly, and asked, "Is my birth mother still alive?"

"No, she died, and this is why I had Ivy stay. Your real mother died when you were ten, and her other daughter came to work for us. It was the least your father could do under the circumstances."

Amelia spun around and locked eyes with Ivy.

Sisters. We're sisters.

Amelia rushed to Ivy but stopped short of hugging her. "I knew there was a reason you and I were always so connected."

"I don't know what to say. This is all such a shock," Ivy said.

Amelia grabbed Ivy's hand and sat next to her on the couch. "What do we do now? How do we move forward with all of this?"

"I suppose that is up to you and George," her mother said and got up to leave. "Darling, just be aware, Nick may not want to marry you once he finds out you are a bastard child."

Gasping, Amelia jumped to her feet. "How dare you!"

"Mother, what a thing to say," George said.

"I only say these things because even though you don't believe me, I do love you and want what is best for you, Amelia."

Her mother sauntered out of the room, shutting the door behind her. George started pacing the room. Ivy studied Amelia intently, and Amelia tried to figure out what to say or do next.

"George, I need to hear what you're thinking," Amelia said.

"I'm thinking that our mother is rather cruel at times."

"You said our mother."

"She is our mother. You are my sister. I don't care who gave birth to you, Melia."

"Do you think I should be worried that Nick will reject me? That his mother will reject me? That Tuva will reject me. Oh my god. I may lose everything after all."

She crumpled to her knees, and Ivy moved to catch her. George gingerly wrapped his arms around both sisters, holding them as a range of emotions poured out of all of them.

Chapter Thirty-Seven

IVY BLOCKED THE CRACK in the doorway and was telling Nick for the second time that Amelia wanted to be alone for a while.

When Nick finally left, Ivy shut the door and turned to Amelia. "You can't avoid him forever, you know."

"I just can't face him right now," Amelia said, moving to a seated position on the edge of the bed.

"Kathleen stopped by while you were napping. She is worried about you, too."

"But will their worry turn to hate and rejection once they find out the truth? I'm not ready to face that quite yet."

"Give them a chance. You might be surprised."

"You could be right, but there is a large possibility that for all their talk of just being bay people and accepting everyone, they will no longer be able to accept me."

"I know you will face this head-on when you're ready. Just don't wait too long."

"I won't. Did you tell Henry?" Amelia asked.

"Henry and I tell each other everything."

"Will he tell?"

"Do you think Henry will betray his two favorite people in all the world?" Ivy asked, sitting next to Amelia.

"I suppose not. What did he say?"

"He's excited the two of you will be brother and sister after we marry."

"He isn't one to betray those he loves," Amelia said.

"I would think we could say that about someone else."

"I'm just so scared," Amelia said, as her shoulders drooped and she covered her face with her hands.

"I know, honey. I don't mean to push. I honestly just don't know how much longer I can keep Nick out of your room."

"What should we do about Charlotte?" Amelia asked, resting her hands in her lap.

"You don't need to call her that on my account, silly. She is still your mother. Adopted or not. She raised you. And despite her being unkind at times, she does love you."

"Okay, what can we do about my mother not letting me leave England?"

"I think once the big secret is shared, then we tackle that."

"Could things get any more complicated?" Amelia asked.

"You could be pregnant, I suppose, since you were apparently so loose on the boat."

Amelia smacked Ivy with a pillow.

Ivy chuckled and asked, "Too soon? I'm sorry, sis."

Amelia joined her sister's laughter as they fell back onto the bed. Her delight turned to crying, and Ivy held her until Amelia heaved a long sigh.

"We need to get out of this bedroom. Come on, let's go for a walk," Ivy said, dragging Amelia off the bed and toward the door.

"Some fresh air does sound lovely."

They snuck downstairs to the outside and walked through the gardens. When they saw someone, they would duck behind a tree or bush and sneak away in the opposite direction. It became a game, and they started giggling as they ran across the lawn toward the trees. Their amusement soon faded but was replaced with contented silence while they walked along.

"It's starting to get late. We should probably go in and prepare for dinner," Ivy said.

"I can't go to dinner," Amelia said.

"You haven't been to any meal today. Skipping breakfast or lunch is understandable, but skipping dinner would be suspicious."

"I just don't know if I want to face them yet."

"You have to, Melia. Besides, me, your brother, and Henry will be there for moral support. And even if nothing is said, we will sit with you in your silence until you are ready to talk. It will be fine. I promise."

"Fine."

"Good job listening to your big sister," Ivy said.

Amelia playfully elbowed her sister before linking her arm with hers. They were rambling on about the beautiful day when they entered the house, but Amelia stopped short when she saw Nick.

"Amelia, I'm so glad you seem to be doing okay," Nick said. "Ivy mentioned you didn't want to be bothered. I thought perhaps you weren't feeling well."

"I'm fine, thank you for asking," Amelia said, rushing past him.

"Did I do something?" Nick asked.

Pausing on the staircase, Amelia turned to Nick and said, "I will see you at dinner."

She grabbed Ivy's hand and bounded up the stairs before she could hear a response.

"You can't make him feel like this is his fault or that he has done something wrong," Ivy said as they entered Amelia's room.

"I'm not meaning to. I just honestly don't know what to say," Amelia said.

"Still, you need to be a little gentler with him. He does love you."

"He loves me right now, but will he after I tell him that I'm a bastard child?"

"Don't you ever say that again!"

"I'm sorry. I just have all kinds of confusing and strange feelings."

"Understandably so. Now, I'm going to run and change, then will come back here and go down to dinner with you," Ivy said.

When Amelia was finally alone, she went to study herself in the mirror. She tried to see if she had any features similar to Ivy's. Amelia looked so much like her father it never dawned on her she had no matching features with her mother. She determined Ivy must look like their mother because the only similarity they had was the same color eyes.

She started to unbutton her dress and chided herself on taking so long. She sped up her progress of freshening up and changed into something more suitable for dinner. She coifed her hair carefully, and when Ivy returned, she tried to put on a brave face.

Ivy squeezed Amelia's arm, and they went downstairs. Polite conversation greeted them when they entered the drawing room and Amelia welcomed the cocktail offered to her. She kept a wary eye on Nick, who was in deep conversation with George across the room.

When the butler called dinner a few minutes later, relief flooded Amelia. She was never good at pretending, so was thankful she hadn't been forced to talk with Nick just yet. Violet must have pitied Amelia by placing her far enough away from Nick that it wouldn't appear rude if she didn't talk with him.

Amelia thought dinner was going smoothly enough, but she didn't participate in conversation and barely touched her food. Nick sent worried glances her way, but she pretended not to notice.

"I'm so sorry, but I can't stay quiet. Amelia, are you unwell?" Kathleen blurted out when there was a lull in conversation.

All eyes turned to Amelia. Her mother shook her head and gave a look that Amelia understood very well.

"It's been a rather tiring day, I suppose," Amelia said, taking a sip of Bordeaux.

"If you say so, but Nick and I are a little worried about you."

"Mother, please. It's okay," Nick said.

Amelia played with her food and sent a pleading look to George.

"We're just trying to figure out what we're going to do with this Willow Bay situation, and since nothing is resolved, it's causing some upset," George said.

"I don't see why this can't be resolved," Nick said.

"Could we not talk about it now?" Amelia asked.

"But how long do we need to keep pushing this topic aside?" Nick asked. "Gram's health continues to decline, and I will never forgive myself if she passes while we are gone. Plus, Mother and I can only be gone so long before the business side of things suffers."

"Then perhaps you should just go home without me," Amelia said.

She shoved back from the table, threw her napkin on her plate, and stormed off.

"Melia," Nick said, but she was not deterred.

She ran up to her bedroom and flung herself across the bed. A few minutes later, her bedroom door opened and shut.

"I don't want to talk, Ivy," Amelia said.

"Well, I don't see how I can understand what is going on with you unless we talk," Nick said.

Amelia shot up to a sitting position. "Who said you could come in here?"

"What's happened, Melia?" Nick asked.

"My mother won't let me leave. So, I believe it's best if we just part ways. Which is difficult for me to do. I just need some time away from you to wrap my head around what must happen."

"I'm willing to help figure this out, although I don't understand why this is so hard. Let me or my mother or both of us talk to your mother."

"It won't matter."

Nick studied her. "There's something else, isn't there? I can tell when you're holding something back."

"Please, Nick. Trust me. It's nothing you will want to know. And once you do know, you will change your mind about me, and won't ever want to speak to me again."

"It can't possibly be that bad."

Amelia decided she didn't have a choice but to tell him. She loved Nick too much.

"My mother is not my real mother."

"What do you mean?" Nick asked.

"Apparently, my father had an affair with a servant. I'm the product of that affair. My father wanted to keep me.

My mother adopted me. And I was raised as a Campbell with a prestigious lineage. But I'm the child of a servant and a father who didn't love his wife. I am a bas—"

"Don't you dare," Nick said. "Don't you dare say it."

"It's true, though," Amelia said. "And get this. Ivy is my half-sister. Just like George is my half-brother. I'm only partly something. Not really whole."

"Stop saying things like that about yourself. That isn't like you, Melia." Nick ran his fingers through his hair and walked across the room to lean against the wall. "Whenever you're ready, you can tell me everything. But I am not leaving this room until you do."

Amelia studied her hands in her lap, inhaled deeply, and started from the beginning. Nick listened to her explain everything her mother shared with her. She included the gossip, the love affair her father had, and her birth mother's death. She went on to explain the fears her mother had and how she was pushing to make sure Amelia married someone quickly, before the truth came out for all to hear.

"Can't you see? You and I can never be together. I couldn't do that to you. Besides, you don't want to be tied to a disgraceful past like mine."

Nick bounded across the room and grabbed her, forcing her to look directly into his eyes. "You listen to me, Amelia Campbell. I love you. I don't care who your father is. I don't care who your mother is. I'm excited you have a sister. And I won't lie and say I'm not shocked by what you just told me, but none of it, do you hear me, none of it changes my love for you. I want to marry you. And I want to spend the rest of my life showing you how whole and amazing you are."

Tears filled her eyes. "You mean it?"

Hugging Amelia to him, Nick stroked her hair. "I loved you from our first moments together. And I will love you until I take my last breath. Yes, I mean every word."

Amelia pulled Nick's mouth to hers and kissed him. The kiss grew with intensity until Nick stopped them.

"I could take you right here, Melia," he said, desire shining in his eyes.

"And I could let you. But we mustn't. Not right now," she said.

"We will have our chance another time, my love," Nick said.

"I'll be looking forward to it."

A knock at the door spurred them apart. Amelia slowed her breathing and asked whoever was there to come in.

Ivy opened the door and said, "Gracious, you two. If I didn't know any better, I would say you were trying to start a fire in here."

"Very funny, Ivy," Amelia said, but winked at her sister.

Nick kissed Amelia on the cheek, indicated they would talk more the following day, and went to leave. Before shutting the door, he paused. "I love you, Melia. Never doubt that. Goodnight."

"I love you too, Nick."

When they were alone, Ivy turned to her. "So, big sis was right."

Amelia laughed and threw a pillow at her.

"Your cheeks are bright red, Melia. Did I interrupt some passion?"

"Some kissing, but nothing more."

"Make sure you're careful. I would never be one to try and tell you what to do. Just be careful, especially while you're still here. Your mother would never forgive you."

"Speaking of my mother, what am I going to do about Willow Bay?"

"George and I talked about it, and we came up with a plan."

"Which is?"

"We're going to insist that you be allowed to go. That's it. That's the plan. Your father would want you to be happy and loved the way Nick loves you. The way your father loved my mother. The way you love Nick. He would choose your love over any scandal. I know it. And so does George."

"Do you think it will work?"

"She won't be allowed to have a say, so yes, it will work. Now I'm off to bed. I'm happy you resolved things with Nick."

"Should I worry that Kathleen will care?"

"No, I don't think so, but if you want to wait to tell her after we are homeward bound, I can understand that. I can see Nick sharing the information with her, though, because that's the type of relationship they have."

"Should I tell him not to say anything?"

"I think we should embrace my new philosophy with our family."

"Which is?"

"No more secrets."

Chapter Thirty-Eight

THOUGHTS OF THE LAST time Amelia was on the lake flitted through her mind as they sailed across the beautiful blue waves. The sun shined brightly above them without a cloud in the sky. Ivy had suggested they go by land this time, but Amelia insisted she had to go by water. Entering Willow Bay by way of the lake was her favorite way to go, even after surviving the storm.

Nick put his arm around her, and she nestled her head against his shoulder.

"Are you okay?" Nick asked.

"I am. I was just thinking about…"

"I know. It's hard not to think about that night and about him."

Amelia pulled away and looked into Nick's eyes. "Are you okay? I wasn't thinking. Should we have gone by land?"

Nick kissed her cheek. "No, my love. This is what soothes my soul and pain just as it does yours."

"And your mother? Is she okay?"

"She feels Nathanial here, so yes. As painful as it is for her to lose her son, she loves being on the water as well."

Ivy and Henry walked across the deck to stand next to them.

Henry raised his arm and pointed. "There she is."

"Yes. There she is," Amelia agreed. "Home."

Nick hugged her before excusing himself to help navigate the boat to the marina. Henry pulled Ivy away to point out something he saw in the water, and Amelia was left to stand alone. She was sure the joy she felt radiated on her face.

"It truly is my favorite place in the world," Kathleen said, coming to stand next to her.

"Mine as well," Amelia said.

"Which is why you belong here."

"Thank you for saying that."

"I know we haven't had a chance to talk. I was looking for the right time, but the moment never arrived. I wanted to share my heart before we got back, but perhaps the right time is now, as we are sailing safely back into the bay."

Amelia placed a hand on her chest, attempting to steady her frantic heartbeat. "Go on."

"I can't imagine how hearing such news from your mother must have felt. It has no doubt caused you to look at so many things differently. You will forever be changed by her news. But for us. For myself. For Nick. For our family. And especially for Tuva. You have been and always will be beautiful-hearted Melia. Our Melia, whom we love and adore with all our hearts. Nothing can ever change that. And I'm very much looking forward to the day I get to call you my daughter."

Tears rained down Amelia's cheeks at being accepted for who she was, based on her essence alone.

"Thank you, Kathleen. And I cannot wait to call you my mother."

"Come. Let's dry our eyes and embrace the beauty of the day."

"I love that idea."

Amelia took in the sights and sounds, and her cheeks hurt from grinning. Her name was called, and she turned toward the wheelhouse. Nick stood there, the breeze blowing through his hair, with a smile matching her own.

"Welcome home, Melia."

Amelia couldn't keep from laughing and said, "Welcome home indeed."

Sparkles of dust floated through the air as the sunlight poured in through the rear porch windows. A bed had been set up, per Tuva's wishes, so she could spend her last days staring at her love, the lake. Amelia shared everything with Tuva, and Tuva held Amelia's hand, squeezing it occasionally until she finished.

"Quite the story," Tuva said. "Isn't it funny how afraid we are of what may never happen? There is so much turmoil and confusion wrapped up in the fear of the unknown. We want freedom from fear, and yet it is our fear that is keeping us chained. We must gain knowledge by asking questions, by talking about those things which are difficult. It is through this alone that we can combat fear and lies and truly be free to love and move forward in life."

"Ever the wise one," Amelia said.

"Ah, well, life has taught me so much, even in my old age."

"How are you feeling today?"

"Like the end is near."

"I hate the thought of that," Amelia said.

"Death is another unknown, isn't it? Yet we cannot escape it. I look forward to being reunited with my Isak and with my parents. And with Minwaadizi. And, of course, my son Billy, and with Nathanial. All who have gone before me are waiting for me. And yet…"

"And yet what?" Amelia asked.

"I find myself not wanting to leave you, Melia. Your story is just beginning here in Willow Bay, and I would love to bear witness to it."

"Perhaps you will."

"I like the sound of that."

A knock on the doorframe signaled Nick's arrival. "Hello, Gram. How are you feeling today?"

"I am here."

"I feel that," Nick said, winking at Tuva. "I came by to see if Melia would like an escort home with a reminder for you that I will be here for our morning coffee conversation tomorrow."

"I'm looking forward to it. You can bring Melia sometime if you choose," Tuva said.

"Actually, I think he prefers to have that time with you alone. He's selfish that way," Amelia said, winking at Nick.

"She's right, Gram. I can't talk about her behind her back if she's here."

Tuva burst out laughing. "You two remind me of how playful Isak and I could be with one another. It makes my heart happy to see the two of you together."

"My heart is also happy," Nick said, widening his grin. Changing the subject, he asked, "Have you given more thought to our conversation yesterday, Gram? I can make a comfortable spot for you on the boat if you wish to join us. And I will carry you on board."

"I have, and I think I will take you up on that offer," Tuva said.

"What are we discussing?" Amelia asked.

Surprise registered on Tuva's face, and she glanced at Nick before saying, "Nathanial's memorial, of course."

Amelia stood, wringing her hands. "I thought that would have been done long before now."

"Sometimes these things cannot be rushed when one is taken from us in such a way," Tuva said.

"Nick, why didn't you say anything to me about it before now?" Amelia asked.

"I struggled to find the words. Things had been so difficult for you, and I didn't want to add another layer of sadness. I would have shared it eventually, but you have been so happy since we arrived, and I didn't want to spoil it."

"So thoughtful of you, but I wish you would have said something so I could help prepare."

"There is still time to help," Tuva said.

"When will the memorial be?" Amelia asked.

"A week from Saturday, and if the weather isn't cooperating, we will do it the following week," Nick said.

"The weather will cooperate, I'm sure of it," Tuva said.

Amelia nodded and contemplated the memorial service. "I understand not wanting to rush this. His passing was so hard for everyone."

"Honestly, Melia, we were waiting for you," Nick said.

Becoming overwhelmed at the warmth of love and acceptance flowing through her, Amelia squeezed Tuva's hand and went to kiss Nick on the cheek. She was sure the tears were shining in her eyes when she said goodbye to Tuva with promises to come the following day. She gathered Nick's hand in hers and they left Tuva's together.

They walked toward the big house when Nick suggested they continue walking for a while. Amelia readily agreed, and they took the route that would take them to her favorite spot on the point. The lake sparkled like diamonds floating on its surface as the sun rose higher in the sky, and she soaked in the warmth on her face.

Nick stopped walking, so Amelia paused to turn around. He stared at something in his hands while he gently played with it.

"Are you okay?" she asked.

Nick looked at Amelia with so much love on his face that her hand flew to her chest as her heart skipped a beat.

She took a step toward him, but he raised a hand. "No, give me a minute."

Amelia sat on a boulder and waited patiently. Soaking in the sun, she closed her eyes, opening them only as Nick began to talk.

"When Nathanial and I were younger, we often discussed how it would take someone special to join us, not as wives, but as partners here in the bay. This isn't an easy life. The lake is a harsh mistress, but the right woman is strong enough to stand against her or beside her, and beside us."

Nick paused, looked across the lake toward the marina, then back at her and continued. "I had lost my way when I agreed to marry Maddy. I had become so focused on business after Father died that I couldn't see things clearly. Then you walked into that dining room and sat beside me. The conversations and promises I had made with my brother came flooding back. It scared me. And I told myself that my duty and honor had to keep me bound to a promise I no longer wanted to keep."

"You can't beat yourself up over the past," Amelia said.

"I know. Please, though, my love, this isn't easy for me to share, so give me the space to talk."

"I'm sorry, Nick. I promise I won't say another word."

"It's okay. It's very much like you to want to ease my difficulty." He smiled and grew quiet and Amelia struggled not to speak. Finding his words, he continued.

"Nathanial and I often talked about you. He loved you. He always asked me if I loved you. I always denied it, because of duty, because of fear, until you were beaten by Mr. Donovan. He admonished me for not admitting my true feelings and that I needed to face them. He also told me that as much as he loved you, he knew in his heart it wasn't the same as the love we had for each other. Even if we couldn't see it. When I left for Saint Paul after you were shot at, I knew I needed to own up to things, but I wasn't sure how you felt. If you loved my brother, I couldn't stand in your way. I wouldn't."

"When you saw me on the boat that night, you ignored me. Is this why?" Amelia asked.

"Yes, when I saw you standing on deck, the wind whipping your hair around. The strength and determination shining in your eyes. I was more in love with you than ever and yet there you were on a boat, spending time with my brother. I was afraid my feelings would show."

"I'm sure my actions during the storm didn't help any," Amelia said.

"You, kissing me back while we were on the boat, gave me hope, but I wasn't sure how things were left between you and Nathanial as he sailed away on the *Vide Fjärd*. The idea that I would just swoop in after he died made me sick. I had to push you away until I could sort things out in my head."

"I had to do the same, Nick. It's okay."

"When we returned from England, Mother handed me a letter from Nathanial. She told me she had found it in Nathanial's things and had been holding it until the right moment. The letter shared he was planning on breaking things off with you because he knew you loved me. He knew that our love for each other was not meant to hurt him, that it was meant to be, and he wanted us to be together."

Nick paused, catching his breath as tears built in his eyes. "He commissioned to have rings made. He wrote that when it came to the color, design, and sizes, all he could think of was making them for me and you. He started having the rings made even before your first attack. He wrote that in his heart of hearts, he knew you and I would find our way to each other eventually."

Tears dampened Amelia's cheeks as Nick walked closer to her. He kneeled in front of her, placed a ring in her hand, squeezed it shut, and cradled her hand in his.

"I must know, Melia. Will you be my wife? Will you be my partner? I didn't know anyone could love as I love you. Marry me?"

Amelia flung her arms around him. "Yes! Of course, yes! I could never love another as I love you."

Chapter
Thirty-Nine

THE *BAY MINNOW* SLID through the water with ease. Everyone huddled on deck, waiting to get to the right spot on the lake. The blue sky had few clouds, and the sun was warm. Tuva sat on her perch with blankets tucked around her.

Amelia sat beside Tuva and held her hand as they sailed along. It was a beautiful day, and it would be filled with love mixed with sorrow as they remembered Nathanial. Everyone had brought a small stone from the bay to drop into the water as they said their goodbyes.

Kathleen went to stand at the entry to the wheelhouse and yelled, "Let's stop here, son."

"I want to find the perfect spot," Nick said.

"Stop avoiding the goodbye, Nick. This is the perfect spot. We have a perfect view of our bay, the sun is shining, and the water is that beautiful blue we all love."

Nick slowed the boat to a stop and dropped anchor. Amelia stood when he came to stand next to her and Tuva. Everyone else gathered around them and Kathleen started to sing. She sang the same song Amelia had sung the night of the storm when they were being cast about on the boat.

When the song was over, Kathleen said, "We gather here today to remember dear Nathanial. He is one whom the lake has not given back to us. So, we have come to him here. He gave his life that night saving so many. He loved each one of us in the only way he knew how. As I let my stone slide into the water, my message to him is this. Rest easy, my son. You are a hero. Your sacrifice will never be forgotten and you will forever be loved. Goodbye, my son."

One by one, everyone else said their words to a fallen hero. Tuva shared her words of wisdom and love in her way while Nick offered her stone to the water for her. Nick took his turn next and had just finished his offering of remembrance when Amelia realized she was the last one to speak.

Moving to the rail, she stared at it as flashes of the storm ran through her. She flinched when the moment Nathanial bounded over the rail to get on the *Vide Fjärd* danced in front of her eyes. She closed her eyes and gripped the railing. She was unable to breathe until Nick's arm wrapped around her shoulders.

"Are you okay, my love?" Nick asked.

Amelia opened her eyes. "Yes, I was just thinking."

"You were remembering," Nick said.

"Yes. I was remembering that night."

"Do you need a minute?"

"No, I'm okay."

Ivy reached out and squeezed Amelia's hand. "Whenever you're ready, sis."

Amelia nodded. "As I stand here, I see the *Vide Fjärd* sailing into the wall of the storm. Those last moments of seeing him bravely sacrifice everything will stay with me forever. His love for me, for this family, will give me comfort when I miss him the most. And as I slip my stone of remembrance into the water, I say to him, thank you for loving me, thank you for helping me see the truth, thank you for the gifts you continue to give, even today. You are forever loved, Nathanial. Rest in peace."

Amelia moved to sit next to Tuva and cradled her hands.

"What a beautiful dedication and way of memorializing," Tuva said.

"It's so fitting," Amelia said.

"My eyes grow weary. I think I will rest them while we sail back toward the bay. The rock of the boat feels wonderful," Tuva said.

"Enjoy the warm sun on your face and the occasional sea spray," Amelia said.

"Two of my favorite things while resting on her waters," Tuva said.

Nick and the crewman started to prepare the boat to sail back home. Light conversation flitted around, and Amelia sat contentedly next to Tuva. Following Tuva's example, she raised her closed eyes toward the sun. She didn't open them until the sway of the boat shifted as it moved in the direction of the marina. She turned to ask Tuva a question but paused. Something about the way she was lying there unnerved her.

"Tuva, are you feeling okay?" Amelia asked.

Not receiving a response, Amelia shook Tuva carefully. When Tuva didn't move or say anything, she started checking to see if she could feel a pulse or hear breathing.

"Nick. Oh my god, Nick," Amelia yelled.

Everyone gathered around while Nick jumped into action. He gave his own assessment and when done, he looked into Amelia's eyes.

"She's gone."

Amelia flung her arms around Tuva. "Oh, my sweet friend."

The crewmen stopped the boat, and everything grew still except for the gentle sway of the boat. The only thing that could be heard was the splash of water against the side. Amelia went to Nick, and they held each other.

Kathleen kissed Tuva on the cheek and said, "This is as it should be. She slipped away on her own terms, surrounded by the people she loved, with a view of her beloved home on the one thing she loved the most—her beautiful lake."

Amelia went to hug her future mother-in-law and said, "I believe she knew this would be her last ride."

"I agree," Kathleen said.

Ivy brought forth a blanket and covered the well-loved woman. She said her own words of sorrow, honoring the life of someone who loved all people. Henry comforted her as they gave space for anyone else to say a last goodbye.

Nick motioned for the crewmen to get them home. He reached out a hand to his mother and put his arm around Amelia while they huddled around Tuva. Amelia's face softened, knowing Tuva was reunited at last with her Isak and her dear friend Minwaadizi.

The funeral guests milled around the drawing room, offering their condolences and discussing their own sorrow at losing such a beloved figure in Willow Bay. The matriarch of the town was finally able to rest. Amelia didn't know all the faces in attendance but was surprised at how many community members she recognized. News of Nick and Amelia's engagement was mixed in with the conversations of Tuva and the importance of her work in Willow Bay.

As the community slowly slipped away to their respective homes, Amelia breathed a sigh, knowing they would soon be alone to grieve as a family. Nick had asked her if she would like to go for a walk after the last guest left, and she was looking forward to fresh air after feeling stifled inside for most of the afternoon.

The last guest was finally escorted out and the door closed behind them. Kathleen hugged Nick and Amelia, professed a headache, and went to lie down. Ivy and Henry had disappeared somewhere, so Nick suggested they take their walk. She strolled along, holding Nick's hand. The sun was dropping lower in the sky, signaling it would be dinner soon.

"Are we going to have a big dinner?" Amelia asked.

"Mamma set it up so it's buffet style. We can come and go when we get hungry."

"I wondered if she might. She mentioned wanting to eat in her room so that she could rest."

"I worry about her. It's been a rough year for her," Nick said.

"I worry, too. My hope is that it will help her to focus on joyful things such as Ivy and Henry's wedding in a couple of weeks and then, of course, our wedding."

"Such wonderful celebrations to look forward to," Nick said.

"In some ways, today was a celebration as well. Tuva was an amazing woman. I will miss her terribly."

"Yes, she was amazing, and as I have said before, you remind me so much of her."

"Hopefully, I can live up to her standard."

"Just be yourself, Melia."

They started to walk back toward the house when Nick asked, "Have you heard from your mother or George?"

"I had a letter from George, but nothing from my mother. I think she is still angry with me for leaving. George says Violet is pregnant again, which is exciting, but he is still planning on coming to Ivy's wedding. I doubt he has heard of our own announcement yet. The news of our engagement has spread around here, but I don't think it has reached England yet. So, I decided to share the news with him in person and I can't wait."

"Will he be happy for us?"

"He will be happy, especially if I am happy, but also because this means our families will be in business for a long time."

Nick laughed before kissing her softly. Love and desire flared in his eyes while the same heat radiated through her. They moved to go inside when Lars walked around the side of the house.

"Forgive me, cap, Miss Amelia," Lars said. "I wouldn't have come to bother you on such a day, but unfortunately, this can't wait."

"A welcome distraction, I assure you," Amelia said. "Only if everything is okay, though."

"Yes, what's the urgent situation?" Nick asked.

"The *Kathleen* is sinking. I think the repairs are just not able to keep her together. I was going to wait and bring this to you tomorrow, but she seems to be slipping into the water quicker than we realized and thought you better come take a look."

"You were right to come get me," Nick said.

"I agree. Do you want me to come with you?" Amelia asked.

"No, you relax here. It's been a long day."

"Very well, but I'll wait to eat dinner with you."

"This could take a while," Nick said.

"I don't mind waiting. But we shouldn't keep Lars and the *Kathleen* waiting. Go on now. I will sit on the patio and enjoy the beautiful evening."

Nick kissed her. "I love you. Be back as soon as I can."

"I love you too," Amelia said as Nick and Lars walked away.

The sun continued to lower in the evening sky, but Amelia didn't move to go in. She enjoyed the lake breeze and fresh air as she listened to the waves in the distance. She began to wonder where Ivy might be and contemplated going to look for her, but decided against it.

She was pulled to her favorite spot and walked off the porch. She hummed the tune of the lake, picked a flower, and played with its petals as she walked along. She was nearing the rocky shoreline when she noticed a figure sitting on a boulder just ahead.

"Is someone there?" Amelia asked, stepping closer to get a better look.

"I wondered if you might come down here after such a day. I've been waiting for you."

"Maddy?"

"Yes, dear cousin, it is I."

Warning bells sounded in Amelia's head, but she tamped down her fear.

"Where have you been?" Amelia asked. "You all but disappeared."

"Father helped me. He put me up in an apartment in the cities, but I wasn't allowed to ever leave. I grew desperate to get out. He talked of finding me a place in New York or Boston where I wouldn't be known, but I hated that I had to run away from my life like a fugitive. I almost took him up on it, but I fled instead. I think I went a bit mad, really."

"I suppose a part of you blames me for that."

"Of course, it's your fault," Madeline said as she slid off the boulder to stand.

It was then Amelia noticed she was holding something. "What do you have in your hand, Maddy?"

Madeline lifted her arm, and the light from the sunset shimmered across a large knife.

"I think I'm going to return to my house. Perhaps you should move along and take your father up on his offer. I won't tell anyone you were here," Amelia said.

She started to walk away but paused when a rock flew past her head, crashing against another boulder just ahead of her.

Spinning around, Amelia said, "Maddy, you don't want to hurt me. You really don't. I know you are in pain and confused, but injuring me won't fix things for you."

"It may not fix things, but it will make me feel better."

"No, it won't. Trust me."

"Trust you? Why would I ever trust you?" Madeline asked, moving slowly toward Amelia. "You came into my life and stole it from me."

"I didn't steal anything from you."

"You stole the business deal away from my father. You stole my fiancé. You stole the role in the Nilsson family that should have been mine. Everything that was mine is now yours, and you took it from me."

"I know that's how it must look to you, but that's not how it happened. I had nothing to do with your father's business. That was between Tuva and George. And Nick and I didn't come together until we were both free."

"But you loved him, and he loved you while he was still mine."

"He is not a possession, Maddy."

"He was mine."

"You told me you didn't love him."

Madeline lunged, wielding the knife, and screamed, "He was mine!"

Amelia moved, but the blade caught her dress, snagging her skin. She clutched her arm and Madeline pounced, knocking them both to the ground. They rolled over pebbles, coming apart when the lake splashed over them.

Scrambling away, Amelia stumbled over rocks up the side of the ridge. Madeline rushed behind, yelling for Amelia to stop. Reaching the top, Amelia started to run, but Madeline's hand snaked around her ankle, forcing her to the ground.

Screaming, Amelia clawed at the dirt as cold steel sliced her leg. She moved away, pain radiating through her thigh. Madeline jumped on her and the sting of the blade caught her again. Amelia bounded up and twirled around. Madeline stood only a few feet away. Breathing heavily, they stared at each other. Amelia tried anticipating her cousin's next move when Nick and Ivy shouted her name.

Madeline turned to look in their direction, then back at Amelia, took several steps, and jumped off the side of the point. Amelia screamed and ran to the edge. Nick and Ivy got to Amelia just as blood pooled around the back of Madeline's head. Her mangled body lay lifeless as a wave rushed over her.

Henry and Lars reached Madeline before her body was pulled into the lake. Henry looked up at Amelia. She could barely see the glint of moisture on his face before the sun completely disappeared.

"Henry?" Amelia yelled into the growing darkness.

"She's dead."

Chapter Forty

THE BANDAGE WAS TIGHT around Amelia's leg. She fiddled with it and stumbled on the walkway. Ivy rushed to her side, pressuring her to go sit down.

Amelia waved her away. "I'm fine. Really, I am."

"Are you sure? Should you even be walking such a long distance?" Ivy asked. "If Nick was here, he would be yelling at you, then me, for not making you rest longer."

"It's been several weeks, and my leg is all but healed. My other wounds are scarring nicely as well. None of the cuts were too deep. I suppose I had my thick funeral outfit to thank for that, I guess."

"I'm just thankful she didn't have a better aim. I don't think I could bear losing you so soon after finding out you are my sister."

"How is Henry with all of this?" Amelia asked.

"He is managing things as best as he can. He loves you. He loved his sister. In some ways, though, he mourned her loss when she disappeared after she hurt you the first time."

"And his mother, my aunt Lucille?"

"It's my understanding that she has isolated herself in a small lake cottage somewhere close to Saint Paul. She has very little to do with Henry or his father. Henry has tried to visit her on several occasions, but she has refused to see him."

"I suppose my uncle has turned a little mad with all this."

"We're actually not sure how he is doing. Henry refuses to have anything to do with him. And most of the family business has transitioned to Henry to handle. Henry will have to travel back and forth from the city to here at times, but he is working to move everything to Duluth or Willow Bay so that we can be close to you and stay here."

"I'm sure conversations of helping each other with business will come up as time goes on."

"I know Henry would love that, but under the circumstances, is going to let Nick bring it up if he ever chooses to do so. We're happy to just be near you all," Ivy said. She paused and changed the subject by asking, "Have you heard if your mother is with George or not?"

"No, he never said, and I was afraid to ask."

"We will find out soon enough. I see your car heading to the house."

"My car?"

"Okay, Nick's car, but it will be yours soon enough, silly," Ivy said.

"I suppose so. Maybe I can finally learn to drive it," Amelia said, giggling at the thought.

Amelia and Ivy rushed back to the house just as the car slowed to a stop. Amelia stopped just short of the car as George climbed out of the back seat.

"George, I didn't realize how much I've missed you until just this moment," Amelia said, walking toward her brother.

"I've missed you too, sis," George said and turned to extend his hand to the back seat.

Her mother emerged with a smile that faltered when she locked eyes with Amelia. Amelia paused even though she wanted to rush into her mother's arms. She wondered if they would ever be able to have a close relationship with all that had happened in the past couple of years.

Plastering a smile on her face, Amelia moved to give her mother a polite hug. "It's wonderful to see you. I'm so glad you came."

"Are you happy to see me, then?" her mother asked.

"Why wouldn't I be?" Amelia asked.

"Perhaps we should discuss this later," her mother said and walked by Amelia. "Ivy, so lovely to see you too, darling."

George hugged Amelia tightly. "Nick told us what happened with Maddy. I'm so sorry you were the target of such cruelty once again."

"Thank you, George. But I'm okay," she said.

"I have no doubt you are, but I'm sorry just the same."

Nick hugged Amelia and kissed her on the cheek. "Missed you."

"You were gone for only a few days, picking up my brother and, apparently, my mother," she said, laughing. "But I missed you too."

Glancing over at her brother, she noticed his questioning look. "What is it, George?"

"Something else has happened. Some news that should be shared soon, I would imagine."

"What makes you say that?" Amelia asked.

George chuckled, but didn't say anything else.

Nick grabbed Amelia's hand as they all walked toward the house. "I would wager he knows."

Dinner was just wrapping up when Kathleen clanged her wine glass with a knife. The table went quiet, and all eyes turned to her. Amelia sent a questioning look at Nick, who just shrugged.

"I would like to propose a toast," Kathleen said. "These last couple of years have been filled with love and tragedy, but we have carried on as we Nilssons do. So, it brings me such pleasure to be hosting such a joyous occasion as the marriage between Ivy and Henry."

"Here, Here," echoed across the room as glasses raised in the air, followed by sips of wine.

Henry stood as everyone settled and said, "I, too, have a few words. We are here to celebrate the love that Ivy and I have. And it brings us joy that we are all together. But I know there is news my wonderful future sister-in-law has to share."

Amelia looked over at her mother and knew the moment her mother caught the sister-in-law reference. She turned to glare at Amelia, excused herself, and left the room.

"What did I say?" Henry asked. He looked over at Amelia just as realization struck. "Oh, Melia. It slipped out. I wasn't even thinking. That's just how I see you now, so I didn't even think."

Pushing away from the table, Amelia said, "It's okay, Henry. She just needs to get used to people knowing the truth."

"Still, I shouldn't have said anything."

"There isn't a person at this table who doesn't know, Henry. It's okay," George said.

"Perhaps, but maybe next time I give you the option to announce your big news, I won't make such a blunder," Henry said.

"What announcement is this?" George asked.

"I'm just going to sit down and shut up now," Henry said.

"Amelia, do you want to share or wait?" Nick asked.

"I'm sure he's probably already guessed, but I'm excited to say the words anyway. George, Nick, and I are officially engaged to be married," she said.

George cheered and went to hug her. When he returned to his seat, Amelia started to leave the room.

"Do you want me to go with you?" George asked.

"No, it's time she and I made peace, and we need to do it on our own," she said and went in search of her mother.

Knocking on the bedroom door, she asked, "Mother, are you in there?"

The door swung open. "What do you want, Amelia?"

"I'm sure Henry's words caught you off guard, so I wanted to make sure you're okay."

"They did more than catch me off guard. I was never more humiliated in my life than I was this evening."

Amelia moved further into her mother's guest room but didn't sit. She wanted to make sure her mother was willing to discuss things. She didn't want to push.

"Get comfortable, Amelia. I suppose we need to clear the air," her mother said, shutting the bedroom door.

Amelia complied but waited until her mother was seated before jumping into the conversation.

"I know you are mad at me for leaving England. It's just not fair that you are trying to punish me with your silence."

"I wasn't trying to punish you with silence, Amelia. I didn't know what to say, so I didn't send any correspondence."

"So, you're not angry with me?"

"Well, maybe a little. But it hurts that once you found out I wasn't your real mother, you were so desperate to leave."

"You know I wanted to leave before then, so that statement isn't fair."

"Perhaps. I guess I feared that since you knew the truth, you would stop trying to be in my life."

"I wrote to you several times sharing things that were going on here."

"Yes, but you are not one to just write about picnics and parties, especially when things were said between us. I thought your letters were a way to pacify me. You were fulfilling your obligations to me, so to speak."

"Don't be ridiculous, Mother."

"My feelings aren't ridiculous."

"You're right. That wasn't fair for me to say either. I'm sorry."

Her mother walked about the room a couple of times. Amelia had never seen her mother look so distraught and struggled to know how to help her.

"Why did you come, Mother?"

"I had to know if I lost you forever," she said. "I know I don't always handle myself well with you, and that I can come across as cruel. I never had a good role model of a loving mother. And believe it or not, despite you not being born from my body, you were my child as soon as you were placed in my arms. A part of me felt guilty for not allowing you to be raised with your own mother, so I promised myself I would love you as if you were my own. Loving you was always easy for me. Showing my love was always the hard part."

"Is that the reason you let Ivy come to work for us?"

"I'm ashamed to say I fought against it. When Ivy's, and I guess your birth mother, died, your father insisted Ivy come to live with us. He wanted her to become his ward. The idea of it terrified me. I was so afraid people would find out our dirty secret."

"Is that how you see me? A dirty secret?" Amelia asked.

Her mother rushed to sit by Amelia, grabbing her hands. "Never. I never looked at you that way. On the contrary, you were mine and I had to protect you at any cost. Your father's betrayal was the dirty secret, and I feared Ivy being his ward would cause people to question. I couldn't face it. In the end, we compromised, and Ivy came to work for us."

"Did it ever bother you to see Ivy and I growing so close?"

"I tried to stop it, at first, but you always did do things in your own way, and I had to learn to accept it."

"This all couldn't have been easy for you. The constant reminder of Father's infidelity, in not just keeping me, but in letting Ivy come."

"Thank you for that, Amelia."

"I'm sorry if you thought I didn't want you in my life. That has never been the case. I just love Willow Bay. It's interesting. I never felt like I belonged in the world you brought me up in. And yet here, I feel like I'm at home. I feel like I'm where I'm meant to be. I feel like myself."

"I can see that, Melia. I would be lying if I said I didn't."

"It just goes against the life you thought you were preparing me for."

"Yes, and it's so far away. I honestly and truly just miss you more than anything. Despite our disagreements and rarely seeing eye to eye, you, my child, are the one that taught me what true love is. You captured my heart like no other. Don't get me wrong, as I've said before, a mother does not have favorites. I also love your brother, George. But with you, somehow, it's different. A mother can love her children equally and yet so differently."

A quiet settled over the room and Amelia thought about leaving. They had more to talk about to heal the wounds between them, but they had taken a large step in the right direction. And she didn't want to push it.

"You don't seem to be affected too greatly by your wounds. Physically, I mean. But how are you emotional-ly?" her mother asked.

Stunned by the question, Amelia said, "I'm feeling better every day. Maddy and I were so close when we were children. It pains me she grew to hate me so much."

"Bitterness and anger can do that to a person."

"It just dawned on me that I haven't even shared my good news with you. You were the first person I wanted to tell. I'm sorry you're the last."

"Well, you just saved the best for last," her mother said, showing a rare silly side to her. "What's your news?"

"I'm engaged."

"That is the absolute best news. I'm so happy for you, Melia."

No longer caring about her mother's protocols and rules, Amelia flung her arms around her.

Wrapping her own arms around Amelia, her mother said, "You truly have been my forever gift."

Chapter Forty-One

THE SUNLIGHT PEEKED THROUGH the curtains, blinding Amelia as she was shaken awake. Ivy stood over her with a ridiculous smile on her face. Amelia sat up, feeling Ivy's happiness, and wondered at her sister's exuberance.

"I have the absolute best idea, Amelia," Ivy said.

"Which is?"

"I want you and Nick to get married this weekend, along with Henry and me."

"What? No, I don't want to take away from your special time," Amelia said.

"You will be adding to it," Ivy said. "We would get married on one day, and you would get married on the next."

"What does Henry think?"

"He loves the idea. He is searching for Nick as we speak."

"Hopefully he isn't shaking Nick awake the same way you did me," Amelia said, laughing.

"I doubt it. You're the only one that slept late, you lazy bones," Ivy said.

"Hey, I had a late night."

"I know. It makes me happy that you worked things out with Charlotte."

"It makes me happy too."

"Melia, we really do want you to use this time while your mother is already here to get married. I know you had been talking about doing it at Christmas, but that would mean she couldn't be here, and neither could your brother. I know Violet isn't here, but at least they are."

"I suppose I should go talk to Nick about it. But if he doesn't object, I don't see why we couldn't."

Ivy squealed and ran to the door. When she flung it open, Kathleen, her mother, and Nick came bustling in to join her excitement. Amelia grabbed her robe to cover herself and was swept off the bed into Nick's arms.

"Are you sure?" Nick asked.

"I have never been more sure about anything in my life," Amelia said.

Nick kissed her soundly, said goodbye for the day, and went off to work.

Amelia turned to the women and said, "I guess we have a second wedding to plan."

Ivy started shouting suggestions while Amelia got dressed behind her screen. Her mother and Kathleen interjected their ideas, and any time they asked for Amelia's opinion, she said she just wanted it to be simple.

The last-minute wedding preparations didn't take much to pull together, but the extra work made the days go by quickly. As the day dawned for Amelia's wedding, she woke up early, bathed, dressed, and sat staring out at the lake.

George came to see her and when he was settled in a chair, he asked, "How are you? I know you were never fond of the idea of getting married."

"It wasn't getting married that I hated the idea of. It was the idea that I had to be bound to someone like a business transaction."

"But you love Nick."

"I love Nick. Which is why this is different."

"Okay, well, if you change your mind, you just give me the signal and I will rush you out of here, Melia."

"Ha, you wouldn't dare. Mother would kill you."

Laughter erupted between the siblings as Ivy entered the room.

"We thought you would be in your marriage bed, sister," George said.

"George Campbell, such a crude thing to say," Amelia said. "You better not let Mother hear you talk that way. Although I love that you have accepted Ivy as your sister, too."

"It's a joy to have two sisters instead of just the one pesky one," George said.

"Very funny," Amelia said.

"As much as it is fun to gang up on Melia, you should run along, George. It's time for her final preparations."

"See you down there, Melia."

"See you down there, George."

Ivy was joined by Amelia's mother and Kathleen several minutes later, and the final touches were made. Amelia embraced the craziness before being swept downstairs to the aisle. She walked toward Nick, who stood under an arch with the point and lake as the backdrop.

Their words of love were shared, and they were introduced to the audience as husband and wife just as quickly as the ceremony had begun. Amelia danced with her husband, speeches were made, and when it was over, she thanked Ivy for suggesting the last-minute wedding.

Nick ended the evening by telling Amelia they would be spending a few days and nights on the water for their honeymoon. He promised a bigger trip the following summer, but for now, they would get some privacy on the lake they both loved.

When Amelia followed Nick across the dock, she was surprised when he brought her on board a boat other than the *Bay Minnow*.

"What's this?" she asked.

"This is my gift to you," Nick said.

"What?"

"She is yours, my love. Walk around her. This boat is all your own."

"You can't be serious. How did you find this so fast?"

"I had already made plans to get her for you before we were even engaged. It was a bit tight, but I managed to get her here in time."

"She's beautiful."

"Come with me, let me show you around and then we will cast off."

Nick took Amelia through all parts of her present. She took special interest in the room he had done up as the honeymoon suite. When they got back on deck, she realized Lars and a few other crewmen were preparing the boat for her maiden voyage.

"You look disappointed. Do you not like your boat?" he asked.

"No, I just thought we would be alone," Amelia said.

"They are only helping us cast off," Nick said, chuckling as he pulled her into his arms. "Trust me, I want you all to myself."

Heat grew between them, and Amelia pulled Nick into a passionate kiss. When she finally let go, he turned to his crew and told them to hurry up so they could get on the water. Lars and the men laughed and scurried about to finish.

Thankfully, it wasn't long before they were pulling away from the dock and out toward the edge of the bay. They sailed peacefully along the water until Nick slowed the boat to a stop and dropped anchor.

"I thought perhaps our first night could be here with the view of our home in the distance," Nick said.

"I love that idea," Amelia said.

"Besides, I'm not sure how much longer I can wait—"

Nick's words were cut off by Amelia's lips on his. They moved to the honeymoon suite, helping each other out of their clothes and tossing them aside.

As they lay together for the first time, Amelia said, "I think a part of me longed for this the first time I saw you."

"I know I longed for you," Nick said.

Amelia kissed him lovingly and rode the waves of desire with him, long into the night.

Amelia woke with a start, and after getting her bearings, she went out to the deck. The moon was high in the sky and the stars twinkled above. She pulled the blanket around her bare shoulders and listened to the music of the calm waves.

Hearing movement behind her, she turned and smiled as her husband walked toward her with nothing on his body.

"As much as I am enjoying the view, won't you be cold?" Amelia asked.

"On the contrary, I thought perhaps you would share your blanket with me," Nick said, wrapping his arms around her naked waist.

Giggling, Amelia kissed her husband softly and turned to enjoy the night sky reflecting on the water.

"Are you okay?" Nick asked after a few quiet moments had passed.

"I was just thinking about the first time I rode up here on a different boat."

"That was a fun day. I couldn't keep my eyes off the joy I saw on your face. You fell in love with the lake that day, I think."

"I did fall in love with her that day, and with you, I imagine," Amelia said.

Biting her lip, she shifted her gaze to stare at the deck.

"What is it?" Nick asked.

"I was remembering—"

"The storm."

"Yes."

"Nathanial."

"Yes."

"I thought about him often today. I wish he could have been there for it."

"I do too."

"It's funny how things work out, isn't it," he said.

"It is."

Amelia started humming and Nick chuckled before he started to sing the words, "The crash of her waves in the cold dark night."

"I love that song," she said.

"I know you do," Nick said. Changing the subject, he asked, "Have you thought of a name for your boat?"

"I get to name her?"

"She's yours, so you get to name her."

"How about *Song of the Lake?* We can paint *Song* on the side if the name is too long."

"I love it. It suits you. It suits her. *Song of the Lake* it is."

Nick kissed Amelia and urged her to come back to bed. She stepped away from him, letting the blanket pool around her feet. Nick let out a gasp, and she beamed at the desire she saw in her husband's eyes. He gently grabbed her hand, and they started walking across the deck.

As Nick ducked inside the wheelhouse, Amelia let go of him, pausing in the doorway. She glanced once more across the water, allowing waves of love and belonging to rush over her. Humming, she smiled lovingly at the lake and followed her husband to bed.

A Note to Readers

Thank you for reading *Song of the Lake*.

If you enjoyed it, I would appreciate a review on your favorite retailer website.

And I'd love to hear from you. Drop me a line at: esther@theestherschultz.com

My website is theestherschultz.com

Acknowledgements

To my husband, thank you for your never-ending support in me following my dreams. I want to thank my four children who inspire me and encourage me to keep going every day. Your pride in the work I do warms my heart every day.

To the YaYas: Megan, Ruth, and Denise. You listen to me vent, and you give me strength when I feel like I can't keep going. You validate my feelings, especially when I come to you in tears, and then push me to keep going. Thank you for your belief in me. I can't forget my amazing friends in WomenLead. Thank you for reassuring me through this process.

Thank you to my proofreaders, who jumped at the chance to help. Thank you, Sarah Hanley, for your amazing help with my book cover. And finally, I must honor and thank my editor, Jeanne Felfe. Your continued faith in me and your immeasurable feedback and wisdom are beyond appreciated. I am so thankful for you for working with me and helping me through another book project.

About the Author

Esther Schultz lives by her personal motto of, "be kind always and spread joy every day." She believes everyone can live a peaceful, joy-filled life and attempts to spread that message in her work and daily life. Her favorite things include spending time in nature, especially along Lake Superior, and advocating for mental health. Esther lives in central Minnesota with her husband, four children, her dog, and horse.

www.ingramcontent.com/pod-product-compliance
Lightning Source LLC
Chambersburg PA
CBHW021237190726
48289CB00005B/1369